A PLACE OF FORGETTING

a novel by

Carolyn J. Rose

2011

A PLACE OF FORGETTING

a novel by

Carolyn J. Rose

2011

A Place of Forgetting

Copyright © 2011 Carolyn J. Rose

www.deadlyduomysteries.com

ISBN: 978-0-9837359-1-5

Cover design by Dorion D. Rose, Broken Cork Photography
Interior Book design by Boulevard Photografica/Patty G. Henderson

Digital editions produced by Booknook.biz

For Elizabeth Lyon, friend and mentor

And for all those friendships that transcend time and

place

CHAPTER 1

I was raised in the cautious years following a terrible war and brought up with a legacy of loss among prudent people in a town snug against the Catskill Mountains. Disciplined by my grandmother's doubt and disapproval, I found comfort in my father's faithful devotion to me and the memory of my mother, even as I chafed against the restraint of his fears.

Ben's affection, like sweet wine, gave me confidence to alter the course they set.

But it was his betrayal of our future that made me bold.

And so, that September afternoon in 1966 when my grandmother barged into my room, I no longer cared about the consequences of speaking my mind. With deliberate care I shoved my chair back, stood beside my desk, and matched her glower for glower. No stinging lecture was worse than having love—or what I'd believed to be love—snatched away without explanation.

"I won't go to the vigil." I slapped my three-ring binder shut. "And I'll never pray to the same power that allowed this war and set Ben down in the middle of it."

And then put that girl in his path.

Gertrude Gorman—that's how I always thought of her because one name didn't suffice for a force of nature—

planted her fists on sturdy hips and pursed thin lips, making it clear I'd crossed one line too many. Living with her was like playing an endless game of hopscotch. Even when I tried—and since April pulled out that engagement ring from Ben I'd stopped trying—I landed in the wrong space or lost my balance.

"That's quite enough, Elizabeth Roark, quite enough."

My full name *and* a repetition. Signs that I was way over that line.

With blunt fingers she snapped off the record player, strangling the Rolling Stones in the middle of "Paint It Black."

Ben's album. *Aftermath.* The last one he bought before his leave ended. I'd smash it before I turned it over to April.

"You can't presume to know God's plan." Gertrude Gorman's false teeth clicked and her breath smelled of butter rum candies—her only vice.

Back in the spring, the cover of *Time* magazine questioned whether God was dead, but my grandmother's faith was rock solid. I pushed the chair into the kneehole of the desk that no longer faced the window overlooking Ben's house. I'd turned the desk, but still tortured myself by peering over my shoulder every few minutes. "Whatever the plan is, I know I'm not part of it."

"Man supposes but God disposes," Gertrude Gorman said with smug cadence. Without platitudes her vocabulary would be no longer than the weekly grocery list.

"So you always say." I spread my fingers across the astronomy text open to a star chart of the northern hemisphere. "There's a test tomorrow. I have to study."

"You're not studying, Liz, you're sulking. Hold your head up and go to the service and pray for Ben with the rest of us. Sulking solves nothing."

"I'm not sulking."

That word didn't even begin to cover my emotional state since April announced that the boy I loved for most of my life proposed to her two days after they met—minutes before he shipped out. I could talk for a week and not define the length and breadth of his betrayal. But my words would be wasted on Gertrude Gorman. She had little time for emotions—her own or those of others.

I touched the cool, slick pages of the text. "I have two chapters to read."

"Read them when we get back."

Prowling to the tall maple dresser, she aligned the silver brush, comb, and mirror that had belonged to my mother, her daughter. "I know you expected Ben Hoyt to marry you when he got out of the Marine Corps but, like most men, he'd rather have a hussy than a decent girl." She rounded on me, leveling a knotted, arthritic forefinger at my forehead. "Better you found out now instead of . . ."

Her voice caught and I knew she was referring to the man who deceived and abandoned her long years before; I lowered my eyes so she wouldn't detect a flash of empathy. Gertrude Gorman might—on rare occasions and in a back-handed manner—offer sympathy to others, but she would tolerate none for herself. We had that stubborn pride in common and, although I ached to admit it, I suspected we'd both lost love for similar reasons.

The more I thought about it—and I thought about it every moment—the more I recognized that Ben chose April because she was everything I was not—beautiful, spontaneous, comfortable inside her skin, and willing to give herself without reservation.

Not that I hadn't tried.

Cringing, I jerked the chair out of the kneehole, dropped into it, and bent over the textbook, remembering that night before his leave ended—his birthday. I'd flung myself across a dingy white chenille bedspread in a chilly motel room that smelled like an ashtray, offering myself the way Gus Heinz, the butcher, offers chuck roast on waxy brown paper. Raised to be a "good girl," I couldn't open my eyes when Ben touched my goose-pimpled skin.

"And now he's gone." My grandmother wiped the top of my bookcase with the hem of her pink-flowered apron. Dust to dust.

"Missing in action," I muttered, holding fast to the flimsy hope in those words. He might be chained in a dark hole, eating wormy rice. Or crouched in the undergrowth hoping for rescue. Or trying to work his way back to his base. If he was dead I'd feel numb emptiness instead of feverish jealousy and roiling anger. Wouldn't I?

You can't be dead, Ben. I deserve an explanation.

"Gone," my grandmother repeated without a sliver of doubt or an ounce of optimism. "Rotting in that jungle without a decent burial." She strode to the desk, blinking from behind gold-rimmed bifocals. "Your prayers might save his immortal soul."

The tremor in her voice surprised me but the guilt she wielded like a cudgel didn't. "All right. I'll pray. But I'll do it here." Where I didn't have to run the gauntlet of the 728 residents of Maplekill, New York.

Most of them had been as certain of Ben's fidelity as I had from the day he walked me to my first-grade classroom until the day last week—my birthday—when April got off the bus. The scrawled note in his handwriting asked me to help his mother look out for her. He'd promised to explain when he had time to write more. I still watched each day for that letter even though I feared it would confirm the obvious—I'd been his best friend, but he'd never loved me any other way.

"I'll pray here," I repeated, staring at a white dot on the star chart. Polaris. The North Star. There would be no moon tonight. What constellations would Ben see in a sky so much farther south than the one we charted together as children? Could he see the sky at all?

4

"You'll pray in church with the rest of us." My grandmother's voice softened, but the words were no less of an order. "Put on a dress, comb your hair, and come downstairs. I made pot roast." Her forefinger prodded a nearly empty bag of cheesy snacks atop a stack of books at the corner of the desk. "And vegetables."

I preferred potato chips, but the crunchy disks with the bright orange filling had been Ben's number-one indulgence. Quoting his favorite science fiction tale, *Stranger in a Strange Land*, he'd often said he grokked them, but not as much as he grokked me.

Not loved.

He never said he loved me.

With tears in my eyes, I slid a crunchy disk from the crackling plastic bag, put it on my tongue like a communion wafer, and let it dissolve against the roof of my mouth with a grainy burst of salty, fatty, hyper-fake-cheese taste. "I'm not going to church."

My grandmother shrugged and spread her hands as if to say I left her no choice. I expected the as-long-as-you-live-under-this-roof lecture, but she went right for the heavy artillery. "Your father thinks you should."

I shook my head, trying to swallow the cracker that stuck to my teeth like library paste. My father gave so much and asked so little. But this? Why not request that I wear a scarlet letter? *L* for laughingstock. *D* for dared to dream it could turn out any other way.

"Some of life's lessons are hard, Liz. Almost too hard to bear." Gertrude Gorman stretched out a hand as if to pat my shoulder, then shrugged again and plodded to the door. "But we go on."

Yes, I thought an hour later as the rest of the congregation bowed their heads in silent prayer for Ben's deliverance, we go on. Even if there's no reason.

I folded my arms and glared at the giant cross beyond the pulpit, challenging the will of the almighty power that had taken Ben from me twice. My grandmother released a soft tut of disapproval and I squirmed on the oak pew and frowned at Reverend Campbell's bald spot and then at each of the eight stained glass windows with their lambs and saints and angels. If I was going to pray in this stuffy church—and I wasn't—I'd pray for a quick end to the service.

My grandmother tutted again, and I turned my head and studied my father's gentle face. As always, he'd nicked himself shaving and a flake of dried blood marked the point of his chin. His faded blue eyes were webbed with red and the creases bracketing his mouth seemed deep enough to hold a dime. His lips moved, and I made out Ben's name, felt both guilty and glad of his prayer.

A pew creaked, fabric rustled, and April rose from her seat across the aisle beside Ben's mother. Shrugging Jo's hand from her arm, she stepped onto the burgundy runner between the pews and began to dance to music only she could hear. Heads tilted up, necks twisted, eyes widened, and a whisper rippled through the congregation.

Gaping, Reverend Campbell watched her dip and sway, her frayed pink ballet slippers circling with intricate steps. Her fingers tickled the over-heated air, the tiny diamond on her ring finger glittering, the bells on her bracelets tinkling.

An image bloomed in my mind: Ben and April in bed—his hands stroking her soft curves, her gleaming honey hair cascading across his chest, her wide brown eyes reflecting his pleasure. She would make love exactly the way I did in my dreams, flawlessly, with breathy moans and sighs and not a second of tense hesitation or a shred of self-conscious embarrassment.

I wanted to leap to my feet, throw my camel's hair coat over her head, and suffocate her. Instead I clenched my fists, twined my legs at the ankles, and tried to imagine myself on another planet.

"Tramp," my grandmother hissed, pinching her tatting-trimmed collar tighter as if protecting skin revealed only during her morning shower and for those few seconds before she shrugged a flannel nightgown—always pink—over her head at night.

"She should be ashamed." The whisper came from behind me. I didn't need to look to know I'd see Madge Eakins, her lips clamped into a pale scar between her thin nose and knobby chin.

"Madge should tend her own glass house," my grandmother huffed.

I nodded before recalling I was too young by my grandmother's standards to know that the man who drove the bread delivery truck on Tuesdays and Fridays didn't pull into Madge's driveway simply to get off the road and sip his coffee. At nineteen I shouldn't know that the gardener who tended Madge's flowerbeds on Wednesdays planted the kind of seed that wouldn't sprout into pansies or chrysanthemums. I suppressed a snicker and feigned innocence. "What glass house?"

"Never you mind. There's no point in growing up too soon."

Or at all. On that other planet, I'd be ten forever. Or six. Six had been a good year. I got straight As in first grade, Ben and I decided chocolate cupcakes were the greatest food ever, and Dad let me keep the puppy Ben found wandering along the highway.

Despite my grandmother's dissent, I named him after my favorite teacher, Mr. Sebastian. He was an old dog now—ninety-one in people years—and he smelled like aged bacon grease, but he was still a loyal friend. He was the only one I told about that motel.

April reached the pulpit and rotated before it like a top, her flowered skirt belling around her ankles, her

7

white peasant blouse dipping across the swell of her breasts, her arms stretched toward the pressed-tin ceiling that spattered down echoes like hailstones when we sang about those Christian solders or that rugged cross. Reverend Campbell gawked and his sister Edna pressed her chin to her chest and drew in her arms like a turtle. No one even pretended to pray.

"Take her outside, Elizabeth," my father whispered. "Take her back to Jo's."

I shook my head. How could he ask that? Wasn't I tortured enough knowing that April slept in Ben's bed, listened to his records, and ate his mother's potato pancakes? I folded my arms tighter. "No."

"Please." My father patted my arm and offered a sad smile. "Jo has enough to bear already."

Fighting a pang of sympathy, I canted my head and glanced at Ben's mother. She'd yanked her wispy brown hair back and bobby-pinned it behind ears flaming as red as embers in a draft. Since Ben's father ran off six years ago with a woman they met on a weekend at Saratoga Springs, Josephine Hoyt blamed herself for almost everything. She apologized for rainstorms, heat, and even the Japanese beetles nibbling on our rosebushes.

But she never apologized for Ben. Not even when they said he defied orders, running from the landing zone to help a wounded buddy. Not even when April brought out that damn ring right after we got word Ben was MIA.

I stayed put. Jo had also betrayed me.

My father's thick fingers kneaded my shoulder, a shoulder I knew was too broad and too strong. "Please. It's what your mother would have done."

My mother. A creature more myth than memory.

For a moment my fists clenched tighter, but then I stood—manipulated but still longing to be worthy—and tugged at the hem of the beige wool jumper my grandmother had made. She chose the bland color because everything must be practical; she cut it a size too large because I refused to wear a girdle like she said a decent woman should. Gertrude Gorman practiced what she preached about "foundation garments." She wore corsets: amazing feats of engineering with stays, hooks, and garters stitched fast to flesh-colored fabric resembling no flesh I'd ever seen.

I squeezed past my father's knees, my eyes on the carpet so he wouldn't see the depth of my misery and so I wouldn't glimpse his. Avoidance was a game we'd played since that wind-whipped March day when he told me my mother went to sleep and would never wake up. As we stood beside the white coffin with shiny brass handles, Gertrude Gorman sniffed into an embroidered handkerchief, raised her chin, and ordered, "Pull yourself together, Gene. The child needs you to be strong, be a man."

So, although I'd often heard him sobbing deep in the night, my father never again revealed his grief, and I spared him mine. Life, as my practical grandmother too often said, was for the living. But living was defined by more than heartbeat and breath. I was bitter proof of that.

The soles of my penny loafers slid on the runner and I clutched at the back of a pew, feeling the eyes of the congregation swarming over me like bees. Reverend Campbell hooked an index finger, urging me on, and I rolled my eyes. Concerned with the next world, he never confronted the difficulties of this one. Last fall half the choir quit—going over to the Presbyterians—because he wouldn't support their fund drive for a better organ. He'd called them prideful and pleasure seeking, but it seemed to me he defined his holiness by what he denied others.

April's eyes were bright but unfocused, her cheeks flushed. "Dance with me," she commanded.

"No." The first word I'd spoken to her since the day she arrived. Fitting. I smelled alcohol on her breath, but couldn't tell what kind; my knowledge of that was as limited as my sexual proficiency. Gertrude Gorman didn't allow "spirits" in the house and, even though I was a year past the legal age, I'd never had more than an occasional beer. I gripped April's bare arm. "Let's go outside."

"No." She twirled away, bells jingling, trailing the vanilla scent of perfume. "Dance with me. Dance for Ben."

Dance? While Ben struggled to survive or lay dead? I wanted to slap her. "No one dances in church," I hissed.

"Why not?"

"We're Methodists." Explaining nothing. And everything.

"Then we'll dance in the street. Like Martha and the Vandellas."

I imagined myself with teased hair and a slinky dress, swinging my hips to the beat. Almost laughed. Almost cried. "Yeah. Sure."

"Okay." She grasped my hand. I heard Reverend Campbell let out a long breath as I towed her toward the vestibule.

"Put this on her." My father stood, shrugged out of the jacket to his navy blue suit, and thrust it at me. "It's cold out there."

The jacket smelled of aftershave and cigarettes, his tangy, smoky scent; I wanted to hide myself within it and scuttle into the dark. But I settled the jacket around April's shoulders, pushed her through the archway, and opened the door. The crisp September air smelled of dying leaves and a few crunched beneath our feet as we descended broad stone steps quarried on Maplekill Mountain by my father's great uncles and hauled on wooden sledges pulled by plow horses. Like those stones, I'd been set in this place on the earth.

"Stuffy old stuffed shirts," April mumbled. "Church isn't my bag."

Not mine either.

I shook off the thought, didn't want us to have even that much in common. "Come on. You're going . . ." I bit my tongue. I'd almost said "home." "You're going to Jo's house."

If Ben somehow got back and married April and they lived next door for fifty years, I would never think of that house as her home.

"Dance." She held her arms to the star-spangled sky. "Dance me there."

"No." I pulled my coat tighter, forced a woven leather button through its hole.

April pirouetted along the sidewalk, stopped at the corner, fumbled in the folds of her skirt and drew out a silver flask. "I need a drink." She unscrewed the top and tipped it to her lips.

The streetlight cast a yellow glow on her smooth throat, and I remembered my mother holding buttercups beneath my chin, telling me the spot of yellow meant I liked butter. I'd clapped my hands at nature's confirmation of my preference. I'd been special then.

April held the flask an inch from my lips. "*You* need a drink."

I shook my head. "No."

"Trust me," she giggled, "you do. You're so uptight. You need a drink more than anyone I know."

How much more of this can I stand?

"You don't know me!" I swatted at the hand that held the flask. "You don't know anything about me."

"Yes I do." She smiled, a cat-like simper that set a blaze in my brain. "Ben told me everything."

Gagging on a howl of shame and despair, I ripped my father's jacket from her shoulders and bolted into the night.

11

CHAPTER 2

Still seething the next afternoon, I reported for work at the bridal shop and shoved a basket of half-price nylon panties to the edge of the glass showcase, making room to study. At fifteen, when I believed sexual confidence was a direct result of filmy underwear, I would have sifted through that basket even though Gertrude Gorman insisted I wear white cotton. "More hygienic," she contended. "Cotton is your friend."

I bent to dig the geography text and a notebook from my satchel. Nylon would have been a slick whisper beneath my slacks. Cotton caught, bunched, made my hips and waist feel bigger.

Some friend.

The text fell open to the map of North America, and I ran my index finger along the spine of the Rockies. Someday I would drive to Colorado and hike to a crystal lake beneath a sky like a bluebird's wing, but now I had morning classes and afternoons behind this counter. While I forced smiles for customers, my grandmother sewed wedding gowns and bridesmaids' dresses in the back room. My father ordered lingerie, sorted stock, kept up with the mail-order side of the business, and made deliveries in a black van with a long-trained wedding dress painted on each side.

The business made us a good living, but I would rather dig ditches.

The shop was long and narrow with a show window at the front where a dozen dolls stood at attention wearing replicas of the frilly and fanciful gowns my grandmother created. Those gowns were the only evidence that she had an imagination. Brackets on one long wall held rolls of silk and satin in a dozen shades of white; across the way were cabinets and drawers stuffed with bras, panties, girdles, garter belts, and stockings. Racks of peignoirs, slips, and bed jackets clustered in the center of the room They whispered of desire but smelled of fabric preservative. On the rear wall hung framed pictures of brides wearing my grandmother's designs.

Unlike the dresses she sewed for me, not one was too large.

I opened the notebook, blocking my view of tiaras made of pearls and rhinestones displayed inside the showcase on a frothy billow of veiling—scratchy stuff I hated to touch. Flipping pages to the chapter on deserts, I plucked a pen from the cup beside the register. The pens were black with tiny, white wedding dresses. Everything about the shop reminded me of what I'd lost.

"Last load." My father trundled from the back, arms piled high with white cardboard boxes. "I'm off."

Off up the Maplekill to deliver gowns for an eighteen-member formal wedding my grandmother had been sewing for since early August. I dropped my pen and raced ahead to hold the door and then open the back of the van, thinking of the road winding among mountains creased by ridges splashed with scarlet. Summer had been dry and the chilly September nights were already burnishing brittle leaves. "I could come. If you want company."

He shook his head, his smile salving the sting of refusal. "Your grandmother"—he never called her

Gertrude when talking with me— "has a headache. She went to lie down. Someone needs to hold the fort."

As if the contemplation of marriage was a military operation and my grandmother the general.

"I could make the delivery for you." My voice sparkled with eagerness. "You could work on plans for the gazebo."

My father's eyes looked inward and I knew he was visualizing the gazebo he planned for the backyard. In the years after he returned from the war in Europe, up until the day my mother died, he was a carpenter and stonemason, sought after for his skill. Sometimes even now he'd slow as we drove on some errand and gaze at the bulk of a chimney or the slant of a roof the way I imagined Michelangelo might have gazed at that chapel ceiling. But, as my grandmother pointed out at the funeral, building meant long days spent miles from home. Who would care for me?

Jo had volunteered. Ben and I, with only a year between us, had been inseparable, running in and out of both houses, never knocking. But my grandmother swept that aside, sold her brownstone in Brooklyn, and relocated her business to Maplekill, moving into our house to "bring some order to our lives."

We'd had fifteen years of Gertrude Gorman's order— three meals a day, clean sheets every Saturday, neat lists of chores to complete and check off.

Order outlined each day.

And yet, the space within that outline seemed empty.

My father twisted a tuft of hair above his right ear and scuffed the toe of one brown oxford on the stone sidewalk. "Thanks, Elizabeth. But it's not easy to find the Hanover place."

I swallowed hope, but didn't give up. "You could draw me a map."

His eyes flicked toward the shop window, then to the stack of boxes in the van. He winced and cleared his throat. "There's a balance due and . . ."

I nodded. The weddings my grandmother sewed for were expensive affairs, often financed with IOUs and promises—neither of which she accepted.

"Cash. Half now and half on delivery. If you can't afford me, don't hire me," she'd tell the mother of the bride in a clipped voice.

But time and again that woman would call to plead that other expenses had been greater than expected. Would my grandmother mind waiting until the end of the month, until the holidays were over, until the income tax had been figured?

"A bargain is a bargain," Gertrude Gorman would recite into the tiny holes in the handset of the chunky black telephone beside the cash register. "No money, no dress." Often she'd repeat that several times, dentures clicking for punctuation.

When I was younger, I used to pity the bride-to-be, her perfect day tarnished by what I perceived as money-grubbing greed. Today I felt a jolt of vengeful joy. Let this bride learn perfection is an illusion, just like happiness.

My father sighed and I patted his arm. The money always materialized. It would today, too, counted out in tens and twenties and slapped onto a table or the hood of a car, as he were an extortionist or a member of a caste so low the slightest contact would contaminate. I saw it happen once, saw him stare off into the distance and wad the bills into his pocket when the counting was done. He told me that it was just business, that he didn't take it personally. My stomach spasmed with rage. How could he not?

He kissed my cheek, wrenched the rear doors closed on grating hinges, slid behind the wheel, and drove off with a pungent puff of exhaust.

15

Watching until he was out of sight, I thought about the many times I pointed out that I could take care of myself and he could go back to doing what he loved. "Your grandmother depends on me" was his habitual answer, all he would ever say.

I trudged back into the shop and yanked my hair—long, straight, and the color of bread left too long in the toaster—into a ponytail. Hunched over the counter, I jotted notes about desert wind patterns, rainfall, and vegetation. The sooner I finished reading about landscapes as barren as my life, the sooner I could move on to Henry David Thoreau and his house on Walden Pond. Glancing at the finery on display, I thought of Thoreau's warning against enterprises that require new clothes. I imagined he might detest this shop as much as I did.

The tiny bells above the door chimed and I felt a swirl of cool air around my ankles. Marking my place with my index finger, I glanced up to see April flow into the shop wearing a fringed red wool poncho, jeans, and black leather boots. I took a step back, feeling last night's humiliation burn my cheeks. Then I squared my shoulders and scowled. To hell with my grandmother's mandate to bestow a welcoming smile on every customer.

April either didn't notice or wasn't fazed. She studied the battalion of dolls in the window, and then drifted among the racks, letting her fingers trail across midnight-blue satin bed jackets, sea-green baby doll pajamas, cherry-red silk robes. Her diamond sparkled, her nails brushed the fabrics, and I caught the floral scent of perfume—Jo's just-for-special-occasions extravagant perfume.

Rage spiked behind my eyes. Ben and I bought that for her last Christmas. Jo kept the blue bottle in the exact center of her dresser and dabbed it on with the tip of her pinkie. April smelled like she'd splashed on half a cup. She

16

had no right to wear it—even if she had asked, which I bet she hadn't, hoped she hadn't. I wanted her to be a thief, not a guest. Wanted, as usual, more than I could have.

I slammed my book shut. April revolved around the rack of pettipants and floated to a stop, fingering the panties in the basket, smiling, her long eyelashes fluttering the tiniest bit. "I'll bet it's fun working here."

I gritted my teeth. "It's a laugh and a half."

Her smile didn't fade. "Your grandmother makes beautiful dresses."

Don't even think she'll make one for you. Not if you were the last bride on earth.

I moved the basket a few inches toward me. "They're expensive."

April shrugged. "I'm going to be naked when I get married."

I winced at an image of April and Ben before a flower-decked altar. He stood at attention, head back, shoulder blades jutting, stomach tight and flat.

"Marriage should be all about total honesty." Diamond flashing, April dismissed other conceptions with a flip of her fingers. "If you're naked, you have to be totally honest."

Or tense and frightened. Like in that motel room.

But Ben, honorable even as his eyes darkened with desire, chose to recognize that as honesty. "This isn't what you really want, Elizabeth." He sat up and reached for his shirt. "And if you don't want it, I don't either."

I'd stared through tears at a brown water stain on the ceiling, too miserably self-conscious to dress until he turned his back to step into his jeans. It was apparent now that he *had* wanted it. Badly. In the few days between the end of his leave and the time he shipped out, he found someone willing.

April held up a pair of lavender bikini panties and peered at me through the filmy fabric. "I wasn't honest last night."

I blinked myself back to the fort I'd been ordered to hold, at the enemy now inside the walls.

"All Ben told me was that you lived next door and were his best friend from the time you were little kids."

I wanted to cry with relief and scream with rage. Relief because April didn't know about that motel room. Rage because he called me a best friend—a designation no more interesting or exciting than a pair of cotton panties. I bit my lip until I tasted blood.

"Is that your car?"

I blinked again. "Car?"

"The faded-out red one with the scabby fenders."

Her words, accurate though they were, cut me. I bought Buggy with money saved from the wage my grandmother paid me: $1.50 an hour for twenty-eight hours a week. That car, rust-eaten fenders and all, represented independence.

April dropped the lavender panties and plucked out a pink pair with tiny red hearts. "Jo says you're going to college to be a teacher. You drive up to Oneonta every morning." She twirled the panties on her finger. "Ben said you really want to go to school in Chicago and be a reporter."

I folded my arms across my chest as if that might halt this desecration of my fragile dream. When I revealed it in the fall of my senior year, Ben, training to be an electrician, said Chicago would be full of opportunities for both of us. My grandmother, however, carped that journalists were prying gossips and claimed it was a man's profession besides. She insisted I learn bookkeeping or hairstyling or become a teacher. Those trades would support me if I didn't marry or if my husband died or left in a less responsible manner as hers had—imprisoned for

18

smuggling bootleg liquor and divorcing her to marry his lawyer's secretary when he got out.

That was another story I was deemed too young to know, but as children Ben and I thrived on discovering what adults hid from us—like the faded letters inside a mothball-scented box that opened with the twist of a hairpin.

It was rare for my father to buck Gertrude Gorman's opinion, but he blessed my aspirations, saying the world was changing, women would have many opportunities in the years ahead. If I won a scholarship, he promised he'd take a loan for the rest. But the next evening I overheard him telling Jo that he dreaded letting me go so far, but hated himself for wanting to hold me close.

I ran to my room, aching because this thing I yearned for would hurt him so much. For two days I clung to my dream, but then shoved it deep into the future. At breakfast I announced that since I didn't like big cities and enjoyed books more than newspapers, I'd decided to be a teacher and study near home. He hugged me so tight I thought my spine would crack and I wondered why, if I'd done the right thing, I felt such churning resentment. Not toward my father, but at whoever made the plan that took my mother away.

"My school was a drag," April said. "The subjects were boring and the teachers were old and grouchy."

I'll bet they didn't like you either. You have the intellect of an earthworm.

If this was what Ben wanted I was glad I found out before I made more of a fool of myself. I bent to stash the geography text in my satchel beside *Walden*, understanding what Thoreau meant about lives of quiet desperation.

April stretched the elastic like a rubber band and shot the panties at the photographs behind the counter. I ignored my grandmother's voice in my mind demanding that I retrieve them immediately.

"Jo talks about you all the time." April twisted the diamond ring on her finger. I tipped my head and studied a crack in the plaster ceiling. "All the time when she's not talking about Ben."

Resentment encased her words the way hoarfrost shrouds a lawn in winter. I matched her tone. "Don't you enjoy talking about him?"

"Yeah, but not *all* the time." April lifted a handful of panties—orange, beige, pink, blue, polka dot—and let them trickle back into the basket. "I need to go somewhere for a few days."

Good. Go.

"Maybe to Niagara Falls."

Fall in. Drown.

"I'm going crazy telling Jo fifty times a day that Ben can take care of himself."

In a strange land swarming with enemies?

I snatched the basket of panties from her grasping fingers and slammed it to the floor behind the counter.

April pouted, then studied her ring, fluttering her fingers. "So I thought, because you were Ben's best friend, and because you never go anywhere on the weekends, that maybe I could borrow your car."

Not a chance. Ben and I had kissed in that car, shared dreams in that car. It was sacred. I gave April a glare worthy of Gertrude Gorman. "No."

She twitched her perky nose. "Well, maybe we could go somewhere together."

A screech of a laugh burst from my throat. "Not in a million years."

April's pouty lower lip plumped a little more, but then she shrugged and gave me that cat-like simper again. "Just think about it."

She walked out, fringe swaying.

20

When she was good and gone, I retrieved the panties and returned them to the basket.

The polka dot pair was missing.

CHAPTER 3

While I brooded about whether to call the town constable, confront April, or just get on with my homework, Diana Price bounced in, long, straight blond hair swinging, lips in a half smile that revealed a glint of perfect teeth. Diana had seven mirrors in her bedroom and a closet stuffed with trendy clothing. Ours was a tenuous friendship based only on proximity and population size.

"I'm trying to find my true self," she'd told Ben a year ago. He laughed and asked how copying movie stars would help. Furious, she'd stopped speaking to us both for a month. In a weird way, I'd missed her and realized I depended on Diana to explain the mysteries of womanhood that Gertrude Gorman was too old to remember and Jo found too painful to mention.

"They're as dumb as they come," she said, unbuckling her beige trench coat.

"Who?" I asked without much caring, wondering if April would deny the theft and hide the panties. Did I have proof? I hadn't actually seen her pocket them, so it would be my word against hers.

Diana bent and checked her reflection in the glass showcase. "Two tourists from the city."

That would be New York City. Art, theater, culture, wonderful food, looming buildings, hurtling subways, and exhaust-laden air.

I pushed the images aside, wondering if I should ignore the panty incident. Would Gertrude Gorman notice one wisp of missing inventory?

Diana smoothed her fuzzy pink sweater over 36D breasts. "They stopped me at the gas station and asked why we killed the maples."

Everyone in Maplekill had heard that before. The word "kill" went back centuries, to Dutch settlers. It didn't mean what I'd like to do to April; it meant a stream. If you studied the map, you'd find Sawkill, Fishkill, Wallkill, Catskill, and more. I shoved the basket another inch along the counter, thinking Gertrude Gorman might conclude I destroyed the panties and blamed April in a petty act of revenge.

"The real story's boring," Diana continued her breathy delivery. "So I told them this was Maple Valley until a blight struck and the army was called in to kill every maple within a dozen miles to save the rest."

I eyed the price tags on the panties in the basket—49 cents. Twenty minutes out of my paycheck.

"You're not listening," Diana pouted.

"I am," I lied.

"Well, you're not listening much." Her tone made it clear the fault was mine. She gathered her hair into a ponytail and then let it drop. "Here's the best part. The woman said she heard the fall leaves were gorgeous and how could that be if there were no maples?"

Even as I awarded imaginary points to the tourist, I realized Diana wouldn't tell this story if she hadn't squirmed out of that trap. In my grandmother's words, Diana had more nerve than a broken tooth. She wouldn't waste two seconds on this panty problem.

23

"I told her the color is courtesy of local art students, led by yours truly," she boasted, "who paint oak leaves."

I groaned. "And they believed you?"

"Not at first." She splayed her fingers and studied pearly nail polish. "But then I begged them not to tell I let that slip or my father would be voted out as town supervisor and I'd have to leave college."

Diana's father worked for the phone company and if she left college it would be because she went to class only twice a month. As I shook my head, she worked a hand into the front pocket of jeans tight enough to cut off circulation and drew out a ten-dollar bill. "They gave me a donation," she whooped.

I blinked at the bill. It represented six hours and forty minutes worth of torture behind this counter, and she'd collected it for lies and embellishment. What would Thoreau have thought?

"Maybe we can take in a movie this weekend."

I felt a shimmer of warmth and pleasure. "That would be fun."

Diana preened her hair. "If I don't have a date, that is."

Humiliation scorched my cheeks. I should have seen that coming. "Sure." I bent to retrieve *Walden*. "Just let me know."

Diana massaged the skin along her jaw, firming, tightening. "You should start dating again."

Metallic fear needled the back of my mouth and I gripped the book with both hands. Ben and I had never "dated." We'd just always been together.

"I could probably fix you up." Diana licked her pinkie and smoothed her brows. "Guys would like you more if you let them think they're smarter than you are. But you have beautiful eyes."

She said the last almost as if it surprised her. Deep violet when I was born, my eyes, now an everyday blue,

24

were the reason I'd been named Elizabeth—after Elizabeth Taylor. I hated people making comparisons where I fell far short. And I hated that almost everyone shortened my name to Liz. Why not Betsy? She sewed flags. Or Beth who died so young in *Little Women*? Why not Bess after the queen? Why not Betty or Eliza or Ellie or Liza or Libby?

Because my mother named me, I never said any of this to my father, but when I was thirteen I told Ben. He laughed and said it could be worse; people could call me Lizzie after the woman with the ax. After that, he always used my full name like my father did or called me by a nickname I loved because it made me feet petite— Littlebit.

But Ben was gone and I was far from petite.

I opened *Walden* to the index card that marked my spot. I'd skimmed the book the day I bought it, but now was underlining and making notes.

"You need more makeup." Diana cocked her head. "And different glasses. Those horn-rims are ugly."

My shoulders slumped. I picked them because they went with my hair. "Thanks for the advice." My throat tightened with swallowed tears.

"You're welcome. I don't mean to brag, but when it comes to clothes, makeup, and men, I'm an expert. Remember when I told you the rule about waiting until Ben told you he loved you before you said it?"

I nodded, half glad I'd stuck to that rule, half wondering what might have happened if I hadn't.

She preened. "Imagine how much more embarrassing this April thing would be if you'd blurted out your feelings."

As if "this April thing" could be worse. I tapped the book. "I've got a lot of reading to do. For class."

If she noticed the hint, Diana didn't take it. "Hey, speaking of April, I saw her come out of here a few minutes ago." She leaned across the showcase. "What did she want?"

I glanced at the basket of panties, imagining the missing pair riding low on April's hips. "Nothing. She's bored."

"Aren't we all?" Diana, beautiful and named for a goddess, took a compact from a black leather sack of a purse and powdered her pixie nose. "Was she drunk?"

I snorted. "It's the middle of the afternoon."

Diana threw her head back and hooted. "Liz, you're as dumb as those tourists. Drunks don't check the clock before they hit the bottle."

"She wasn't drunk."

"Okay, well, did you tell her to take a hike?"

"No, I—"

"Of course you didn't," Diana sneered. "I bet you were as nice as you were at church last night."

Nice. A sharp little word. Like ice and slice. A word for cloaked emotion, intention held in check. "I wasn't nice."

Diana sucked in her cheeks. "Did you tell her to leave?"

"No."

"Did you tell her to throw herself under a truck?"

"No."

She smiled, condescending as a queen before the French Revolution. "Then you were nice."

"I wasn't! I told her—" I bit my lip. Saying I told April I wouldn't go on a trip with her was admitting we had a conversation and I didn't want anyone to know that I'd stood here like a stump while she prattled and pilfered. I'd pay for those panties and say nothing. April would steal again. And when she did I'd—

"You told her what?"

"Huh?"

26

"What did you tell April?" Diana sucked at her cheeks again. Finding her true self through suction. "What did she want?"

"Nothing."

Diana shrugged. "Okay. If you— Wait! I know!" She snapped her fingers. "She wanted your grandmother to design a wedding dress."

Her eyes sparkled and she licked her lips, probably already savoring the joy of sharing the latest installment in the "poor Liz" soap opera. "Didn't she?"

"No. Besides Ben is missing in action." The words ripped my lips like fishhooks.

"Oh, he's so levelheaded, Liz. He'll find his way back." Diana spoke in an offhand way, as if she was talking about the chances that the Beatles would have another hit, and then that sly smile twitched her lips. "Did April have the nerve to ask for a *white* dress?"

I gagged at the sexual reference. "She. Didn't. Want. A. Dress."

"Liar," Diana taunted. "Stop being so nice, Liz, or she'll ask you to be the maid of honor." With a flutter of her fingers, she waltzed off to broadcast her fictitious news. "See you later, alligator."

After the door closed I grabbed the basket of panties and flung it across the room. "Don't come back," I yelled, not sure if I meant Diana, April, Ben, or all of them. "Don't ever come back."

CHAPTER 4

On the stroke of five I locked the cash register, put the bar across the back door, and used my key to set the bolt on the front as I went out. Golden light dribbled along the ridges like clover honey, but the slanted rays of the declining sun skipped across the narrow valley of the Maplekill. Dawn came late to this hollow, and twilight early, but the folded ridges offered shelter from winds whipping out of the icy interior of Canada, snow-laden storms surging up the Appalachians, or stealthy nor'easters hanging off the coast of New England and delivering sodden backhanded squalls. The first settlers set their cows and pigs loose on the ridges and planted corn and rye on the more gentle slopes, but they built their homes down along the stream curling out of the Catskills.

In two hundred years, little had changed.

I hunched my shoulders and crossed my arms, striding along the stone sidewalk, wishing I could draw darkness around me like a cape to hide my misery. My satchel bounced against one hip and my purse against the other, coins jingling: change from paying for those panties. The sound fanned the coals of my anger. No matter the consequences—Jo's embarrassment, my grandmother's assumptions—I should turn April in.

I smiled at the thought of her behind bars and, as I passed the hardware store with its dusty displays of hammers, planes, and screwdrivers in the bay windows, I embroidered my fantasy, chopping off her hair, stripping her of beads and bangles, and dumping her into a dowdy denim dress. As I approached the village green, I mentally scrubbed off her makeup, bleached her summer tan, and carved wrinkles into the skin around her mouth and eyes.

A bell jangled and I caught the mingled scents of vanilla, talcum powder, and rubbing alcohol. The drugstore.

"Liz?"

Fingers clutched at my sleeve. I whirled and saw Jo, a white paper bag tucked tight against her green wool coat, her pale blue eyes misted with despair. "Liz." Her nails scratched the weave of my sweater.

I cringed, heard my father's voice saying Jo had enough to bear, and swallowed hard. Touching her hand, I felt the knotted knuckles that forced her to wear mittens instead of gloves, to have her wedding and engagement rings sawed off when the divorce was final.

"Hi, Jo." My voice was as thick as peanut butter from the back of the fridge. "How are you?" Meaning, "Have you heard anything?" Meaning, "Is this just a bad dream?"

Jo shook her head and sighed, a wisp of sound almost lost in the whirring tires and rattling fenders of a passing truck. "I'm sorry about last night. About April."

I imagined a string of Jo's apologies stretching into a future as bleak as a January night. Had anyone ever interrupted her atonements and told her to stop taking blame for what wasn't her fault? Not Reverend Campbell. He would see those *mea culpas* as humbling confessions. Not my grandmother. She apologized for nothing while encouraging penitence from others. Only my father might have broached the subject, but in such an oblique and tentative way that Jo would have been left wondering what the conversation had been about. "Why are you

29

sorry?" I challenged. "You're not responsible for April's behavior."

Jo blinked. "But I—"

"No." With two fingers I touched a shoulder no more substantial than those padded hangers covered in white satin on which my grandmother hung her gowns. "You didn't force April to drink. You didn't make her dance. You didn't—"

You didn't make your son fall in love with her. You didn't make him dump me like his father did you.

I felt a hot sickness in the pit of my stomach. Ben had followed the example set for him. Dumping me had been inevitable, whether I'd slept with him or not. Fate couldn't be changed. Or so I might tell myself.

Jo frowned. "But she's . . . my guest."

I gritted my teeth on that sugarcoating, hating myself for being grateful Jo hadn't said, "She's Ben's fiancée." Fate or not, that word cut like a razor.

"She's old enough to have some manners."

My grandmother's words. Was that my future? Growing into Gertrude Gorman?

Jo nodded but her eyes focused on something far beyond me. "I don't understand." The pharmacy bag crinkled in her fist. "Why couldn't they wait for him?"

"They were under fire." I repeated the official story and touched her shoulder again. "He went back against orders."

That hadn't surprised me. One spring when the Maplekill was running high, rusty red from slashing at its clay banks, rumbling with rocks rolling in the current, Ben ignored Jo's cries and plunged in to rescue what he thought was a cat. He emerged a hundred yards downstream with a gash on his leg, a twisted ankle, and a scrap of brown carpet.

"He told me he'd take care of himself. He promised he'd come home." Another betrayal.

30

She extended a quivering index finger, the nail bitten to the quick, and touched my cheek. I caught the scent of the perfume April had appropriated, swallowed bile, and stood like a statue as Jo pressed a dimple into my cheek, her skin rough and cold. "And I thought you two . . ."

Shame and rage burned my cheeks and her sympathy was like kerosene on the fire. "That's not your fault either." I jerked away, saw sunlight retreating up the slopes of Maplekill Mountain. Another long day nearly done; another long night ahead. For both of us. My eyes prickled with tears. "I have to go."

Jo's finger dropped, trailed along my arm, and curled into a fist. "I wish that—"

I thought again of the lonely night coming and all the others to follow, and then I wrapped my arms around her as I had when I was small, before Ben and I had secrets between us that made me blush beneath his mother's gaze.

Jo gasped and then leaned into the hug; her fine hair tickled my ear and I caught the scent of lemony shampoo. I hoped that if she hugged April the embrace was brief and formal, more duty than devotion. I hoped April sensed that, but suspected she was too self-centered to notice, or care if she did.

Jo snuffled and her arms tightened around my waist. "I have to go," I repeated, twisting from her arms and bolting away. "I have to go."

Except for the ticking of the clock hanging above the stove, the whoosh of the furnace, and the gasping wheeze of Sebastian's breathing, the house was still. But I felt my grandmother's presence and knew she was sleeping in the upstairs room my mother and father had once shared. That room stretched across the rear of the house, larger even than the living room. It had windows on three sides, built-in bookcases, and its own bathroom. My father had

31

put years of love and labor into that space, but abandoned it the day my mother died. Since then he slept on a convertible sofa in the cramped room off the kitchen that had once been his office. He crammed his shoes under the narrow desk, stuffed his socks and underwear into its drawers, and hung his few shirts, jackets, and slacks in the hall coat closet.

For a year after she moved in, my grandmother used the guest room across from mine at the front of the house, but one night at dinner she staked her claim. She began without preamble, without testing our reactions: "I need quiet when these headaches strike, Gene. And I need space to work at home so we don't spend money heating the shop evenings and Sundays." She finished with a nod toward the upper floor.

"Mom's room," I'd gasped. It was just the way she'd left it and at five I found solace in that. I'd often lie with my face in her pillow, breathing in her faint scent—oatmeal soap and roses. Or I'd rock in the chair where she'd read to me and imagine that she was just down the hall, picking out a book or finding my teddy bear.
"But . . ."

My grandmother had speared me with her eyes. "She's gone, Liz. She's not coming back."

A sob broke from my chest. I felt as if my mother had died again. As if my grandmother had killed her. My father's fork fell from his fingers and clinked against the plate. In a moment he folded his napkin, and stroked my hair. When he spoke, his words were cold as winter ground. "She's right." He stood, his face without expression. "She's always right."

My grandmother answered from between gritted teeth. "Building a shrine won't help you build a life."

Harsh words. Practical advice.

I pondered it as I peered through the window above the sink at the lilac hedge along our property line and, beyond it, the upper story of Jo's house. The shade was drawn on the window where Ben had often appeared to put on puppet shows or act out book titles as I washed and dried the dinner dishes. When I completed my chores I called with answers—seldom correct because Ben's tastes ran to science fiction and mine to poetry and classics.

Sebastian grunted and staggered to his feet, rumpling the quilt beside the heat vent. Until last fall he slept at the foot of my bed, but age had clouded his vision and made his muscles limp and stringy. When each stair step drew a whimper, I carried him up to my room, staggering beneath his forty-five pounds. The day he tumbled going down, my father bought me a new quilt and folded this one into a bed beside the refrigerator. Sebastian was comfortable here, but I missed pressing my toes against his warm back, watching him run in his sleep, and trying to imagine where his dreams took him.

"Hey, boy," I murmured, scratching behind his ears. "Did you have a good day?" He licked my wrist, his dry tongue snagging the skin.

I filled a glass with water and poured some into my cupped hand. He lapped at it, then hobbled to the door and raised his muzzle toward the worn leather leash hanging from a hook.

"You want to go for a walk?" On a good day he wobbled only a few feet onto the lawn, relieved himself, and lurched to the house again.

He whined and nudged the end of the leash, making it sway so the clasp clanked against the side of the refrigerator. I clutched at it. The least out-of-the-ordinary sound might wake my grandmother. The end of Sebastian's tail vibrated, and then swung into a full wag when I hooked the leash to his collar. "Did you dream you were young again?"

Careful not to open the screen door so far the hinges squealed, I led him across the low stone porch and down a carpeted ramp my father had built. At the bottom he tottered to a halt and lifted his nose to the wind, eyes closed. Snuffling, he ambled toward the lilac hedge. The year I was ten, Ben and I had cut an archway through the dense branches. The route saved thirty steps for him, thirty-five for me, crucial seconds that we wouldn't have been together if we'd used our front doors and the sidewalk. Next spring I wouldn't clip the new sprouts. Nature would fill the gap.

I pulled back on the leash, but Sebastian lunged, jerking it from my hand and shambling through the notch. Head down and hoping to appear casual should April raise the shade, I followed. When he reached Jo's half-moon-shaped deck, he put a front paw on the lowest step, sniffed, and then backed away, clouded eyes brimming with confusion.

I seized the trailing leash. "Ben's not there. Let's go home."

Sebastian barked once and headed for the rear of Jo's property at a trot. Surprised, I followed through a break in a stone wall that marked the dividing line between her lawn and the remnants of an apple orchard planted by farmers gone for generations. The trees were bent and gnarled, riddled with holes, crusted with rot.

Witch trees I called them when I was young, frightening myself so that I wouldn't eat the bright globes they produced. When I rejected her Waldorf salad, my grandmother told me there were no witches, no spells cast on the fruit. But my father understood and made up a charm to protect me: "Apples, apples, red and sweet, are you safe for me to eat? Cross my heart and say well, well, that's the way to break a spell."

Crossing my heart with my free hand, I chanted the charm as Sebastian and I plunged beneath the trees. The ground was littered with brown apples fumbled loose by the wind. Yellowjackets crawled among them, feasting on the pulp, and I watched where I placed my feet until we reached the bank of the Maplekill.

The stream was low, pooling among mossy rocks. A rough trail ran beside it, beaten down by fishermen seeking trout, kids searching for swimming holes, and hikers bound for the top of Maplekill Mountain.

Sebastian whined and plodded along the rocky path. "Far enough." I tugged at the leash. "You're too old for a hike. And I'm wearing loafers."

Giving no sign that he heard, he trudged on, stumbling over roots and once bumping into a sapling close beside the path. The trail grew steeper and he stopped, panting. "Good boy." I stroked his head. "Let's go home now."

He whined again and staggered on, over tumbles of broken shale the color of rust and through drifts of fallen leaves that riffled like new money. His tongue hung from the corner of his mouth and his chest labored, each breath coming out with a wheezing huff that made me wince. "Come on, Sebastian. Let's go get dinner."

Heedless, he planted his front paws on a slanting slab of bluestone and scrabbled at the edge with his hind feet, snarling as if he could make the rock back down and clear his path. I blotted my eyes on the sleeve of my sweater and gave him a boost, his hip bones sharp against my palms. "Let's go back. Let's get a dog biscuit."

Without a flick of an ear, he churned on, a constant whimper in his throat. Gentle natured and usually obedient, he also had a stubborn streak. Knowing nothing would turn him, I unsnapped the leash and gripped his collar, drawing him along with me.

Maplekill Mountain was little more than a hill with aspirations of greatness and in a few more minutes we reached the top, emerging from a tunnel of birches into a grove of oak, leaves lustrous with sunlight. Trembling, Sebastian wove through wild blueberry bushes toward the

35

rock ledge that overlooked the valley. Ben and I had often sat there, me reading aloud while he chipped away at our initials and the heart that enclosed them.

"No." Wary of the rattlesnakes that often crawled out to sun themselves on the ledges, I stomped on the ground and thrashed at bushes as I hustled to get ahead of Sebastian. "I won't go there."

He tilted his head toward the last of the sun.

"No," I repeated. "It will hurt too much."

He whined and nudged my leg.

I slung the leash about my shoulders, dropped to my knees, and wrapped my arms around his neck, rubbing my chin against an ear still velvety though the rest of his coat had grown coarse and stiff. "Why do you want to go there?"

He pushed against my shoulder, his whine splintering to a baby's yearning cry. My heart chilled and I flung my arms wide. "Go on then. Go."

He broke into a lopsided lope, sun dappling his coat, silvering the white splotches and tinting the brown a cinnamon red. His claws scraped against the jutting rock near the edge.

I held my breath. Did he intend to leap out to meet death?

But he flopped to his stomach, his front paws outstretched like those of the Sphinx, lips drawn back in a grin, breath coming in gulps. Eyes on the valley, I marched to the ledge and solved the problem of that heart by sitting on it.

Just rock. Nothing more.

When a gusting updraft showered us with golden birch leaves, I brushed them from Sebastian's back, fingers stuttering along the knobs of his spine. He grunted, and then pointed his muzzle into the valley as if he wanted to be certain I saw the houses and shops of

36

Maplekill huddled below, clinging to the gray road like doll handkerchiefs pinned to a sagging clothesline.

From up here I couldn't see April or Diana or my grandmother. And from down there, they couldn't see me. I felt as if I'd been jolted from my orbit, sent spinning far from their gravitational pull.

I tilted my face to the sun and let it wash me like warm rain. A shadow passed. A hawk canted its wings and banked in a tight circle, riding a thermal toward a tatter of cloud. "Thank you, Sebastian."

He licked my hand. I watched his head drop to his paws and his chest compress. It didn't fill again.

"No!" I threw myself beside him. "Don't go. Don't leave me."

His tail thumped once against my knee and his muscles went slack. Sobbing, I stared into his eyes until they were as empty as my dreams.

CHAPTER 5

I couldn't bear to leave Sebastian up there alone, even for the time it would take to get Dad, so I knelt, bent my neck, and laid him across my shoulders. Bowed beneath the weight, I almost fell several times as I staggered down the shadowed trail.

Dad was pulling the van into the driveway as I stumbled, panting and slick with sweat, through the gap in the lilac hedge. He cut the lights, killed the engine, and ran to me. "Elizabeth! What happened?"

"Sebastian died on the mountain."

Dad lifted him from my shoulders and cradled him like a baby. "You should have come to get me."

"I didn't want to leave him." I rubbed the back of my neck. "Besides, I managed on my own."

"You always do," he said in a tone shaded with both admiration and exasperation. "Why did you take him up there?"

"He took me." I pressed my fingers against Sebastian's lids, closing his vacant eyes. "He . . ." I wondered if my father would understand the last gift Sebastian had given me, then decided to keep it all my own. "I think he wanted to die on his own terms."

"That's a hope we all have."

There was a tremor in his voice, and when I raised my head I saw his eyes focused beyond me, into the gathering dusk. Was he thinking of my mother? Or was he pondering his own end? With chill horror I realized that he, too, would leave me.

As the years passed and my mother's memory faded, my idea of death became linked to the demise of fictional characters like those in *Wuthering Heights*, *A Tale of Two Cities*, or *Romeo and Juliet*. I had often contemplated my own departure—taking a bullet as I crusaded for civil rights, or perishing in a spectacular fall from Mount Everest—imbuing my death with noble significance. Since Ben's betrayal, those visions were bleaker, more in the vein of jumping from a bridge or standing in front of a train.

It hadn't occurred to me that my father had considered the shape of his own passage to oblivion. But I couldn't ask. Our unspoken pact made that forbidden territory.

He blinked, then carried Sebastian to the porch. "He was a fine dog. A good friend." His fingers trailed along Sebastian's jutting spine. "He's nothing but skin and bone."

And willpower. Studying the ribs arching above his concave belly, I was amazed he'd been able to walk beyond the orchard, more amazed that he hadn't felt weightless across my shoulders.

Dad's fingers combed bits of leaf from Sebastian's tail. "We don't have to do it right away, Elizabeth. You should think about where you want to . . . bury him."

Bury! That brutal word punched me to my knees. How could I put Sebastian in a hole in the ground and cover him with dirt?

I felt Dad's tentative hand on my shoulder. "We could take him back to the mountain if you want."

I shook my head. Too many memories of Ben. Visiting Sebastian's grave would take me deep into a tangled thicket of withered hopes and dreams.

39

"How about in that clump of birches at the bottom of the yard by the creek?"

No, not there, either. I had peeled strips of chalky bark from those trees and written notes to Ben. He'd once braided their twigs to make me a crown on May Day. I curled my fingers around clumps of grass and tore them from the ground. There wasn't a single place in Maplekill that was mine alone, where Ben wouldn't haunt me.

"Maybe around the far side of the house near the laurel bushes?"

I drew in a shuddering breath and touched Dad's fingers. That side of the house offered three acres of privacy: a wide stretch of lawn ran up against a line of maples backed by a battalion of white pine and hemlock. Only the windows in the seldom-used guest room and his office-bedroom looked out onto this yard where, each March, on the anniversary of the day my mother died, Dad went out alone with a shovel to transplant a wild mountain laurel bush from the woods.

He'd built a bench—barely large enough for two—and set it among the shrubs. Even on bitter winter nights he often sat there with his right arm stretched out as if to draw my mother close against him.

As a child, warned that the pale blossoms and waxy leaves were poisonous, I wondered why he chose laurel and not roses or forsythia. Later, when I studied Greek mythology and learned about Daphne's flight from Apollo, I thought I knew. But I never asked.

"I think Sebastian would like to be there."

Dad squeezed my shoulder. "Why don't you get his quilt?"

And his toys. And a can of dog food, and the biscuits he sucked at until they were soft enough to chew with the nubs of worn-down teeth. Supplies for the afterlife. Whatever and wherever that might be. "Okay."

Feet dragging, I crossed the porch and lingered at the door, conscious of the soft thud of the van door, and the crunch of Dad's feet on the gravel path to the toolshed. I wanted to avoid Gertrude Gorman, but expected she'd be standing by the sink, peeling, chopping, or mashing some defenseless vegetable. Although she'd never been mean to Sebastian, she never petted him, either. For her, his passing meant only less sweeping, vacuuming, and dusting.

I knew she wouldn't mention that—at least not for a while—but that's what she'd be thinking and it would color anything she might say or do. I told myself that my grandmother's attitudes had been shaped by loss and there was a lesson there for me, but this was a time for mourning, not lessons.

Trembling with suppressed rage, I opened the door. The kitchen was empty, but I heard footsteps on the floor above. Like a thief, I gathered what I came for, bundled up the quilt, and escaped. As I set it all on the edge of the porch, I saw Dad pacing off a spot by the light of a guttering kerosene lantern. "Measure twice, cut once," the motto he'd lived by as a carpenter, spilled over to life in general. I guessed his deliberate caution, like my grandmother's chilly practicality, had been molded by the irrevocable.

Dad gripped the handle, set his foot at the top of the blade, and drove it through autumn-browned grass, cutting loose squares of sod. I thought of Thoreau equating grass to our lives, saying that we die down to a root that sprouts green blades into eternity.

Something else to ponder later.

The shovel scraped against pebbles and stones that choked the thin soil. Glaciers, wind, and water carved the Catskills from an ancient plateau, leaving tumbles of boulders, slides of broken shale, and loaf-sized rocks that farmers lugged to the edges of their fields and wedged

41

together to build walls. This patch of lawn had once been a vegetable garden, but the best that could ever be said of the soil was that it drained well. Each winter the relentless frost thrust up rocks and each spring we plucked buckets of them from newly turned earth. Summers we weeded and watered and gathered a scanty harvest of corn, tomatoes, beans, onions, and carrots. Ben once joked that Dad had to put a pipe wrench on those carrots and screw them out of the stony ground.

I bit back a moan. Even this spot held a memory of Ben.

Turning from the grave, I spread the quilt on the grass and carried Sebastian to it. I tucked him up for his last rest with half a box of biscuits, a faded red rubber ball, a gnawed squeaky frog, and a frayed bit of knotted rope he liked to tug on.

Had those sad and tired toys once been new? Had I once been happy?

The punch and scrape of the shovel ceased and I shivered, thinking of Sebastian's dark bed, of sodden autumn days and vicious winter winds. I breathed in dew-heavy air and held it while we knelt beside the grave and settled him into the raw earth. "Thank you," I whispered. "I'll never forget. I'll always love you."

"He had a sweet soul," my father said. "He'll find another good home."

"I know."

I believed that. But I couldn't watch as Dad filled the grave.

"We'll get a stone from the old quarry tomorrow," he said. "And I'll carve his name on it."

The porch light came on, hinges creaked, and my grandmother called out, "Dinner's ready." Another creak and the screen door shut with a snap. Gertrude Gorman wasn't one to wait for a response to a message delivered. She'd assume we'd come right in because we always had.

Resentment burned my throat like vinegar. "I'm not hungry."

"Neither am I." My father sighed. "Especially not for beans and franks and canned peaches." The quick-and-easy meal my grandmother always made after a headache laid her low. No matter that I offered to cook or my father suggested we go out to eat, she martyred us all to swollen slices of hot dog and slimy beans in a sea of ketchup. It was her job to cook, ours to eat.

"Let's go up to the Lamplighter," my father said, his voice brightening, "and have a cocktail."

I blinked. A cocktail? I'd never thought of my father as the cocktail type, couldn't imagine him ordering one inside the restaurant with green shutters where Maplekill residents went to mark special occasions. "Really?"

He brushed a hank of brown hair back from his forehead. "If you want." He shrugged and fitted the last square of sod. "Or we could go to Donnie's, shoot a little pool, and have a burger and a beer."

"Beer," I repeated, marveling at this new dimension to my father.

Or was it new? I'd been so tangled up with Ben and school and lately my own misery that I hadn't wondered where or how he passed his evenings. Had he been building a life while mine was slipping away? "Pool?"

"I know you play." He kept his head down. "You're pretty good at it, too."

I felt my cheeks flame and was glad of the deepening night. How could he know that? Ben taught me, but I'd never mentioned it to anyone, not even Diana. Pool halls, according to my grandmother, were smoke-filled and sinful places populated by hustlers and loose women. The tobacco haze at Donnie's was almost part of the décor, but I never noticed much sin besides an occasional bet, and the only hustler was Donnie herself, a woman with gray-blond hair and a voice like crushed gravel. Sensing my grasp of the geometry of the angles and the physics of the collision of balls, she made fifty dollars betting the regulars I would clean Ben's clock the second time we played.

She gave me half and, when I turned it over to Ben as a consolation prize, threw back her head and roared with laughter. "Hang on to her, boy. They're not making 'em like that anymore." Then she patted her hair and, in a voice that was almost a purr, told me to say hello to my father.

My breath caught in my throat. Dad and Donnie? Laughing, touching, kissing? My heart thudded in my throat and I gasped for breath.

Dad didn't seem to notice. He picked up the shovel and tucked a few straggling blades of grass into the crack between squares of sod. "I met your mother in a poolroom, you know."

I swallowed air as thick as pudding. Now he was rewriting history. The story I heard as a child contained a soda fountain, a malfunctioning milkshake machine, and a man so smitten that he didn't mind lumps of ice cream and a crust of malt powder. Was he changing that now to make it seem natural, even inevitable, that he and Donnie would . . . ?

"They had a sandwich and beer place in the back and she was behind the counter. She had on a pale green dress with puffy sleeves and a white collar."

"A beer place," I gasped. "You lied."

"Only to keep that from your grandmother," he confessed. "But there *was* a machine malfunction. I ordered a draft beer and got a glass full of foam." He gazed into the darkness. "And didn't mind a bit." His voice cracked. "There will never be anyone like her. I'm glad for every moment we had."

Was that the point? Was I supposed to be glad for every moment I had with Ben? Was I supposed to forget

44

that my moments had been tarnished, cheapened? Should I be happy my father was going in search of more moments to be glad about?

The hinges creaked once more. "Dinner is on the table," my grandmother called, her voice shrill on the cooling air. "Are you two out there?"

"We're around the side." Dad thumped the shovel against the ground. "Your call," he whispered.

I felt dizzy, drained, rootless. I couldn't face Gertrude Gorman or that ghastly meal, but I couldn't bear to see my father with Donnie, either.

"Let's go somewhere. But not to Donnie's, okay? I . . . I used to go there with Ben and . . ."

"I understand," he said, bending toward the lantern. "I know how it feels to be ambushed by the past." He turned down the wick. The flame flickered and died like my mother had, bringing darkness down on the fifteen laurels, the bench built for two.

"But I just happen to know of another pool hall." Dad leaned the shovel against the edge of the porch, picked up the lantern, slung an arm across my shoulders, and marched us to the driveway. "Put our dinners in the refrigerator," he called to the silhouette in the doorway. "We'll eat later."

The silhouette stiffened. I did the same. "Suit yourselves," came a voice laden with disapproval.

"We will," he whispered.

The door slapped shut. The porch light went out. As we groped our way to Dad's old truck, I relaxed and felt a tingle of delight. We'd conspired together against Gertrude Gorman.

"Maybe you should get a puppy," he said as we rolled past the sign that proclaimed Maplekill's population.

No!

Sebastian had set me free up on Maplekill Mountain, and I wouldn't dilute his sacrifice. "I don't want a puppy."

45

"Don't worry about what your grandmother will say." In the dim light from the dashboard I saw his hands tighten on the wheel and guessed he was imagining the campaign against dog dirt and odors, accidents and gnawed shoes. "I'll have a talk with her."

"It's okay." I touched his elbow, felt the moist heat of his skin. "There will never be another dog like Sebastian. And besides, you'd be stuck taking care of a puppy. I'm going away to college next year."

I surprised myself, both with that statement and the fact that I spoke without hesitation.

Something else to think about later.

If he was startled by my pledge to leave, he didn't show it. "I wouldn't mind having another dog around. And I know how much you need—"

"I'll think about it," I lied, not wanting to hear his assessment of my need. I squirmed to face the dark hulk of the mountain. Tears blurred my vision and night flowed around us like dark water. I wished I could lift my feet and drift away on it.

Hours later, after Dad tiptoed out to the stone wall and left our dinners for the raccoons, I crawled into bed with a handful of tissues.

When tears didn't come, I took stock of my situation— always a surefire way to prime the pump of pity. I had no mother, my father was dating, my grandmother didn't love me, my boyfriend had abandoned me and might be dead, his fiancée was a thief, my girlfriend was no friend at all, and my dog was dead. I repeated the list, added that I was too heavy and too awkward, and then repeated it all again.

Not a single tear emerged.

Perhaps I'd cried them all.

Was that possible?

46

I wadded the tissues and tossed them to the floor, thinking about that dark current of night I'd longed to drift away on, and knowing that I'd drifted too long. It was time to swim. Dad had Donnie. Why shouldn't I be a journalist?

And why should I wait a year?

Sliding from bed, I studied the calendar on my desk. If I got busy filling out forms and writing letters, I might be able to transfer for the next term.

I gazed out the window that looked toward the street and saw star-washed birch branches nearly bare of leaves. If I waited too long, I might settle back into my rut smack in the middle of the path of least resistance.

The birches shivered in the wind and a flutter of leaves pelted the window.

No more ruts.

I'd go next week. Find a place to live. Get a job. Pay my own tuition. It would be the ultimate test of independence.

A floorboard creaked. Every muscle tightened and I held my breath, as if my grandmother could hear my plans. "A girl your age on the road alone? Like some floozy? Absolutely not!" She'd demand that my father impound my car.

My teeth clenched. I couldn't put him in the middle of that fight, so I wouldn't tell him.

I'd leave on Monday morning, setting off at 6 a.m. as I always did to make my early class with time to spare. Then I'd keep going, past Oneonta, on to Rochester, Buffalo, Cleveland, Toledo, Chicago . . .

I shivered. A little voice in my head told me if I got scared I could always turn back.

I told the voice to shut up.

CHAPTER 6

On Friday, instead of taking notes in geography class, I made a list of what I needed to do in order to make my escape under Gertrude Gorman's watchful eyes. Before I left Oneonta I stopped at a branch of my bank.

The teller, a washed-out redhead with lines bracketing her lips, noted the withdrawal from my savings account and snapped fifteen twenty-dollar bills onto the marble counter. "Can I help you with anything else?"

That question seemed to refer to more than a banking transaction—it seemed to indicate I needed help with my entire plan.

"Is there a problem?" the teller asked. "You did say three hundred, didn't you?"

I nodded. It seemed like such a paltry amount. I opened the thin green bank book, thumbed pages smelling of ink and stamped with dates going back to my fifty-cent deposits in first grade, and checked the new balance: $453.48. Was that enough to launch a dream? Yesterday I would have said "no," and put this scheme on the shelf. But today . . . "I think I'll close the account."

The teller raised eyebrows in need of plucking.

My mouth went dry. Would she notify the manager? Would she tell my father? His name was on the account beneath mine—had been since I opened it. "Can I do that?"

"It's your money." She glanced toward the manager's desk and gave me a faltering smile. "But we hate to lose your business. If you're unhappy with our service . . ."

"Of course not," I assured her, wondering if she'd be called on the carpet for letting my skimpy account get away. "I, uh, I'm probably buying a car tomorrow," I fabricated. "And trading mine and I'm not sure exactly how much I'll need and the bank won't be open."

She narrowed her eyes and wet her lips as if she was about to call me on my pathetic lie. I gripped the edge of the counter. *It's my money. So what if I'm not telling the truth. It's still mine.*

She wet her lips again. "If you left a few dollars, you wouldn't have to close out the account and then open another if you have money to put back after you make the deal." Her eyes cut toward the manager again—a puffy man in a brown suit shiny at the knees and elbows and a wrinkled tie that failed to hide buttons straining in their holes.

I riffled the bank book pages. A few dollars wouldn't make much difference. "How much would I have to leave?"

Her shoulders lifted and she scanned the final notation. "How about twenty-three dollars and the change?"

That gave me $730. I nodded.

I stuffed the whole wad into my purse, but on the way home I pulled over and slid $500 inside a rip in the seam on top of the sun visor. At the gas station with a flying red horse sailing above the pumps, I filled up the tank, and then stopped at a market for supplies: nuts, apples, cheese crackers, six bottles of cola, and a flashlight with spare batteries. That evening I wrote a letter to the registrar and asked for any refund to be sent to Dad.

Packing a suitcase and lugging it to the car would be like putting a notice on a billboard, but under the guise of collecting for a clothing drive I persuaded Gertrude Gorman to give me two frayed flannel shirts, a sweater with a few tiny moth nibbles, a pair of mittens, a plaid coat I outgrew when I was twelve, and two dresses she held up against me twice before admitting they no longer fit. I stashed my clothes and toiletries at the bottom of three cartons, then laid the castoffs on top. I couldn't take much, but Thoreau—who believed we become burdened by our possessions—hadn't either.

That left the hard part—getting blankets and a pillow out of the house. Except for that abortive hour with Ben, I'd never been inside a motel, and didn't think I had the guts to spend a night in one alone. I heard stories—mostly from my grandmother—about women raped and murdered in motels. Safer to sleep in my car.

As it turned out, my grandmother gave me the break I needed when she came down to the shop at four on Saturday. At the sound of her footsteps—more stomping than stepping—I turned from a copy of *Seventeen* left behind by a shopper who had dog-eared an article about complexion care and watched as she circled her work table and peered beneath it. Lips crimped, she plunged her hands into drawers packed with lingerie delivered just that morning and sorted by size and manufacturer.

My father glanced up from the inventory book. "What are you hunting for?" His voice had a sharper edge than I'd ever heard. "No point in tearing everything apart if I've seen it."

Wondering about the limits of his patience, I spun back to the counter—there was peril for bystanders when my grandmother was in one of her moods.

"I had another card of pearl buttons. It was right here Thursday morning."

I heard the slap of flesh on wood and knew she'd smacked the long wooden cutting table. My father and I never touched anything on that table, no matter how

50

much that something might appear to be trash. A snip of thread might be needed to finish a hem; a shred of fabric might become a bow or the loop to hold a button; a slice of cardboard might measure the width of a sash. "A white card with eight pearl buttons?"

"I haven't seen it," Dad said, the edge on his voice blunted, "but I've been busy with new inventory. Six boxes yesterday and five more this morning."

"You didn't set those boxes on my table, did you?"

"Of course not. I never do."

"Are you sure?"

My fingers clenched around the magazine, my nails digging into the slick cover. *Stand up to her, Dad.*

"I'm certain," he said, his voice quiet but all edge. "I'm well aware of the rules about your table. So is Elizabeth."

You tell her, Dad.

Silence. I imagined my grandmother's face, swollen and bright with angry blood. Waiting for her explosion was always the worst part. My fingers tightened until the knuckles ached. And then my father spoke once more, his voice as soothing as warm honeyed lemonade.

"You had another headache yesterday, remember? Sometimes when you get two in a row you forget—"

"I never forget a thing." Another slap. "That card was here Thursday."

"And now it's not," Dad said, calm as if he'd commented on a change in the weather. "And all the talk in the world won't make it appear again, so why don't I go buy the buttons you need?"

Silence, then, "You'll get the wrong kind." As sulky as a child denied a treat.

And my father responded just as a parent long on patience might. "Then perhaps you'd better ride along."

"I don't have time. I have a dress to finish." Petulant.

51

"And if you work too hard and get another headache this afternoon you could have a stroke. When you're paralyzed, you'll have nothing *but* time."

I gripped the magazine even tighter, my pulse pounding in my fingertips. A stroke! Paralyzed! Was my father just speculating, or was Gertrude Gorman truly sick?

I wanted to stride into that room and demand the truth. But I also wanted to remain in the dark. Shielded by ignorance, I could drive away. Burdened by truth I might feel obligated to stay.

"It's a beautiful day," my father said as if he were talking to someone waiting in line behind him at the fruit stand down the road. "The leaves are turning on the mountaintops. We won't get many more days like this before the snow flies."

I drummed my fingers on the case, hoping she'd agree. I needed just five minutes to load the car.

Silence, profound. Then, "No dilly-dallying along the way," my grandmother warned.

"I'll only slow down on the curves. The van's out back."

"I'll need to comb my hair and get my purse." Peevish.

"We'll stop by the house on the way."

I heard the back door creak open and Dad raised his voice. "We're going to run an errand, Elizabeth." As if that had been his plan for the afternoon all along. "We'll be back in an hour or so. Unless your grandmother makes me stop for ice cream."

I turned to see her by his side, one hand in the crook of his arm. Although her posture was as stiff as ever and her chin was as high, she seemed diminished, almost fragile. "Do you think the cold might make my head feel better?"

"Couldn't hurt." Dad winked at me and ushered her out.

For a long time after they drove off I marveled at how he dealt with her anger, confronting and deflecting, like a boxer bobbing and weaving around the ring until he exhausted his opponent. When had he developed such skill? Why hadn't I noticed?

Right then, I loved him more than ever—maybe because I was leaving him, and he was leaving me. I wanted to lock the shop and race after him, sit beside him at the picnic table outside the ice cream stand, offer him the best bite, the curlicue bite, from the top of my chocolate-dipped cone, and tell him how much he meant to me.

Then I thought of Gertrude Gorman's reaction. How could I explain that I'd broken the rules and closed the shop an hour early because of love?

I laughed out loud. To her, love and money were mutually exclusive. Money was generated by business, and business was conducted with conditions that weren't tossed aside for frivolous reasons. Love, real love, didn't have conditions.

An image of that miserable motel room flashed into my mind.

No, real love *shouldn't* have conditions. But there was a condition set in that room and I hadn't met it, hadn't even known about it.

And if I had . . . ?

I flung the magazine to the floor. How many times would I relive that shameful night? How far would I have to go, how long would I have to live, to dilute the pain of that memory?

I retrieved the magazine and set it beside the basket of panties April had pilfered from. My love had always been conditional too. The condition had been that Ben wouldn't give himself to another.

Was unconditional love real? Or was it romantic myth? I glanced at the copy of *Walden* jutting from my purse but doubted Thoreau had the answers. From what I'd read so far, nothing indicated he'd fallen in love— conditional or otherwise.

Sunday evening a chill fog slunk through the valley and toward morning I heard the gush of rain in the downspout at the corner of the house. I was careful to do everything as usual: shower, dry my hair, and dress in brown slacks, a pale blue broadcloth shirt, and a tan sweater. Collecting my books, I went down to the kitchen to measure coffee, fill the percolator, and set it on the stove. Avoiding even a glance at the space where Sebastian once slept, I drank a small glass of orange juice and dropped a slice of whole wheat bread into the toaster.

I'd left my note of explanation in my room. It was brief and factual: "Went to Chicago. I'll call you when I get settled." It would be hours before they found the note and by then I'd be two hundred miles away, maybe more.

The thought of all that distance squeezed my heart. "You can't be homesick until you've left home," I lectured myself as I poured half a cup of coffee and filled it to the brim with milk—the way I always drank it. I'd stop at the college and use a familiar ladies room, because after that …Well, that was uncharted and frightening territory.

"Don't worry until you have to." But in case I ended up squatting in the brush beside a road, I took a roll of toilet paper from the pantry and stuffed it in the brown leather purse my father said reminded him of a horse's feed bag.

The rain had diminished to a sputtering drizzle when I stepped out onto the porch in a green hooded raincoat with my books cradled against my chest. Buggy gleamed in the graying light like a beacon. I dashed across the sodden lawn, unlocked the door, opened it on squealing hinges, and slid inside.

"About time you got here," a voice whispered.

54

CHAPTER 7

I recoiled, slamming my elbow into the door and thumping my knee against the bottom of the steering wheel. "Oww!" My feet tangled with the clutch and brake, holding me hostage. Books tumbled to the floor.

"I've been waiting fifteen minutes," the voice complained. "Let's get going."

"April?" My pulse hammered in my ears as I peered at the murky shadow. I locked the car last night. I did every night. "How did you get in?"

"With this." Something thin and hard poked my shoulder. "I found it in Ben's desk."

Snooping bitch! Did she have to appropriate everything? I thrust my hand out, palm up. "Give it to me."

"No." I heard the jangle of her bracelet and guessed she'd snatched the key away. If the interior light worked, I could make a grab for it and twist it from her fingers, but dark as it was, I made no attempt. I didn't want to touch some private part of April.

"If you lose yours, you'll be glad," she informed me. "Besides, it will make it easier when I drive."

"I told you before, I'm not loaning you my car."

"I know." Sulky. Snotty. Like a kid hogging a playground swing. April and Gertrude Gorman had a lot in common. "I'm coming with you."

Like hell you are.

"To school?" I managed a shrill, one-note laugh. "Why? You hate school."

"That's not where you're going." Her voice grew smug. A cat claw-combing canary feathers from its whiskers.

"I am so."

"You're not. I saw you load those boxes and stuff in your car."

Spying on me from Ben's window, stealing his key, stealing those damned panties, probably wearing them right now. I gripped the wheel. "I'm going to school. Get out of my car."

April laughed, a vicious, nasty sound, more of a snarl. "You're not and I won't."

I wanted to rip out a double handful of her glorious hair. Instead, seething, I untangled my feet and swung them to the ground. "Then I'm going into the house," I said over my shoulder, "to call the town constable." Paul Schoonmaker. And wouldn't he love this. A catfight he'd call it when he checked in for coffee at the drugstore. By the end of the day everyone in Maplekill would be clucking over the latest installment in the story of poor Liz and the girl Ben dumped her for.

"Looks like your grandmother's awake."

Canting my head, I spotted soft white light glowing behind the sheer curtains in the back bedroom.

Damn.

In a few moments Gertrude Gorman would be downstairs in her red plaid bathrobe and crocheted slippers, making oatmeal or cream of wheat. She and my father would eat their hot cereal with butter and maple syrup or brown sugar and raisins. Maybe she'd say it would stick to their ribs and my father would chuckle and make a comment about sticky ribs.

I felt a heaviness on my heart. I missed him already.

"She'll wonder why you haven't left yet," April

prompted. "In another few minutes she'll come out to see what's wrong."

I chewed on my lower lip. The rock and the hard place.

With a sigh, I chose the least familiar of my tormentors, swiveled into the car, gathered my purse and books from the floor, and stuffed them into the back. I pulled the balky door exactly as hard as I would on any ordinary morning, snapped the lap belt Dad had installed, and pumped the gas pedal. The engine chugged to life and I smacked the gearshift, wishing it was April's face.

She had the good sense not to say another word as the car clattered through Maplekill and climbed steadily up the valley. The tires churned through sodden leaves brought down by last night's rain and my mind churned through ideas, mostly worthless, like appealing to the better nature April didn't possess.

The eastern sky turned a muzzy gray, shot with veins of pink, and I lingered for a few delicious minutes over a vision of stopping where the highway crested through Wildcat Notch and yanking her from her seat—easy to do because she hadn't snapped her belt. I'd toss her into the deep ravine, savoring her shrieks, the sound of splintering branches, and the shattering rumble of loose rocks I'd kick down after her. Jo would report her missing, and the men of the valley would turn out to search, but it might be weeks, even years, before a hunter came across her remains.

I sighed. For reasons I'd never understand, Ben loved April. And much as I wished I didn't, I loved Ben. For his sake, I couldn't deliberately harm her.

But that didn't rule out death by accident.

I smiled at a faint glimmer of gold in the east. April was self-centered and she drank. Things could happen. I consoled myself with visions of her dancing across a highway in the path of a speeding truck, or falling into a river when she tipped her head back to sip from her flask.

"So where are you going?" Casual, wheedling. I could grow to hate that voice. Yet my heart felt lighter and I smiled at a shaft of sunlight gilding the treetops. She had no idea where I was bound. Perhaps she'd believe the clothing-drive explanation. Perhaps I could ditch her when we reached the college, or drop her at the bus station or an intersection where she could hitch a ride to . . .

Peering into the rearview mirror, I surveyed the back seat and spotted the lumpy army-green duffel bag she arrived with sprawled atop my boxes. She was set on more than a day trip.

Her bracelets clinked. "Where are you going?"

As if I would share my dream with her. I threw the question back like a trout too small for the legal limit. "Where are *you* going?"

"South. West." I caught her shrug from the corner of my eye. "This place is so boring."

"Does Jo know?"

"No. Does your grandmother?"

"That I'm going to school? Yeah, I only go five days a week." I nodded toward the back seat. "That stuff's for a clothing drive."

"And the food is for a food drive."

Not even a question. She must have been watching when I packed the car while my father and grandmother were gone. "That's right. A food drive." Diana could have pulled off that lie without a quaver, but my voice had all the authority of the pan of mush my grandmother would be dishing up about now.

"What about the soap and shampoo? And the toothpaste? You can't give half-used stuff to a food drive, can you?"

Fury lit my brain. She'd gone through the boxes.

I forced a breath and then another. "Of course not.

58

That's going in my gym locker." She didn't know that I wasn't taking PE and had no locker. Or did she? How much of my life had she pried into?

April chewed at the cuticle on her thumb for a few moments and my galloping heart slowed. I was just about to congratulate myself when she flashed that feline smile again. "And the blankets and pillow? Are you studying reproduction in biology?"

My jaw tightened at the insinuation that my morals were no better than hers. Maybe I *could* kill her. "No. They're donations for a family that, uh, lost everything in a fire." A lie so lame it needed a brace and crutches. Why had my father stressed honesty when deceit would have been more practical and enabled me to compete against those who bent the truth like licorice whips?

"Everything?" April marveled. "Wow. That must have been quite a fire."

Her voice was too bright, too filled with manufactured awe, but I stuck to my crippled lie. "Huge. Burned the house to the foundation. They were lucky to get out alive."

She twined a strand of hair through her fingers. "Strange that there wasn't anything in the paper."

Wild ideas careened off each other like pool balls on the break, so loud I thought she couldn't help but hear the collisions. "It, uh, just happened yesterday. I got a call from . . . uh, from Reverend Campbell." Religion. That might shut her up. April didn't seem to know much about that.

I watched from the corner of my eye as she twined another strand of hair. Just when I thought I was safe she threw back her head and laughed. "If I couldn't lie any better than you, I'd still be living at home, too."

Clamping my teeth, I held back a defense of my life. What was the point? The car hit a chuckhole that made April clutch at the door handle, her bracelets jingling. In the silence that followed, I turned her statement around

59

and looked at it from another angle—perhaps she was saying that because she was such a good liar she wasn't welcome at home.

I realized that I didn't know where she was from, didn't even know her last name. Odd. I couldn't remember anyone mentioning it. Not even Jo. Everyone in Maplekill had a family name, a bit of history you carried with you, a link to the past that, whether you liked it or not, whether you took it or not, established a place for you in the future.

Was the girl who intended to get married in her birthday suit going by one name just to be different? Would she take Ben's last name when they married? Had they talked about that? My curious nature formed questions but I held them inside. I wouldn't want her to think I had any more interest in her than in a parasitic plant.

April twisted her engagement ring. "I'm from Colorado," she volunteered.

Naturally. She had to be from one of the places I most wanted to see. As we rolled into the outskirts of Oneonta I downshifted and broke my vow. "Where in Colorado?"

"Denver."

Crossing that off my mental list of places to see, I pulled over at a diner that advertised free coffee with every meal. The gravel parking lot was packed with trucks of all sizes, unwashed hard-mileage vehicles of college students, and two gleaming county patrol cars. I nuzzled Buggy up to the grill of a dump truck loaded with fill dirt. "You can hitch a ride here."

April folded her arms and pressed herself against the back of her seat. "No. I'm going with you."

"You're not." I turned off the engine, pulled the key from the slot, clicked my seatbelt open, and swung my door wide. I'd haul her out if I had to. Height and weight would be on my side.

"This says I am." She flashed a foil-wrapped square. A

condom. "I found a bunch of these in Ben's desk. If you make me get out I'll go back to Maplekill and tell everyone that you and Ben were getting it on."

I stared at the rubber, a relative of the one Ben had stripped off in that motel room just a few blocks from here. How many had he bought?

Cold horror squeezed my gut. I'd never allowed myself to think beyond a single sexual incident, a boundary we'd cross, a hurdle we'd get over. But Ben had prepared to cross that boundary again and again. I tasted his disappointment, hot and metallic, at the back of my mouth.

"No one will believe you didn't." April crackled the foil between her fingers. "Your reputation will be ruined."

I gritted my teeth. Madge Eakins' reputation had been ruined for years and she seemed to get on just fine. Besides, I was leaving. I wouldn't hear what people said about me. "I don't care," I lied.

"Your father will be so disappointed," April said with phony concern.

Would he? The father I'd discovered Friday night—the man who played pool, drank beer, and did who-knows-what with Donnie—wouldn't have been surprised that Ben and I went to a motel room. He might even have felt it would be good for both of us.

"And your grandmother . . ." April smiled. "Well, you know how she'll react."

My hands gripped the wheel, the key biting into my palm. Gertrude Gorman believed reputation was paramount. My supposed sin would tarnish her reputation beyond polishing and prove that I didn't respect myself or my family. I could almost feel her icy silence, hear doors slam, and pans bang on the stove. In my absence, my father would be forced to endure that.

"It's your call."

Another rock and another hard place. Dad deserved

better. "Okay."

"Good." April slipped the condom into a purse made from a pair of cut-offs with a strap that had once been part of the American flag. "Where are *we* going?"

"Chicago," I muttered.

"Chicago." She fluffed her hair. "I've never been there."

I felt as if I'd betrayed not only my dream but the city itself, Carl Sandburg's city, the crossroads of America. My fingers, icy and stiff, poked the ignition key at its slot; metal chattered against metal.

A tall man in a gray uniform carrying a grease-spotted brown paper sack and a bottle of cola emerged from the diner and climbed into the dump truck. It started with a roar and a cloud of burning oil. Gears clashing, the driver backed away in an arc, pointed the truck south, then idled for a moment, unwrapped something from the sack, and took a huge bite.

Saliva pooled beneath my tongue and I thought of all the foods that gave me comfort: macaroni and cheese made with lots of extra-sharp cheddar, cold milk flavored with sugar and vanilla, crusty bread dripping with garlic butter, chocolate with nuts, black olives, potato pancakes with sour cream. If there was ever a time I needed to feed my misery, this was it. I pulled the key back, tucked it into my pocket, and reached for my purse. "I'm going to get a scrambled egg sandwich and go to the ladies room."

"Well I'm not getting out." April folded her arms below her breasts, pushing them up into the scoop of that damn peasant blouse. "I don't trust you not to drive off."

I rolled my eyes. "April, you've made it clear you'll ruin my life if I do. And you've made it clear I can't lie worth a damn so I can't put anything over on you." The hinges groaned in protest as I leaned on the door. "Besides, I don't trust you, either. What's to stop you from using your key and driving off?"

April's eyes flickered and gleamed. I swung my feet to the gravel lot, shrugged out of my raincoat and tossed it in the back. "Except for the fact that I'll tell the police."

I nodded at the patrol cars, hitched my purse over my shoulder, and headed for the diner, turning my back on April, turning my thoughts to that scrambled egg sandwich and whether I'd have it on rye or whole wheat, with butter or mayonnaise, with bacon or ham. Definitely with cheese and lots of onions. And no gum after I ate. If I had to share the car with April, I *wanted* bad breath.

I placed my order, paid, used the restroom, and then perched on the edge of a red vinyl-covered stool at the end of the counter, hunching as if that could deflect curious glances, telling myself not to be so self-conscious. I concentrated on the scents of brewing coffee, frying onions, and browning potatoes, the sizzle of eggs hitting the grill, the scrape of silverware against thick white plates, and the buzz of conversations that didn't include me. I thought of John Donne's poem and knew that right now I *was* an island. A lonely island far out beyond the horizon.

I swung toward the rear of the diner, noted for the tenth time the pyramid of doughnuts beneath a clear glass hood, and rotated toward the door. April came through in a toss of luxurious hair and a sway of hips. Heads turned. The buzz of conversation stuttered.

April gave me that satisfied smile, settled on the next stool, and waggled a finger at a waitress who could have been the bank teller's twin. "I'll have a scrambled egg sandwich to go." She glanced at the chalkboard over the pass-through to the kitchen. "With Swiss cheese. And bacon. On whole wheat." She tipped her chin at me. "My friend will pay."

Friend? Fury spiked my brain but, blackmailed, I dug for my wallet. I was an island.

"I'll be back in a minute." April spun off the stool.

63

"I'll be right here." An island.

"I know you will," she said in a confident simper. Heads turned in her wake as she sashayed to the ladies room.

To hell with this!

I stood, left two dollars on the counter so the waitress wouldn't be stiffed, and walked out, legs jittering.

Maybe I wasn't a good liar yet, but I was learning fast. I was learning to shed a lifetime of guilt, too. Yes, Dad would suffer for what I hadn't done with those condoms, but he had Donnie to ease his pain. My supposed shame and Gertrude Gorman's sanctimonious fury might finally set him free. Perhaps he'd walk out of that damn bridal shop and go back to doing what he loved.

CHAPTER 8

"Hey," a voice called from behind me. I started, realized it wasn't April, and peered over my shoulder.

The waitress stood at the door, holding a paper sack. "You forgot your sandwich," she called. "And what about your friend?"

"She's not my friend," I shot back. "But give her that sandwich, too." I ripped the key from my pocket, jerked the door wide, and fell into the car.

I didn't take time to snap my seatbelt before turning the key. The starter ground for endless seconds and then caught; the engine chugged to life and I popped the clutch and gunned the motor—something I'd done only once to show Ben I could. The rear wheels spit plumes of gravel that rattled off the fenders and Buggy bounced across the lot and fishtailed into the street. I glanced back; the waitress had gone inside and there was no sign of April. Navigating through town, I chanted: "North, north, north. Find the Thruway and turn west, west, west."

My hammering heart slowed and in a few moments my breaths no longer overlapped. Trembling gave way to intermittent shivers, waves of nausea, a ringing in my ears, and the sour smell of anxiety. And then I was out of town.

I inhaled the scents of cows, mown grass, and crisped leaves, flexed my shoulders, loosened my grip on the wheel, and snapped my seatbelt. To paraphrase Thoreau, I had moved with confidence toward my dreams. But now I had to deal with guilt and fears of inadequacy. So perhaps I wasn't really moving with confidence, just moving.

Would I meet with unexpected success as he projected? Or would I sputter to a stop?

"No!"

I pressed my foot against the gas pedal. The engine coughed and clattered and Buggy lurched, but then the speedometer inched up to fifty, the legal limit. I crested a winding hill and peered into the rearview mirror at the road raveling behind me like a gray wool scarf knitted beneath my wheels.

The ground leveled and the speedometer popped to fifty-five. I feathered the brake, pulling Buggy back, but then let it go. Why not? Diana, who'd dated a cop, swore she always drove a few miles over the limit. Cops, she claimed, were after "real" speeders and people who were drunk and dangerous.

I hesitated, then considered that my cautious adherence to rules hadn't gotten me very far or very fast. I stomped on the gas.

Fence posts flashed by like the tiny movies Ben and I used to make by drawing a series of pictures on the edges of notebook pages, each picture slightly different and offset from the previous one by a quarter of an inch. When we fanned back the pages with our thumbs and let them flip, we saw a bouncing ball, a stick figure shooting an arrow, a dog chasing a cat, a couple running toward each other. Unsophisticated amusement from a simpler time. If only—

A siren wailed. I tapped the brake and stared aghast as the speedometer needle fell from sixty-two. Lights flashed in the rearview mirror. Sick with dread, I eased to the shoulder, wheels crunching across broken glass, bits of cardboard, and windrows of weeds. I hoped the patrol car would shoot past to a problem not involving me, but it pulled in twenty feet back, sunlight flaring off its windshield.

I killed the engine and fumbled in my purse for my wallet and license remembering Diana again. "Flirt with the cop if you get stopped. Joke that your car is powered by a hamster running on a wheel. Then bat your eyelashes and smile and make your voice deep and whispery."

Easy for her to say. Impossible for me to do. I wiggled my license from a plastic sleeve in my wallet, put my hands on top of the wheel, and squinted into the glare off the side mirror.

The door of the cruiser opened and a tall man stood silhouetted in a dazzle of reflected sunlight. He flicked one hand toward the passenger side and then strode toward me with a loose-limbed gait, halting a few feet behind my window. I twisted my neck and gazed up into dark sunglasses. The morning sun bounced off the lenses, splintering into my eyes and making them water.

"Sorry I was speeding," I croaked as I held out my license. "It got away from me on the downhill."

"We'll get to that in a minute," he grunted, gesturing to a shorter silhouette behind him. "Is this the woman who stole your duffel bag?"

"That's her." April's voice, proud and contented. "That's my stuff, right there in the back seat on top of those boxes."

My fists clenched. *No!*

Why hadn't I noticed? My head buzzed with rage. Why did she always win and why did I always lose? I opened my mouth to tell the cop the whole sordid story, then clamped my lips. Why would a cop April had convinced to chase me down believe a word I said?

The cop leaned to peer in the window, his jaw tight. I caught the strong scent of coffee on his breath and choked back a sneeze. He straightened and glanced over his shoulder at April. "That green duffel bag?"

"Yes. The one with the beads and feathers on it," she purred. "I can tell you what's inside if you want to make sure it's mine."

"It's hers," I said in a voice as cool as I could manage. "But I didn't steal it. I forgot she left it there when she got out to hitch another ride."

The lie sounded plausible to me, but I wasn't a fabrication expert like April. "You're not going to cite me for that, too? For picking up a hitchhiker?"

The cop worked his jaw, sunlight fracturing on his glasses. "She says you intentionally drove off with her bag while she was in the restroom."

"I drove off," I admitted, my palms slick with sweat, "because she told me she was headed south. I'm going to Chicago. To get a job and go to college. Like I said, I thought she had her duffel bag and I didn't check the back seat before I left."

Whose word would he take, that of the dowdy girl headed for college in a battered car or that of the flashy hitchhiker with beads and feathers on her duffel bag?

The cop tilted his head to study April. "Is that true?"

"You don't seriously believe that bull?" she snapped, her voice as harsh as bleach. I heard a scuff and a series of pings and guessed she'd kicked gravel against the hubcap.

Bad move, April!

I almost smiled, chewed at my lower lip instead, and didn't glance at the mirror to treat myself to the show.

"Besides, I wasn't hitchhiking. I know that's wrong." Her caustic tone grew syrupy. "Liz is a friend of a friend. She agreed to give me a ride."

I snorted. If you twisted the definitions of "friend" and "agreed" like a rubber band, then that statement was accurate.

The cop sighed and hitched at his belt. "How are we going to resolve this spat, ladies? Can you work it out, or

68

A PLACE OF FORGETTING

do we need to go to court?"

"There's no need for that," April jumped in. "This misunderstanding is all my fault. I was playing the radio so loud I guess she didn't hear me say that if I went with her to Chicago I could find a bus or a train going south."

The cop rubbed his jaw. I glanced in the mirror and saw April's reflection move closer to his; she tipped her head back and, although I couldn't see, I was certain she fluttered her lashes. "I won't press charges against her for stealing my stuff if she gives me a ride to Chicago."

No!

Hundreds of miles with April would be pure torture. But the alternative might be far worse.

The cop tugged at his lower lip, then bent to peer in the window. "How about it?"

Another impossible choice. I shrugged.

"I'll pay half of her speeding ticket," April offered, her voice as sultry as an August night. "Although it's hard to believe this little car could have been going more than a few miles over the limit. The engine's not much bigger than my purse."

Words from Diana's script.

The cop grunted and tapped Buggy's roof. "Watch your speedometer," he told me. "Especially downhill." He straightened and pointed at April. "Don't play the radio so loud you distract the driver."

"I won't. I learned my lesson," she tittered. "And thank you so much for the ride. I've never gone that fast before. It was fun."

Shaking his head, the cop walked back to his car. I heard April rustle through the weeds along the shoulder and then the door opened and she settled in beside me and held out a paper sack. "I brought our sandwiches," she simpered.

"I'm not hungry." I stared into the rearview mirror, watching the cop execute a U-turn.

"Well I am." She tore open the sack, releasing the intoxicating scent of bacon and onions. Saliva pooled beneath my tongue. "Yum." She licked her lips. "Maybe I'll eat both of them." Folding back the waxed paper wrapping, she revealed toasted wheat bread with a yellow and white fringe of fried egg and congealing cheese.

Damn it!

I seized the sack and liberated the sandwich I'd paid for with far more than cash. The bread was rubbery, the cheese had the texture of tar, and the eggs needed salt and pepper, but I wolfed it down. I ate from spite, from stinginess, and from self-reproach. If Ben was alive he might be hungry. If Ben was alive, he might be far more miserable than I was.

And if he returned . . . ?

I gazed at April sucking grease from her fingers. If Ben returned and married her he might find himself in another kind of jungle—a tangle of lies and deceptions where all his skill in remembering landmarks, reading a compass, and building shelters wouldn't help. Ben was naïve. Maybe more naïve than I was. If that was possible.

Back in the spring, when we read articles about anti-war protests in New York and other cities, he said the protesters were misguided. When I said I agreed with them, he shut me down by quoting JFK's credo. I felt small and selfish and gave up the argument.

Ben went to Vietnam intending to do something for his country. But was his country doing anything for him now? Were they searching? Or had he been written off as just another casualty of war?

I gagged down the last cold lump of sandwich, wadded the waxed paper into the sack, fished out a napkin to wipe my hands, and started the car. "Put on your seatbelt."

April opened her mouth, but then complied and, for many miles, said nothing. When she finished her sandwich, she squirmed sideways in the seat and gazed at

70

farms, fields, hills, and valleys, then kicked off her sneakers and put her feet up on the dash. She'd painted her toenails different colors—red and lilac and silver. Mine were pale pink, the polish chipped.

Once she reached for the radio knob, but when I frowned she snatched her hand back as if she'd been burned. A few miles after we chugged onto the Thruway, she cleared her throat. "I'm sorry about your dog."

I gripped the wheel tighter, my grief for Sebastian violated along with everything else. "Yeah," I said, because not responding might make her say it again. Did she mean it? Had she ever had a dog? I vowed never to ask.

Miles rolled away. She huffed out a sigh, and then another. "You might at least thank me for talking him out of the speeding ticket."

"Yeah," I said. That response had worked before.

"So thank me."

"Not in this lifetime."

"But you were going over sixty and—"

"—and I would have paid the ticket." I smacked the wheel with both hands. "Listen, April, I'm stuck with you until Chicago. I know that. So let's get it over with and get on with our lives."

"Okay," she pouted. "But that doesn't sound like much fun."

Fun? Did she think we might find a drugstore and shoplift nail polish, or stop at a department store and try on clothes in the same dressing room? I snorted out a laugh. "You can have all the 'fun' you want after you get out in Chicago."

She sighed and crossed her arms. "If that's what you want."

"It's exactly what I want."

She rocked for a few moments and then poked her chin at the radio. "Could we at least have some music?"

I shrugged. "If you can find some." I seldom listened

71

around home because the mountains made it difficult to pick up stations that played the latest hits; their signals faded in and out and were often laced with static. Local stations came through fine, but the penalty for a clear signal was lazy music from another generation, church talk, or local gossip and editorializing.

April spun the knobs and found Percy Sledge singing "When A Man Loves A Woman." I hummed along for a moment, and then my heart seemed to freeze up. Was this how Ben loved April? Was he so blinded that he'd do anything for her? I wanted to shout at April to turn it off, but suffered instead. I'd had practice at that and I suspected I'd have a lot more before my life was over.

April swayed and snapped her fingers while the Outsiders sang "Time Won't Let Me," and not long afterward, following a few sips from her flask, she fell asleep.

In the early afternoon we stopped for gas and food without speaking and without incident, and when the sun went down we reached Ohio and another truck stop. "I'll be glad to drive," April said when the tank was full. "You look really tired."

I was. I'd gone beyond tired and into the valley of extreme exhaustion—both physical and emotional. Lights of on-coming cars shimmered across the windshield and my glasses and my eyes burned from squinting. Fingers in a death grip on the wheel had ached since we crossed into Pennsylvania, and a muscle in the side of my neck twitched and spasmed, stabbing like a knitting needle every time I turned my head. But I wouldn't admit any of that. I didn't want to relinquish the little control I had.

"I've been sleeping most of the day. And there are lots of signs so I can't take a wrong turn." April took the final bite of a chocolate bar, tossed the wrapper in a barrel beside the gas pump, and sipped at a container of coffee she'd laced with cream and sugar. I cursed her for, in addition to everything else, being one of those people who never had to watch their weight. "If I drive we'll be there by morning. Maybe sooner."

Sipping my coffee, I knew it couldn't touch the weariness that had leached deep into my bones. When I bought the car over Gertrude Gorman's strenuous objections, I promised Dad that I'd recognize my limitations and be cautious, especially at night. If April didn't drive, we'd have to stop so I could sleep. Did she have money for a motel room, or would I be stuck paying for that?

"The sooner we get to Chicago, the sooner I get out."

Even that didn't deliver the jolt of energy it would have a few hours earlier. "What about your flask?"

"I won't touch it," she promised, raising her right hand. "I'll put it in the trunk if you want."

"Okay," I sighed. "I guess."

To her credit, April dispensed with the condescending smile I expected. She simply nodded, set her coffee on the roof, brushed potato chip crumbs from the passenger seat with the edge of her hand, and collected the wrappers she'd tossed to the floor. I folded myself into the passenger seat and buckled my belt, certain that she'd bend the rules of the road like she did the truth and I'd have to take the wheel within minutes to avoid a head-on collision.

Alert for the least sign of carelessness, I watched April secure the flask in the trunk and then walk around Buggy, checking the tires and wiping a smudge off the windshield with the heel of her hand. She adjusted the seat and mirrors, snapped her seatbelt, slipped the pilfered key into the ignition, started the engine, checked her blind spot, signaled, and pulled onto the highway.

As she drove, keeping to the limit and passing with care, my tense muscles relaxed. But my brain still seethed with annoyance. I wanted her to screw up, but she could have gotten an A plus in any Drivers' Ed course. Why did she have to be better than I was at everything?

April tweedled the radio dial through a rash of static and landed on a deep voice delivering the weather report: clear and sunny tomorrow in Cleveland. She turned the volume down when that gave way to a commercial for acne cream and I thrashed in my seat thinking of all the pimples I'd fought since puberty and betting April's skin had been blemish-free from birth.

Eventually, despite my intentions, the thrum of tires, the engine's clatter, and the whoosh of air through the window that didn't quite reach the top of the frame lulled me into a series of fretful dreams. Ben and I were children, rolling strips of pie dough into snakes and sprinkling them with cinnamon sugar. We were in his car, a behemoth he sold to a friend named Tommy when he went into the Corps, sipping soda from the same straw at the drive-in.

I came awake, saw headlight beams carving the dark and April's hands firmly on the wheel at ten and two. In a moment, I plummeted into another dream. Ben was driving Buggy, rattling along beside a creek, searching for a good place to go tubing. I was beside him, wearing a T-shirt, cut-offs, and flip-flops. Sun spangled the stream as it narrowed and threaded itself through a wall of undergrowth. I sucked in sweltering air and the rank odors of rotting vegetation, smoke, and fear. Helicopter rotors thumped the air and I heard a cry for help that could have been my own. "I'm coming!" Ben shouted.

His face was streaked with dirt and blood. His mouth was set in a grim line. I clawed at his arm, my nails scratching against fabric stretched tight and sliding off.

The sky flamed, burned to a barren white, and Ben was gone.

I opened my eyes. I was in Buggy, but the driver's seat was empty.

74

I swung my leg around the gearshift and smashed the brake before I realized the car wasn't moving. Above my labored breathing and the echo of Ben's shout I heard the shuffle of feet, the scrape of metal on metal, and a soft guzzle and ching.

I blinked and the dream gave way to gas pumps and a picture of a green dinosaur. April stood beside Buggy, stretching her arms above her head and twisting her neck. I peered through the windshield at a wide parking lot lit by a row of street lamps swarmed by moths, a metal-sided diner as shiny as a new dime, and a flickering neon sign that read "Louisville's Legendary Hot Dogs."

Louisville? I closed my eyes, remembering all the maps I'd ever pored over. Louisville was . . . in Kentucky!

CHAPTER 9

"How the hell did we get *here*?"

Anger I'd been holding in check for days ignited and spread like a forest fire. I vaulted from Buggy. "You did this on purpose!"

"I had to. I *have* to go south." Palms thrust outward, April backed away, colliding with a gas pump. "I couldn't tell you because I knew you'd be mad."

Making it sound like this was my fault. "I'm not mad. I'm furious." I raised fists clenched so tight my forearms trembled. "I'm leaving you here!"

April jerked her hands in front of her face and cowered between the pump and a trash barrel. A sandy-haired attendant, his oversized blue uniform shirt wrinkled and splotched with oil, gaped. "Earl," the embroidered patch on his pocket read. He didn't look old enough for the name or big enough to stop me from punching April's perfect nose.

"But I don't have money for a bus," April mewled. "And I *have* to get there. I have to."

From the corner of my eye I saw Earl nod in agreement, already under her spell. Well, he could have her.

"And I've got to get to Chicago." I dropped my fists and flexed my fingers. Earl might not be able to hold me back, but he was perfectly capable of calling the police. "And that's where I'm going as soon as Earl is finished filling the tank of *my* car."

Earl started and turned his attention to the nozzle. "But it's not too far out of your way," April whined. "And we're already in Kentucky."

Earl nodded again as if confirming that geographical fact.

"I don't care if it's just another mile!"

"I guess Ben was right." April kicked at an oil can spout lying beside the pump. "You don't like to compromise."

That wasn't true! He couldn't have said that! My brain boiled.

Earl clicked the trigger on the nozzle, hung it up, and replaced the gas cap, then checked the amount registered on the pump, tucked his hands into the pockets of his tight jeans, and raised his eyebrows.

And even if Ben had said that, why should I compromise with her?

April worried the hem of her peasant blouse and chewed her lower lip. "We can be at Hog Run Ridge tonight if we keep going."

"You be careful in a place like that," Earl said. "Them wild old razorback hogs can be mean."

Razorback. A word I'd never heard, yet a word that reverberated in my mind. I flashed on a black and broken ridge thrust up from a green valley. The image clicked away, replaced by a field of head-high grass, elephant grass.

Elephant grass! How would I know that?

I heard the whump of helicopter rotors again and a cloud of dense smoke seemed to sweep over me, burning my eyes and throat. Someone shouted and an explosion shook the ground. I batted at the smoke, trying to see, to find my way to—

"Want me to check the oil, lady?"

In an instant, the smoke swirled away and there was

Earl, rocking from heels to toes, a filthy bit of once-white rag in his hand. With a sharp pop the diner sign flickered out, the word "Home" fading last. Earl fluttered the rag.

"Yes," I told him. I glared at April until she lifted her eyes. "Where's Hog Run Ridge?

"Arkansas."

My mind dredged up what I knew about the state. It was west of the Mississippi, north of Louisiana, and south of Missouri; Little Rock was the capital and nine years ago the governor tried to stop integration.

"Eisenhower will have to do something about this," Dad had said. Each evening after dinner he turned on the radio and told me: "Listen. This is history happening."

"Hog Run Ridge is up in the mountains," April added.

Behind me I heard Earl open the engine compartment. "Why do you *have* to get there?"

She sighed and used that smug tone. "You wouldn't understand."

My hands curled into fists once again and her gaze darted toward them. I took that as fear until her lips twitched into a tiny smile and I realized that she was baiting me. Well, this time I wouldn't bite. "Okay." I shrugged. "If I can't understand, then I'm going to Chicago. You can stay here with Earl. I'm sure he'll help you find someone to take you to Arkansas."

Grinning like a jack-o'-lantern, Earl slammed the rear hatch. "Oil looks good." He stuffed the rag into his back pocket and did his heel-toe dance again, his eyes on April who stared at me, lips in an O, a deepening furrow between her brows.

"Thanks." I checked the numbers on the pump, bent into Buggy and dug three ones from my purse. "Keep the change," I said as I slapped them into his grimy hand. "Buy April a soda."

I reached into the back seat and wrestled her duffel bag to the concrete apron, then fished her flask from the trunk and laid it on top. "Here you go. Good luck hitching a ride." Feeling light and calm and certain, I levered the driver's seat back so I could fit behind the wheel.

"There's a man there who sees the future," April blurted.

The future.

Like a stone tossed into a still pond, that word sent ripples through my brain. Did I want to know how my life would unfold? Flipping the key in my fingers, I decided I wasn't sure. Knowing the future seemed more frightening than living toward it day by day—and that was scary enough. But I *did* want to know about Ben's future—if he still had one.

That thought made me feel sick all over.

The antidote was contempt. "A fortune-teller?" I scoffed. A man with vague visions like the women with enormous hoop earrings at carnivals—caricatures of themselves who talked in general ways about dark strangers, love, and found money.

April crossed to Buggy and gripped the top of the door. "No, Liz, he's not a fortune-teller. He's a psychic. And he's always right."

Not even Gertrude Gorman was always right—although she'd surely argue that point until your ears sheared off your head in desperation. I pushed the key into the slot.

"I think I've heard of him," Earl said, "from some people who filled up last week—or was it two weeks ago." He scratched at his chin, leaving a smear of grease. "What the heck was his name?"

"Ezekiel," April said.

"That's right." Earl snapped his fingers. "Ezekiel. Like from the Bible."

I recalled Ben once claiming that Ezekiel's wheel of fire had been a UFO. I'd laughed, told him he'd been reading too much science fiction, and dared him to tell

79

Reverend Campbell. He hadn't taken me up on it, but Ezekiel had come up again a few months later in a sermon about a valley of dry bones, and on the walk home Dad had sung about connecting toe bones and foot bones. Gertrude Gorman had pronounced the song frivolous, not appropriate for a Sunday.

"He's got a farm on top of a mountain," Earl said. "People come and work on it and he drinks some kind of a magic potion he brews up and then sometimes he gets these visions."

"Sometimes?" I snorted. April and her shiny little flask would be right at home with a sham psychic who drank magic potions. But I couldn't see her working in trade for what she learned. Rumor had it she hadn't lifted a finger at Jo's house.

"Please, Liz," April pleaded. "I have to know if . . ."

I expected she'd say Ben's name next, but instead she smiled her self-approving smile and finished the sentence with, ". . . I'll make a record. If I'll be famous."

I shook my head, disgusted with her self-absorption even as I wondered if that very self-confidence had attracted Ben.

"You're a singer?" Earl marveled. "Like rock and roll?"

"Not yet." April released the door and tossed her hair. "But people tell me I have the look."

Earl licked his lips in agreement. "You been singing with any bands?"

"Not yet. But I want to."

And I want to walk on the moon. I turned the key. These two deserved each other. The engine sputtered and died.

Earl inched toward April with an eager smile. "Ezekiel's never been wrong."

I pumped the gas pedal and twisted the key again. The engine turned over with a groan of apology. I slammed the door and slapped the gearshift into reverse. "Have fun in

Arkansas."

"Wait!" April flung herself at the car, clawed at the side mirror. "What about Ben?"

I forced a casual shrug. "What about him?"

April's brow furrowed. "Don't you want to know what happened to him?"

I gave her another shrug. "Don't you?"

She gnawed at her perfect lower lip and twisted her ring; the diamond glittered in the harsh light mounted above the gas pumps. "Of course. We're engaged." She leveled a forefinger at my face. "But you've known him forever. He said you were his best friend. How can you just drive away?"

My busy brain reminded me that I'd decided Ezekiel was a fraud. But my anguished heart felt as cold and heavy as the sod on Sebastian's grave. It seemed to thud to a halt even while my brain bustled on, reminding me that I had a plan and a schedule. My heart beat again, asking, "What would Ben do if you were the one who was lost?" My brain countered: "What would he do *before* he met April, or *after* he gave her that ring?" My heart, clinging to the past, insisted that Ben was a true friend; he would hunt high and low—even see a phony prophet in Arkansas—to find out what had become of me. My brain argued that a true friend doesn't—

"Enough!" I yelped, yanking at my hair. "Get in the car. We'll find Ezekiel. On condition that you get out of my life after we do and that you give me back the car key right now."

She fingered her pocket and pouted. "But what if you want me to drive?"

"I won't." I stretched out my hand. "Give me the key."

She held out for a second, but then gave it up. I tucked it in the bottom of my purse. "You won't regret going to see Ezekiel," she said as she heaved her duffel bag into the back.

81

"I already do," I muttered.

"You'll need maps." Earl scuttled into the service station and emerged with folded offerings. "These are the really good ones. Don't tell anyone I didn't make you pay. Here's Tennessee and Arkansas." He thrust those toward April and handed two more to me. "And you'll want Missouri and Illinois so you can get to Chicago after you see Ezekiel."

I thanked him and pushed them under the seat, reminding myself that it had been only a day since I'd set out for that city, and soon—maybe even the next morning—I'd point Buggy in that direction again.

The day passed in a blur of road signs and interchanges, rolling hills and rivers, colas and chips. The air was warm and moist. I stripped off my sweater and rolled up my sleeves; we drove with the windows down, the wind rushing in our ears, and the radio turned up. My hair grew slick with grease, road dust packed into every pore, and my lips cracked. At rest stops my legs wobbled and I drank water like a camel at an oasis and wondered why I was doing this—because I wanted to close the book, because I wanted to prove I could compromise, or because I was crazy?

We dipped south through Memphis because Earl said we'd make better time that way, crossed the Mississippi, and sped through what I later learned was the Arkansas Delta: level miles stretching to the horizon, towns huddled beside railroad tracks under an enormous sky, shacks bleached by the sun.

When we stopped for gas, April dug through her duffel bag for a map drawn on a paper napkin in red ink. She directed me west and then north into low rounded mountains that reminded me of home. As the afternoon grew tired, rain began to fall, a drizzle that muddied the dusty windshield, and then thick drops that splattered like bugs against the glass. In another hour, we turned west

82

again at a town called Stony Ledge.

There I spotted a flagpole and beside it a miniscule brick post office and a phone booth. That note I left for Dad promised I'd call when I got settled. I imagined he had computed distance and average driving speed and was waiting in the living room beside the phone with Gertrude Gorman circling nearby listing the many errors of my ways lest he omit one in the lecture she'd primed him to deliver. It hurt that he might be worried, but it hurt more to think about her barbed comments. A phone call would reassure him, but a written message would spare me a lecture.

"I've got to send a postcard," I told April as I pulled into a narrow graveled parking lot. Darting through the rain, I yanked open a door painted the color of morning glories and found myself facing a polished wood counter and a gray-haired woman with a brown dress, a lace collar, and a welcoming smile.

"You caught me just two seconds before I closed up." She cocked her head and looked past my shoulder. "New York, huh? You must be going to Hog Run Ridge." Her voice seemed to trail off at the end of every sentence, making it sound wistful, regretful.

"Yes. I need a stamped postcard."

She opened a drawer and slid it across to me. "Expect you've been out of touch for a few days."

I nodded, fumbling pennies from my wallet, coins clattering on the counter, one rolling off the far side and falling to the floor behind her. "Sorry."

"Don't think a thing of it." She retrieved the maverick penny and corralled it and the others in the drawer. "I expect that in a few weeks I won't see but half a dozen cars a day going up that road and I'll know every one."

I nodded again, using the pen chained to a staple at the edge of the counter to scrawl Dad's name and address on the front and a single line on the back: "Took a detour

83

south but will be in Chicago soon."

"I'll put that in the sack," the woman said. "It'll go out first thing in the morning."

"Thanks."

"You be careful in that little toy car. It's blowing up a toad floater."

I smiled as I dashed back to Buggy. I'd have to remember that expression and share it with Dad—after he got over being angry.

The road beyond Stony Ledge wound along a stream, climbing higher and higher on the shoulders of a long ridge marked by the jutting ledges I assumed gave the community its name. A faint sloping from the center toward ditches on either side indicated that the road had been graded once, but hard rains had left it looking like the old washboard Gertrude Gorman kept to grind out grass stains.

April sucked at her flask and held the map close to her face. "It's not far now. We count six mailboxes—there's one—and turn at the seventh."

Trees closed in around us after we passed the sixth mailbox and the road became a pair of ruts filled with rushing water and rounded stones that shifted beneath the wheels so Buggy lurched and faltered like a drunk. Twice we scraped bottom so hard I thought something would tear loose and we'd be stranded. I longed to give up and turn back but now the road was so narrow and the ditches so deep and abrupt that turning would be risky.

I thought about the card and the days it would take it to arrive. An idea formed in my mind. If April called Jo, she'd tell Dad I was safe. I took a shot at an off-hand tone. "Are you going to call Jo soon?"

April turned to me, her face a blank. "No. Why?"

Because you're her future daughter-in-law. "She might be worried."

April shrugged. "I guess."

84

I waited, counting seconds to thirty, forty, fifty. "What if she's heard something about Ben? Don't you want to know?"

"Ezekiel will tell me. There!" She pointed through the gloom at a listing mailbox heaped around with sodden roses and zinnias. It had once been painted a deep sky blue and decorated with a golden moon and silver stars, but the paint was chipped and faded, the moon had waned to a sliver, and the stars were dim. Beside it, a constricted lane threaded between an enormous pair of willows, their trunks twisted around with rusty barbed wire, their thin, dangling branches like tattered curtains in a long-abandoned theater.

Maybe Ezekiel would tell me something about my future that I could pass along to Dad—something to make up for all his worrying.

I turned the wheel and Buggy clawed its way over the center hump. We rumbled across a series of sagging pipes and April grabbed at the door handle. "What's that?"

"Cattle guard."

"Huh?"

"Cars can go over it, but horses and cows won't cross it."

"Why not?"

I shrugged, remembering how my father had explained it. "I guess it's sort of an optical illusion. What you see is influenced by what you already know. Animals learn that when the ground drops away it's dangerous. They can't see much under the pipes and they think that's a big hole they'll fall into."

April craned her neck and looked back through the pelting rain. "But it's not big at all. All *I* see is a little ditch under those pipes."

"That's because you're not a cow."

April fluffed hair that had managed to retain bounce and body in spite of dust, wind, and rain. "If I was, I'd be

85

smart enough to figure out there isn't a big hole there."

And maybe you'd get your feet caught between the pipes and break your legs. And the other cows would laugh. I opened my mouth to make a snide comment, but just then the road seemed to stand itself on end and charge at the hillside, so all I said was, "Maybe."

Buggy slewed from side to side as the wheels alternately bit on slabs of stone and slid in deep pockets of oily mud. Branches raked the roof, water cascaded at us, and I felt as if I was driving up Niagara Falls. "How far is it to the farm?"

April peered at her napkin map. "It doesn't say. But it can't be—"

Something cracked like a gunshot. April screamed. A branch slammed into the windshield, blinding us. I stomped brake and clutch pedals to the floor and the engine strangled itself.

April put a hand over her heart. "That scared the shit out of me." She took a long pull at her flask and peered at the leaves plastered to the glass. "What do we do now?"

"Get out and pull it off."

"In the rain? We'll be soaked."

No doubt about it, she was the smartest cow in the herd. I folded my hands in my lap and used the sarcastic tone I'd perfected for Gertrude Gorman but never had the nerve to employ. "Oh. Right. I guess we better wait for the rain to stop."

April peered at the leaves again, then twisted her neck in an attempt to look up. "But it might rain all night."

"Yeah, it might." I stretched my hand into a bag of barbecue potato chips and stuffed a few into my mouth, relishing the burst of salty sweet flavoring. "I'm glad I brought my pillow and blanket."

April scowled. "What about me?"

I gave her and innocent look. "You didn't bring a pillow?"

"No, I didn't bring— I thought— Damn it!" She unfastened her seatbelt, flung the door wide, and stomped into a torrent of muddy water. The leaves against the windshield fluttered loose for a second and then fell back. "It's heavy," she yelled. "Come help."

I rolled my window down a few inches. "Break it up," I advised and helped myself to another handful of chips. I felt a sense of pride; I was figuring out how to handle April like Dad had handled Gertrude Gorman.

Above the thrumming of the rain I heard a series of scrapes and cracks. April cursed and the leaves fluttered again. Annoyed by her helplessness and her crack about my inability to compromise, I reached for the door latch just as the branch slithered from the hood. April dove into the passenger seat, her hair pasted against her cheeks and neck, her nipples outlined through the thin fabric of that peasant blouse. "Why didn't you help?"

I answered with a question of my own. "Why should we both get wet?"

She frowned, perhaps realizing that comebacks like, "because we're friends" wouldn't fly. Then she pouted and wrung out her hair.

I grinned and turned the key. The engine glugged as if it was chugging a beer and I heard a grinding screech. The wiper blades, bent by the impact of the branch, arced across the glass like fingernails on a chalkboard, trailing shreds of rubber rubber.

"Crud." I hit the knob. They skreeked to a halt.

"What do we do now?" April asked.

Just like a broken record.

"I'll have to drive without them." Waiting in the middle of this hill for the rain to stop, no matter what I'd told April, wasn't safe. I moved the seat forward until my nose was over the wheel and peered through sheets of rain.

Foot by foot Buggy crawled up the ridge. My legs

ached, my eyes burned, and the road seemed endless. Then, with a final surge, we emerged onto a sloping meadow glazed by a beam of sunlight knifing between roiling clouds.

"There are the cows." April pointed to two bony creatures huddled beneath a clump of trees. "And there's the farmhouse."

It, too, huddled close against a dripping grove and its tin roof was as swaybacked as the cows' spines. Sun played across its windows like flame and made the dark rocks piled around the porch glow. The rain pattered to a stop and I nosed Buggy in behind a pickup truck so ancient and abused it looked like a long-buried casket on wheels.

"We're here!" April ran her fingers through her hair. "I can't wait to see Ezekiel." She bounced from Buggy and skipped up three stone steps to a broad porch surrounded by a bowed railing that might once have been painted green but was now a moldy gray that matched the door. I peeled myself from the seat, muscles twitching.

Before April could knock, the door opened and a woman as thin as an axe handle and as dark as midnight stepped through. She folded long arms and glared at April. "Ezekiel's gone."

"Oh." April retreated a few steps, touched the railing, and snatched her hand away as if she'd burned it. "Well, we'll wait for him to come back."

The woman shrugged. "Suit yourself. But you'll be waiting 'til eternity. He's three days dead."

CHAPTER 10

"Dead?" April staggered, clutched the railing.

The woman nodded toward the setting sun. "Buried yesterday."

"I'm sorry to hear that." In a flash, I understood what the woman at the post office had been hinting at and wished I'd asked just one simple question. I thought of the hard miles I'd put on Buggy since Louisville, hard miles on a detour I regretted before I took it.

All for nothing. All for longing to see behind a closed door.

"But he can't be dead." April shook her head, damp hair lashing her cheeks. "We came all the way from New York. I need to know my future."

"Sure you do." The woman rolled her eyes. "And I bet if he'd known you was on the way, his heart woulda beat another few days."

I smothered a grin while April chewed her lip. "Well, I didn't *really* know I was coming until last night. And the guy who drew the map said Ezekiel didn't have a telephone. But I thought he could see the future so—"

"You thought he'd wait on you?" The woman threw her hands in the air and rolled her eyes again. "The idea of it! Never once did any of the pestilence of pilgrims on this ridge say he musta knowed they were coming."

April preened her hair, so involved with herself she

couldn't detect sarcasm and disdain. I shuffled my feet, thinking that I was just the opposite—I saw put-downs where there were none.

"Gift of gab," the woman said. "That's the only gift Ezekiel had. He could no more see the future than I can fly to the moon."

April gawked at her. "But everyone said he—"

The woman snorted. "Even a blind hog finds an acorn now and then."

"But everyone—"

"No one wants to admit they was made a sucker, do they?"

So Ezekiel was a fraud, like Dorothy's wizard. And April wouldn't get even a consolation prize, a medal, or a diploma. Pouting, she slumped to the steps. Unlike Dorothy's companions, she didn't already possess what she'd come looking for.

I gazed at my loafers. And I had no ruby slippers to click together three times. Not that I would do that. There was nothing for me back in Maplekill.

"I suppose y'all be needing a place for the night." The woman hitched a thumb over her shoulder. "Drive on through the orchard and squeeze in amongst the others. And tell them to get that cow milked before long or she'll start bawling and be at it all night."

April glanced toward the pasture. "But I don't know how to—"

The woman melded herself into the dark rectangle of doorway and I heard a latch click.

Leaping to her feet, April confronted the weathered door. "I want to know my future! If Ezekiel can't tell me, who can?"

"Let's go," I said.

"I don't know how to milk a cow," April yelled. "And why should I if he's dead and can't tell me anything? Why should I?"

Disgusted, I stepped to the edge of the porch and spoke up, wanting to make it clear to the woman inside that I was above this. "You're tired, April. Let's go find a place to sleep."

"She's lying." April stumbled to Buggy and threw herself inside. "Everybody said he saw stuff. Everybody said that! He wasn't a fake."

It was pointless to prolong this, so I started Buggy and we followed winding tracks gouged into tall, wet grass through an orchard of apple trees as gnarled as the ones in Jo's yard. A chicken coop, its door hanging on one hinge, hunkered among the trees, but no chickens scurried before us. Beyond the orchard a barn slumped like a tattered clown waiting to enter the ring at a third-rate circus. Its roof was a patchwork of shingles, tar paper, flattened coffee cans, and even license plates; at one corner chunks of weathered siding had fallen away to studs locked in a losing battle with gravity. Still, if the rain returned, even this sorry shelter was better than none.

I wedged Buggy in among a pack of aging vans and beat-up cars painted with daisies, swirls of bright color, peace signs, and the word "love" in fat, stylized letters. As we climbed out, I heard a guitar and voices struggling through "Mr. Tambourine Man." Two dogs—one a German shepherd and the other looking like a cross between a Dalmatian and a beagle—bounded up and sniffed our legs. I bent to scratch their ears, felt a pang of disloyalty to Sebastian, and thrust my hands in my pockets.

"Welcome, strangers." A man emerged from the double doors, lank blond hair brushing his shoulders, a string of bright beads around his neck, his tanned chest bare and streaked with dirt like the feet protruding from frayed jeans. "Have you come a fair piece?"

"From New York," I volunteered.

"For nothing," April pouted.

The man smiled, teeth glistening. "No journey is for nothing, little sister. Each path changes us even as we walk it."

I blinked. Thoreau might have said something like that.

April shrugged it off. "I'm hungry," she whined.

As far as I could tell, our journey hadn't changed her one bit.

"Then you shall be nourished. Come." He led us into the barn where, in the grainy light through the broken walls, I saw perhaps twenty people sporting a profusion of colors like a garden in late summer, their long hair laced with flowers, ribbons, and feathers. They clustered on moldering bales of hay arranged to avoid holes in the roof that dripped water through smoky air onto a packed earth floor littered with empty bottles, wadded sacks, and crushed cans. "Wenches, bring food for these travelers," the man called.

The song sputtered to a halt. "Who died and left you in charge?" A stocky woman in a flowing green velvet dress rose and planted her hands on her hips. "We're not wenches." Her voice gritted like sandpaper. I didn't think we'd like each other much, but I agreed with her sentiment. "Besides, we ate all the chicken and corn and Delia stripped the garden early this morning. All we have left is oatmeal and the apples we liberated from the orchard. We're saving most of those for breakfast."

"But we still have plenty of wine," the man said with a grin.

"Wine?" April ignored the woman's frown and favored the man with a flutter of lashes and a simpering smile. "Wine sounds delicious." She offered her left hand, fingers cupped downward, as if she expected him to kiss her ring. "I'm April."

"I'm Jason." He clasped her hand in both of his, bowing his head as if he were praying over it. "That's

92

Miranda." He jerked his chin toward the glowering woman. "And these are all travelers on roads much like your own. Join us."

April gave Miranda a haughty glance, twitched her hair over her shoulders, and plopped beside a bearded man in a red satin tunic who sat cross-legged, a dark green jug between his knees, a lumpy cigarette wedged in his lips. With his eyes directed at the breasts outlined beneath her damp peasant blouse, he unscrewed the top and presented the jug like an offering at a shrine. April favored him with a smile, tilted the jug, and took several long swallows. A girl with a guitar winked at the man in the tunic and strummed a bit from "Do You Believe In Magic?"

"And you, sister." Jason plucked an apple from a basket nailed to a roof support and offered it. "Will you eat of Delia's forbidden fruit?"

"No." I raised my hands, warding off the biblical image, Miranda's baleful glare, and a dozen scrutinizing stares. I felt awkward and out of place in my baggy brown slacks, and grubby blue blouse. "I'm fine. I, uh, ate not long ago." If, unlike Gertrude Gorman, you defined potato chips and soda as food. I smiled, both at my grandmother deciding how to classify those snacks and the idea that her image could sustain me in this strange land.

Jason gestured with his whole arm, taking in the depths of the barn. "Make yourself comfortable—any place that isn't claimed is yours."

In the fast-failing light I saw sleeping bags and quilts spread beneath lengths of green and brown canvas suspended above rough stalls that reminded me of the charge we'd been given. "The woman at the house said to milk the cow."

"Delia?" He snorted. "That old witch can't give us orders."

I frowned. "But don't you . . . I heard that you help

with the chores."

"We did when Ezekiel was alive," he snorted. "There's no reason now."

No reason? These people, with peace and love painted on their cars, were supposed to be caring, sharing—a new and better breed. "What about because you're sleeping in her barn and that you 'liberated' her apples?"

"Aren't you the preachy one," he chuckled wagging a finger and raising his voice. "Miss Up-Tight. Miss Do-What's-Right."

A spatter of derisive laughter rose from his audience. Degraded, I stalked from the barn. I'd seen people milk cows. I'd do it myself.

The sun had set, leaving a froth of pink and gold at the western rim of the world and a faint star in the east. I wondered if Dad was sitting on his bench watching over Sebastian in the dusk. No. It was later in Maplekill, full dark.

A thousand tiny sounds surrounded me: the drip of water from the eaves, the strumming of the guitar, the rustle of leaves in the orchard, the whine of a mosquito, the squeak of some small creature. Was Ben also alone? In that country half a world away where time was more than half a day ahead of me, was he looking to the sun to find his way?

Shivering, I hurried to Buggy for a flashlight. I might never know what had become of Ben. And if he did return, he belonged to April.

I heard the clatter of metal behind me and turned. By the light of a lantern held before him, I saw Jason and a woman with long braids heading toward the pasture with a bucket. The dogs followed, only their heads and the points of their tails visible as they zigzagged through tall grass. "We're going to milk Clover," the woman called with a smile. "Do you want to come?"

I smiled and took a step toward them, feeling warm,

included, until Jason shot her a look that made her flinch. "We don't want your help, Ruthie Righteous. We're only doing this because we need milk for breakfast."

Tears sprang to my eyes, but I held onto the smile in defiance until he turned away. Then, feeling cold and empty, I collected my blanket and pillow from the trunk. I considered making my bed in the orchard, but another rustle in the grass and a jagged bolt of lightning on the horizon made me think again. Shoving the seats back as far as they would go, I reclined them the few inches they'd give, then stuffed some of the contents of the boxes into the passenger side floor space to extend my cramped bed.

I had little hope of sleep, but it came within minutes.

The sound of an engine woke me and I raised my head to see a dust-covered car pulling away. A red bandanna fluttered from its antenna and bits of fraying clothesline lashed a motley collection of suitcases to the roof. I unfolded myself, joints popping, muscles twitching, and waded into dew-dappled grass. The sky was clear and the sun already sat well above the horizon. A breeze brought the scent of scorched milk and cooked apples.

Pulling on a pair of sneakers, I wandered into the orchard and found a spot screened by tall grass and fallen boughs where I could squat and then squirm into clean underwear, a pair of too-loose khaki slacks, and a pale green blouse with a Peter Pan collar that I'd packed as part of my clothing-for-charity ploy. I wiped my hands on the damp grass, and dug into the trunk for an apple, a packet of peanuts, and a cola—warm, but wet and loaded with caffeine. I drank down half and bit into the apple.

Sunlight glinting off the windshield reminded me I'd have to get the wipers fixed before it stormed again. Had there been a service station in the last town we passed through? Stony Ledge? I remembered only a jumble of buildings, their contours blurred by the rain. Well, if not, there were other towns. I'd tell April I was leaving for

95

Chicago and—

Nausea squeezed my gut. What if she wanted to come with me?

"Just go," a little voice in my mind suggested. "Go right now. You don't owe her a thing. This tribe will take her in."

I leaned against Buggy and watched a bird soaring in tight circles above the pasture. In his last few lines of communication in that damn note April had in her hand when she got off the bus, Ben asked me to help Jo look out for her.

"He dumped you!" the voice railed. "You don't owe him a thing."

"He could be dead," I whispered. "That may have been his last wish."

A wish I should honor no matter how loathsome because, in spite of it all, I remained certain he would do the same for me. I sighed. Ben had seen something in April that I didn't see. That I refused to?

"What would your mother have done?" my conscience asked in my father's voice. "You told Jo that April should have better manners. Where are yours?"

"Damn it!" I threw the apple core to the ground, swallowed the last of the cola, and wrestled April's duffel bag out of the back, surprised that she hadn't come for it. Lugging the bag to the barn, I set it beside the door, and stepped into cool dimness broken by random shafts of sunlight.

"Look who's here. Little Miss Golden Rule," Jason taunted.

I pasted on the armor of a smile, guessing April had turned them against me with statements like, "She's a stuck-up, inflexible bitch. She doesn't care about anyone but herself. She gets mad for no reason."

Jason stood, placing himself between me and a propane stove where Miranda stirred a steaming pot.

96

"Come to beg for breakfast?"

I lifted my chin so it wouldn't quiver. "Thanks for the offer, but I already ate. I'm looking for April."

He raised his eyebrows at Miranda who smiled, winked, and hooked a thumb toward the rear of the barn. "Back there."

"Behind the plaid blanket," Jason added with a smirk. "With Stash."

I hesitated, wondering about that wink and the smirk, my skin prickling with embarrassment. "Thank you."

"Happy to help, Miss Goody Two-Shoes."

Cheeks burning, I picked my way through a hodgepodge of cast-offs to the plaid blanket sagging on rusting wire. "April," I called in a low voice. "April, are you in there?"

I heard only a muffled snore in reply.

"April. I'm leaving for Chicago now."

The snore broke into a snuffle, then a snort, then subsided to a snore again. I crooked my forefinger around the edge of the blanket and peered inside. Just in front of me, April's peasant blouse lay in a tangle with a red tunic, two pairs of jeans, white undershorts, and those damned polka-dot panties. Beyond them, on a lumpy green sleeping bag, April and the man called Stash lay twined together.

I felt a thrill of vengeance. This was a taste of his own medicine for Ben.

For a moment I savored it, sweet on my tongue, but then hated myself for being vindictive, hated her more for defiling his love, the future he'd intended. I slipped behind the blanket and nudged her foot with my toe. "Wake up."

She groaned and I nudged again. "Wake up. Now!"

Her eyes fluttered open and she curled tighter against the snoring man. "Stop it, Liz. Leave us alone. We're trying to sleep."

Rage flamed through my brain but burned itself out in

an instant, leaving behind enormous sadness for Ben's loss and a swelling serenity. April's actions shattered the bond of obligation. "I'm taking off. Your duffel bag's by the door."

CHAPTER 11

Head high, blood pounding in my ears, I strode through the barn, pretending not to see the smug grin Jason exchanged with Miranda. Outside the sun blazed, burning off the dew, but my icy fingers trembled as I adjusted the driver's seat and excavated the maps Earl provided back in Louisville.

"Wait!"

Glancing over my shoulder, I saw April racing toward me in Stash's red tunic, her bare legs flashing. I slid into Buggy and slammed the door. She gripped the top of the window, panting, breath reeking of stale wine, hair rank with the scent of smoke. "Why are you taking off?"

"Why are *you* sleeping with that man?" I leaned stared into her bloodshot, unfocused eyes. "You're engaged. Don't you love Ben?"

"Of course." April's gaze skewed toward the barn. "But he's not here."

I wanted to slap her until my arm went numb, but gripped the wheel instead. "No. He's dead. Or a prisoner."

April's nostrils flared. "And nothing I do will change that!"

"Couldn't you at least be faithful until . . . we know?"

"I tried." She sniffed and swallowed.

Sure you did! I shook my head.

"I really did. But I'm not as fortunate as you are," she said in a rush. "My mother ran off when I was little and

99

my father never loved me, never gave a damn about me."

I narrowed my eyes. Another lie? I fought it, but the image of my mother's gleaming coffin fanned a spark of compassion in my heart. How different things might have been if my mother had lived, how different for April if her mother had stayed, if her father had cared.

April sniffed again. "That's why I need a lot more affection than you do."

The spark of compassion blinked out, smothered by shame. I studied my ringless fingers. Ben must have told her about that motel room. Hot shame scorched my cheeks.

"I was honest with Ben about the way I am," April said. "I'm lonely and afraid and I need to feel loved. I know he'd understand."

I didn't quite believe her and I doubted even altruistic Ben would "understand" that his fiancée "needed" to have sex with a man she'd just met, but I had grudging admiration for her ability to recognize what she wanted and go after it. Maybe that's what attracted Ben—that and the flattering and flirting I never attempted. Days of hoarded bitterness give way to spiteful satisfaction— the love he'd deprived me of was wasted on April and love he got from her was polluted.

I slipped the key into the ignition. Ben was no more important to April than Stash or any man who was right here, right now. "I hope Stash gives you what you need." Pumping the gas pedal, I turned the key. "I've got to be going."

She frowned. "Going where?"

"Chicago, remember?" The engine chugged to life.

Her eyes flickered toward the barn and she answered as if she hadn't heard. "Stash says there's a neat cave in the mountains. It's not far."

I shuddered. Caves were too confining, too much like— I blinked away the image of Sebastian's narrow

100

grave. "Well, you and Stash can go when he wakes up." I worked Buggy into reverse.

Her fingers screeked on the window. "Well, see, Stash came out here with Miranda and Roger, but Roger's afraid he'll get sent to Vietnam, so he's splitting for Canada."

I snorted. Ben hadn't run. Ben hadn't allowed himself to be afraid.

Or had he? Guilt, cold and greasy, swelled in my gut. I had never asked. Would he have told me if I had?

"So we need a ride," April said.

I gestured toward the vehicles surrounding Buggy. "So get one." I pumped the gas again and let out the clutch. The engine died in a cloud of raw fumes. *Flooded! Damn it!*

April batted air with her hand. "We tried, but only Jason's going to California, and his car is full."

I opened a map and pretended enormous interest in the web of red and blue lines, counting off three hundred seconds until I could try again to start the engine.

"So I thought that after we all went to that cave you could drive us—"

I crumpled the map. "To California? That's more than a thousand miles."

"I know. But that's where I need to be. I just feel it." She put her hand over her heart. "Haven't you ever just felt something?"

I said nothing, refusing to reveal any more about myself, remembering the dream I'd had about Ben. Had it meant he was still alive?

"I was out in California when I met Ben, but in San Diego. That's just a surf town. San Francisco's where it's at."

"And what if Ben comes home?"

She flipped her fingers. "He'll find me. I'll call Jo when I get there. It will only take us a few days and you don't *have* to be in Chicago tomorrow."

I hammered the wheel with my palms. "That's not the point." And April, I was certain, knew that.

"Stash says he'll pay for gas and food and motels. He's busted right now, but he has stuff he can sell along the way."

Stuff? April's dilated pupils and the reek of her hair added up. Marijuana. "I won't—"

"You there, girl!"

April straightened and tugged at her tunic. Craning my neck I spotted the psychic's wife marching toward us. Her graying hair stood out in tufts and twists and she wore a wrinkled tan shirt and a pair of overalls that flapped about the middle of her shins. She lifted her feet high, revealing huge black basketball sneakers that flopped with each step like clown shoes. "You the one let my cows out?"

"No," April bleated, backing away. "It wasn't me. I didn't go near them."

Delia halted and leveled a finger at me. "Was it you left the gate open?"

I shook my head, afraid to speak in the face of her fury, frightened that if I said what I believed—that Jason had done it from carelessness or spite—she would accuse me of lying to protect myself or being a snitch and a traitor to the tribe. Years with Gertrude Gorman made it easy to recognize where an attempt at defense only made me the target of a stronger offense.

Her muddy brown eyes narrowed and I felt a fleeting, knifing pain in my head as if I'd stared into the sun. She nodded and wheeled on April.

"You get those freeloaders out of my barn and hunting for my cows." Her lips twitched into a malevolent grin. "And when they're back in that pasture, I want every last one of you the hell out of my sight inside an hour or I'll go fetch the sheriff. Chigger Johnson's been itching for an excuse to clean this place out and set an example for other

102

road trash."

My stomach jittered. I'd heard scare stories about southern justice.

April swallowed and spun away. Delia watched after her for a moment, then set her hands on her narrow hips and fixed her glare on me. I steeled myself against those flat opaque eyes that shielded her thoughts and emotion. "You carry me down the road," she ordered. "Case they've gone to the spring to wallow."

I felt myself nod, wondering about the verb "carry" and whether she meant for me to hoist her on my back. But she climbed into the car beside me, smelling of sour sweat and coffee, kicking at the stuff piled in the foot well with her enormous shoes. The starter ground for a few seconds and I flipped the key back. "It's flooded," I whispered.

"Try it again," Delia said in a calm and certain voice.

I held my breath and turned the key. The engine caught. *Thank you, Buggy.* We rumbled through the orchard, past the house, and down the hill, wheels skidding on drifts of stones left by the downpour.

"Pull over there." Delia pointed to a grassy spot the size of Gertrude Gorman's work table sidled up to the ditch on the left. I pulled over, wheels sinking into sodden soil. Delia unfolded herself, crossed the road, jumped the ditch with a slap of rubber and a flap of fabric, and pointed into the woods. "Spring's that way."

I leaned over, dragged her door closed, and locked it. From force of habit I grabbed my purse and hitched it over my shoulder as I got out, my feet sliding, squishing in mud at the bottom of the ditch.

"Ain't you the city girl," Delia hooted. "Leave that bag behind. It'll only get in the way."

Embarrassed by her laughter, but remembering Gertrude Gorman's lessons about caution, I removed my wallet and tucked it deep into my pocket, then thrust the purse under the heap on the floor and locked the door behind me. The sun felt like molten metal on my shoulders and Buggy's bumper scorched my fingers when I grasped it to pull myself from the ditch.

"Come on now." Delia plunged into the woods along a pair of faint ruts overgrown with saplings.

I hesitated, glancing back at the car, yearning to be on the way to Chicago. How long would this take? Couldn't she do this without me?

"I'll likely need your help with Pig-head."

My sense of duty and obligation kicked in and I raced after her, branches slapping at my face.

"Don't bother yourself too much over the ticks," she warned, thrashing through a thicket.

Ticks?

"Seed ticks I call 'em," Delia called over her shoulder. "They hang on the leaves. Get up into your armpits and your woman place and suck your blood."

I snapped my arms to my sides, pressed my legs together, and peered at my blouse. There! Something not much larger than a freckle crawling at surprising speed toward my neck. I brushed it off, spotted another on my pants, and went after it.

"They latch on faster than you can knock them off," Delia snorted. "Best get them all at once. They'll be on you as thick as flies on manure by the time we get back."

I shuddered, imagining a tide of ticks washing over me, burrowing into my skin, sucking me dry. Each tiny creature had April's face. Shaking off the image, I hustled to catch up with Delia who strode on, seemingly oblivious to what might be working its way inside her shirt or up her bony shins.

We angled down the ridge, our feet slipping in damp, loamy drifts of last year's leaves. Oaks and pines loomed overhead, but it seemed no cooler in the shade than out on the road. "There you go." Delia pointed to the ground

104

where a double set of prints joined the trail. "Those old cows love a good wallow." She wiped sweat from her forehead. "Don't mind one myself on these hot days. Course snakes feel the same."

I gasped. "What kind of snakes?"

"Moccasins, rattlers, copperheads. And I don't know what-all. I see one, I'm gone the other way." She turned, head down, following the split-toed prints. "We got cows to catch. Make a racket and snakes mostly let you by."

Mostly?

I fell in behind, stomping my feet but knowing I'd never spot a snake camouflaged among rocks, moss, decaying limbs, and low-growing plants with a sheen to their leaves that reminded me of that poisonous laurel back home. I opened my mouth to ask Delia what they were, but decided the hazards I already knew were enough. Panting along behind, I gulped steamy air, scalp itching with sweat that burned into my eyes, shirt damp, legs trembling.

"There they are!" Delia halted and pointed across a clearing. Head to tail, the cows stood belly deep in a muddied pond barely large enough to hold them both. One of them cut its eyes toward Delia and began to low. The sound pinged inside my skull, swelling until I had to strain to hear Delia.

"Pig-head's dry, but Clover's gotta be milked. That's what I was fixin' to do when I found them gone."

The earth shifted under my feet. I reached for the nearest tree, crashing against it, and slipping to the rippling ground. Delia's voice faded in and out, like poor radio reception. "Pig-head. . . willful . . . Clover . . . gentler." I tried to call out, but my tongue filled my mouth.

Delia glanced over her shoulder, then spun, grasped my forearms, and jerked me to my feet. "Lord, girl, you're red as a Christmas ribbon. Gotta cool you down before you tump over."

Half dragging, half pushing, she got me to a narrow shaded ledge above the pond and ordered me to lie in a trickle of water seeping from the hillside. The rock was cool against my spine, but the roar in my head continued to build. Delia dug into the seep with both hands and smeared mud on my forehead, cheeks, and throat. She dug again and coated my arms, flung more across my chest. The rusty mud smelled like old eggs and rotting lettuce. I gagged and flailed at Delia's hand.

"If you're feeling good enough to fight me, then put your mouth up there and drink." She pointed to dark water oozing from the wound she'd opened in the hillside.

I shook my head.

"Don't be stupid, girl. Drink. But not too much." She gripped one arm and the back of my head and pressed me against the seep like a baby to a mother's breast. Water trickled against my lips and, despite my intentions, I sucked at it. It felt gritty on my tongue and I had to steel myself to swallow.

"Enough," Delia said after a minute. "You lie up here while I milk that cow."

I nodded, nasty water roiling in my stomach, the sound in my head down to a distant hum. Delia waded into the wallow and smacked a brown and white cow on the rump.

It lifted a forefoot, then set it down again. "Get on up, Clover, get on up." Delia smacked her again and the cow sloshed from the water. Hunkering on a rotted stump with her knees wide apart, Delia grasped a pair of teats and squeezed with a rhythm that set milk hissing against the earth.

I closed my eyes for what I thought was just a minute, but when Delia shook me awake, both cows stood near the stump. "Roll over and wet down your clothes," she ordered. "Then drink again. Drink more.

I didn't argue. The water had cleared. It was cold and

106

tasted of rock.

"We'll go up the hill," Delia said after I got to my feet. "It's harder, but quicker. Then I'll make you some salt and sugar tea."

That sounded worse than the water. "I'm okay," I grunted.

Delia fixed those inscrutable eyes on me. "You're not. It would be smart to admit it."

She smacked the cows on the rumps, turning them to the slope, and said nothing more as we climbed, casting back and forth across the incline, keeping the cows between us.

We emerged near that fossil of a truck. The sun was high and the smothering heat clamped down like the lid on a pressure cooker. "Get in the shade. I'll be back in two shakes."

I glanced at the road, thought of my car waiting.

"Get in the shade," she repeated, her eyes pinning me like a butterfly to a corkboard.

With a nod of defeat, I wobbled up the stone steps and slumped beneath a curtained window. I reeked of sweat and that rancid mud had dried to a gray crust. My skin itched so bad it was all I could do not to claw at it. I longed for the tub and shower across the hall from my room back in Maplekill, for a fat bar of soap and a coarse washcloth, and then a pitcher of lemonade, and a bag of cheese snacks.

Closing my eyes, I burrowed deeper into my daydream. Except for the buzzing of insects, the caw of a crow, Delia's grunted commands, and the clomp of the cows' hooves, there was not a single sound. No voices. No music.

It took a minute for that to sink in. When it did, I grasped the windowsill, levered myself to my feet, and peered toward the barn.

"They're as gone as last Sunday. Bet they took off like

107

scalded cats the minute we was out of sight down the hill."

I turned to see Delia hoisting herself up the steps. "But you told them to find—"

"And you thought they would?" She boomed out a laugh and slapped her thigh. "How'd you live to grow up, girl? You're as trusting as a newborn chick."

I felt a flash of anger, but couldn't argue. In spite of what I knew about Jason and the others, I believed they would search for the cows.

"Your friend musta got a ride with them." She said "friend" in a way that implied I had poor taste in companions, then pointed to the edge of the house. "Come on around back and let's get you cleaned off."

I followed her to a pump set in a slab of concrete and watched her power the handle up and down until sulfur-smelling water gushed into a washtub. "What are you waiting for?" Delia kicked off her shoes and shrugged out of her overalls.

I turned aside. "I'll wait until you're finished."

"A modest newborn chick," she hooted. "Ain't but us two here, girl. Soap's right there." I skewed my head far enough to see a pale brown mass squatting at the edge of the slab like a mushroom swollen by the rain.

The lure of spouting water overcame my inhibitions. I peeled off my clothes, set my glasses, wallet, and keys on the back steps, seized the soap, and knelt beside the washtub, plunging my head into water so cold it stung like a swarm of bees.

Delia did the same and we traded the harsh soap back and forth, washing ourselves and then our clothes, laying them over a rope stretched between two trees. I felt myself blush just a little when Delia told me to hold still and pinched a tick from my hip and flattened it between her fingernails. What would Gertrude Gorman think of this?

The image of my grandmother's face made me giggle when Delia fingered through my hair and squinted into

108

my ears and then had me do the same for her. To my relief there were only a few ticks and those came loose without resorting to the matches Delia brought from the house.

"You're a game one," she told me as I sat on the steps in my wet underwear eating a slab of grainy cornbread topped with lumps of cold butter and drinking my third glass of tea laced with sugar and salt.

Curious as I was about the interior of her house, I could tell by the way she held the door open just far enough to slip through that she didn't want me to see. I made a point of pretending interest in the view from the steps: an outhouse tilting like the Leaning Tower of Pisa, the pump and washtub, pine trees supporting the sagging clothesline, and the neglected orchard.

"Coming all the way from New York on a fool's errand." Delia topped off her tea with clear liquid from a brown jug. "Running into the woods without a thought for the heat." She drained the cup with long swallows, poured in tea, and topped it off again. "You go after what you want. And you do what has to be done, even if the way isn't easy."

I opened my mouth to correct her, tell her she had me confused with April, that I was the one who stood by and let things happen. But that was a long story and the afternoon was getting old.

And maybe she was right. I *was* going after something I wanted and I'd delayed long enough. I finished my tea, wiggled into damp clothes smelling of brown soap and sulfur water, and thanked her for everything.

"Stay on the shady side of the road," she cautioned, handing me a gallon jug of well water. "And drink more than you think you need."

I thanked her again and then picked my way along the ruts and around potholes, glancing back at the first bend to see her raise her cup as if toasting me. Then I was alone, starting out again. In spite of the treacherous

109

footing, I strode along, swinging the jug, and whistling "Cast Your Fate To The Wind." April had twisted my journey, but dealing with her had given me courage I hadn't possessed when I started. I was no longer concerned about finding my way in Chicago. I had conquered the unknown to get here. I would do it again.

The road unwound ahead of me and I spotted the turnout where I'd left Buggy.

It wasn't there.

CHAPTER 12

No! The jug slipped from my fingers and shattered, water splashing across my feet and up my legs. I bolted down the hill. I must be mistaken. The car must be farther along, around another bend.

But as I drew closer, I spotted sunlight glinting on broken glass and brown cardboard flattened in the ruts. Someone—or several someones—had dumped my boxes and pawed through the contents, leaving behind only a pink flannel nightgown with a drooping hem, a pair of brown suede shoes run down at the heels, patched corduroy slacks that had been my father's, and a pink dress with white and yellow daisies handmade by Gertrude Gorman and, of course, a size too large. Or more. I never weighed except when forced to stand on a doctor's scale each year—the last humiliation had been noted at 152—but there seemed to be less of me than on the day Ben left.

I bent to survey the ditch and spotted my comb and hairbrush, a tube of acne cream, and a compact. My purse was gone. And the spare key had been inside. I'd made it easy for them to steal the car and the money hidden in the visor.

I threw back my head and howled with rage—furious at April, Stash, Jason, and anyone who'd helped loot my car, furious at those who drove past and didn't intervene or stood by while they betrayed me.

No, not betrayed! There had been no bond of trust; I was simply someone they came across and took advantage of. I meant no more than the cow they'd stripped milk from last night.

I seethed, imagining April and her new friends laughing at my foolishness, making fun of my cardigan sweaters and pleated skirts, my plain blouses and sensible shoes, my cotton underwear. That damn old-fashioned, stick-in-the-mud cotton underwear!

Violated and sick with shame, I stumbled across the ditch and sank into the shade of an oak tree. A few moments ago I'd been confident, optimistic, and ready to prove I was self-sufficient and deserving of the independence I'd wrested from my family by stealth. Now I was abandoned, uncertain, and brimming with qualms. If she knew about my situation, Gertrude Gorman would say pride goes before a fall, implying I deserved every bit of this.

And perhaps I did.

If I'd waited until the end of the term, April might have been long gone from Maplekill. If I'd taken a stand and departed with my father's knowledge, I wouldn't have been vulnerable to her blackmail. If I hadn't believed I needed to sneak the money from my account, I might have gotten travelers' checks. If I'd paid attention at the post office in Stony Ledge, I would have asked questions and learned Ezekiel was dead. I would have turned back.

And then there was the biggest fault: if I'd slept with Ben, he might have been immune to April.

I seized a rock and hurled it at the scatter of broken glass.

Or maybe having sex with me in that shoddy motel room would have been so disappointing he might have run to someone like April even faster.

A murmur of a breeze slipped through the tired leaves above my head, making them rasp against each other. I

112

turned my face to catch the spill of air, too bitter for tears, my eyes as dry as the leaves.

Something moved in a clump of weeds at the edge of my vision.

Snake?

I leaped to my feet, heart thudding.

The thing fluttered and I saw it was Thoreau, spine broken, pages creased, stained with dirt and grass. I gathered him to me, smoothing, wiping, feeling less alone.

Settling in the shade again, I thumbed through *Walden*, studying the lines I'd marked. I noted what he said about well-worn clothing. Yes, I had that. I noted his comment about stripping your life. April's tribe had taken care of that. I read what he had to say about not being found until we are lost. Well, I knew where I was although no one who loved and cared about me did.

Just like Ben.

Ben, if he was still alive, would do everything he could to be found, to return to Maplekill. But this place wasn't a war zone. I'd been ripped off, but being "missing in action" gave me new freedom. I'd have to relinquish that freedom and more if I returned to the house where Gertrude Gorman reigned.

"What would Henry David do?" I asked the oak tree.

"Build a cabin by that spring and call it Wallowed-in," a voice in my mind answered. I laughed, thinking of Delia encountering Thoreau at that cow wallow. What would they make of each other?

Well, I wasn't equipped to build a cabin, but I had other options. I could walk to town and find a place to stay for the night. From that phone booth by the post office I could call the sheriff and tell him my car had been stolen. I could tell Dad, in a vague way, that I'd taken a slight detour but would be on my way to Chicago soon to follow a dream I had a right to. I'd ask for the money from my college fund. If he balked, I'd work and earn my way.

113

I stood to collect what the tribe had left me and noticed clouds roiling high at the edges of the sky. Insistent gusts revealed the silvered undersides of leaves. Setting out on foot along that treacherous road was an invitation to more trouble than I'd already acquired. I knotted the bottom of the nightgown, stuffed my few possessions in at the neck, and slung it across my shoulders. Delia had a truck; perhaps she'd drive me to a bus station.

As I trudged up the hill a sweltering wind blundered through the trees, shoving limbs, snapping twigs, and sending clusters of leaves spinning to the ground. I paused only long enough to kick the shards of the broken jug well into the ditch and was drenched with sweat and trembling by the time I reached the house and set my burden down beside the steps. Plodding up them, I knocked.

I was about to walk around to the back when I heard shuffling steps. Something—a chair maybe—crashed against the wall and then Delia snatched the door wide and glared from red-rimmed eyes. "Ezekiel's dead!"

I stumbled to the railing. "I heard. I'm sorry."

She stepped out onto the porch, thrust her fingers through kinked and knotted hair, and ran her tongue across blunted teeth. Her eyes stared past my shoulder. "Dead and gone."

Her breath reeked like the alcohol Gertrude Gorman swabbed on the thermometer before she checked to see if I was running a fever. I wondered how many times Delia had topped off her cup since I left. "I'm sorry for your loss."

"Sorry don't make it right." She gripped my arm, fingers digging for the bone. "What you want here, white girl?"

My father, cautioning me to pull over if I saw Gus Heinz driving on a Saturday night, had said there was no way to predict what a drunk would do, so I forced myself

114

not to show fear or fight her grip. I spoke in a quiet voice that trembled just a little. "Someone stole my car." I cocked my free elbow, and pointed at the sky. "I need a ride to town so I can call the sheriff. I'd walk, but it's going to rain."

Delia released my arm, staggered to the edge of the porch, turned her head, and studied the sky. A jagged bolt of lightning cleaved the base of a towering cloud. "Gully washer," she muttered. She lowered herself to the steps, her knees popping. "Stole your car, did they?"

"Yes, ma'am."

She prodded my bundle with bony toes rimmed by thickened, yellowed nails. "This all they left you?"

"Yes, ma'am." The nightgown looked even more forlorn than it had lying in the road. Was it pathetic enough that Delia would take pity on me? "That and the clothes I have on."

She studied my misshapen outfit, prodded the bundle again, slapped her thigh, and laughed. "That's what comes of keeping bad company. Lie down with dogs and you get up with fleas."

I shook my head. "But they weren't—"

"The Lord helps those who help themselves. Don't expect old Delia to help those who can't manage to do that much."

It took me a few seconds to puzzle that out and then I clenched my fists, anger simmering in the back of my brain. April and Stash weren't my friends. Their actions made that clear. But Delia's mind seemed made up.

"Never mind. I'm sorry I bothered you." I stomped down the steps and seized my bundle. "I'll walk to town." And if I was struck by lightning, then it was what I deserved for making yet another stupid decision.

"Sheriff won't give a damn about your problems anyway." Delia spat into the rocks beside the porch. "White as you are, you got no standing around here. And you're a Yankee, besides. He'll look for that car about as hard as I'd look for the owner of a hundred dollar bill blowing by in the wind."

"But he's the sheriff. He has—"

She flipped her fingers toward the road. "Go on. Find out for yourself. Find out how Chigger Johnson feels about high-minded hobos now Ezekiel's dead and buried."

A chill spread through my chest as I remembered what she'd said about the sheriff looking for an excuse to come up here.

The tears I hadn't cried back on the road burned my eyes but didn't fall. What good would they do? Once again I was between a rock and a hard place. My new permanent address.

Lightning crackled, gusting wind lifted a clump of my hair, and a single raindrop, heavy as mercury, struck my cheek.

"If you've got the sense to get out of the rain, you can stay in the barn tonight," Delia said in a disinterested tone. "But don't expect more. I didn't take you to raise."

She hoisted herself erect, swayed, and stumbled to the door. It closed with a sharp click and I heard the sound of a bolt scraping into place.

A second raindrop struck my arm and a third splashed against my glasses, blurring the left lens. Bundle bouncing against my back, I plodded to the pump and coaxed water from the depths of Hog Run Ridge. While swollen drops pelted my neck, I bent and drank until I could swallow no more, then scavenged four wormy apples from the orchard and trudged to the barn.

Even in the dim light I saw that the tribe, intent on leaving before Delia called the law, had made no effort to clean up before they cleared out. Empty bags, broken bottles, and crusted cans were everywhere on the packed-earth floor and articles of bright clothing lay heaped in the corners like autumn leaves swept by a careless wind. I

116

spotted a few tarps, one still strung across the top of a stall to keep out water already seeping between the patches on the roof and dripping from the rafters.

The clutter made me feel weary, sad, and angry all at once. This was my room for the night and, grim as it was, I'd make it as neat as I could. I gathered armful after armful of abandoned clothing and dumped it all under the tarp to keep it dry. Three other canvas tarps were mildewed and ripped, but I hefted the bales of hay scattered at random, formed them into a sofa of sorts, and overlapped tarps across it. A long-handled rake with wooden pegs instead of tines hung from a spike driven into one wall; I wrapped a burlap bag around the splintered handle and dragged clumps of loose straw and the tribe's leavings into the far corner.

A bottle of shampoo with an inch left in the bottom emerged from a mound of apple cores and beer bottles. Treasure! I pounced on it and set it aside.

I was reminded of the tree house Ben and I had built—with plenty of help from Dad—when I was nine. We'd furnished it with dusty cushions and discarded curtains from Jo's attic and provisioned it with crackers, jars of strawberry jam and peanut butter, two chipped plates, and two mugs without handles. He found a pitcher without a spout and we hauled water and displayed the goldenrod and Queen Anne's lace we picked as summer waned. We'd spend our afternoons aloft, reading or trying to hammer the scraps of wood we pilfered into something resembling a chair, content with just each other.

I slammed the rake against the earth, snapping a tine. How many years would Ben haunt me? When I was old and withered, would he still stalk my mind, still a child, a boy, a young man? Would I still wonder how it might have been with us if—

"Stop it. Just stop it!"

With a last vicious heave on the rake, I finished that

task and set to work sorting discarded finery—trying to distract my thoughts from Ben, my stolen car and cash, and my stillborn dream of Chicago. As I sifted, I found cast-offs that might supplement my own: a pair of nearly new jeans, three T-shirts that were sweaty, but intact, a collection of socks, a corduroy jacket with frayed cuffs, a yellow elastic belt, and a pair of black flip-flops with a gouge out of one heel. I set these aside and formed the rest into a narrow pallet with grimy underwear on the bottom. Folding shirts inside of shirts I made a pillow and designated two long skirts as blankets.

Thunder shook the ground, rain drummed on the metal patches in the roof and spattered on the tarp above my head. In a few minutes the barn grew as dark as my thoughts. I closed the doors and, noting that the bolt had been ripped off, used the rake as a wedge. Stretching out on my lumpy bed, I gnawed around the worm holes on the apples and somehow fell asleep.

I awoke to the deep rumble of an engine and the smell of burning oil. Buggy? I sat up, listening harder, then slumped back in defeat. This engine didn't clatter like an old washing machine.

The rumble ceased with a chugging cough and a backfire like a gunshot. A car door slammed and heavy feet stomped toward the doors.

I leaped from my pallet. Had Delia brought the sheriff?

My eyes strafed the barn, but except for windows too high to reach and jagged gaps too small to slip between, the only way out was through those doors.

CHAPTER 13

"Are you in there?" Delia called.

Don't answer.

I flattened myself against the stall, my heart pounding, visions of handcuffs and jail cells flashing in my brain.

"I brought you some breakfast."

Saliva pooled under my tongue. I swallowed, told myself this was a trick, kept still. Maybe they'd think I left during the night.

Hinges grated. The rake toppled, thudded, bounced. "Are you in there, girl?"

My lungs compressed and my breath caught in my throat. Raising my hands above my head, I held my trembling chin high, and wobbled into the broad rectangle of light streaming through the doors.

"Did you think I forgot you? I brought eggs and grits and fried potatoes with onions." Delia's shadow stretched to my toes. "What the hell are you doing?"

I dropped my hands an inch.

Delia cackled and shambled farther into the barn. She wore the same high-topped sneakers with another pair of faded overalls and a red flannel shirt. "You thought I brought the law."

Cheeks burning, I shrugged and accepted the mounded plate she thrust toward me. The aroma almost brought me to my knees with pleasure, and I seized the

119

fork, stabbed a pile of browned potato slices, and stuffed them into my mouth. They were greasy, salty, and a little scorched, but right then they were the best I ever had. "Thank you," I mumbled.

She acknowledged that with a flip of her hand. "I would no more call Chigger Johnson to run somebody off than I'd stab my foot with a pitchfork." She circled my makeshift sofa, then sat and patted the space beside her. "Sit down, girl."

I stuffed a load of over-easy egg into my mouth. Peppered with a generous hand, but fuel for the hike from Hog Run Ridge to Stony Ledge.

"Sit," Delia ordered. "I don't bite."

The hell you don't. I swallowed more potatoes, barely chewing, afraid she'd take the plate back at any moment.

"You're sure skittish. Is it because I got liquored up yesterday?"

I shrugged, eyeing a lake of white mush with a puddle of butter in the center. Were those grits? I slid the fork into the pile and took a tiny taste. More salt and grease. I loaded the fork as best I could. Grits were slippery.

"Is it the drinkin' that bothers you?" Delia narrowed her eyes.

Thoreau believed the wise man should drink only water, but this wasn't a good time to quote him.

"Or is it the talking I do when it takes hold of me?"

I shrugged again, afraid any answer would be wrong.

She leaned back on the hay-bale sofa and tipped her face to a spangle of sunlight reflecting off a row of raindrops hanging from a rafter like crystals on a chandelier. "Well, if you stick around, you'd better get used to that."

Stick around? Not a chance. I finished the grits.

"I'm bad to drink, I admit that. And it don't take me the way it did Ezekiel. He'd open up with it like a flower in spring."

120

She spread her hands and smiled, the first I'd seen. It transformed her plain face, lighting her eyes like a candle in a window on a frosty night. "He'd get down his banjo and pluck those strings so hard and fast I thought they'd snap and strike at him like snakes. And he'd sing. Had a voice as smooth as quality sippin' whiskey."

Her eyes misted over and the candle in them went out. I bolted the rest of the eggs and potatoes, wanting to be gone before another metamorphosis brought the woman from last night.

"Me, I just get hateful." She stretched out her legs and wiped a hand across her eyes. "Seems to feed my pain 'stead of dulling it. Get so miserable I lash out at anyone who has it any better—and that's almost everyone with white skin or education or a place in the world. Used to go off in the woods when I was younger and wail like a banshee."

She spread her arms along the back of the sofa. "In the winters I'd sit here in the barn and wonder why I was ever born. Should have thought to make me a seat like this. You're clever, girl."

I nodded yet again, feeling as manipulated as a puppet, and scraped the plate clean with the edge of the fork.

"I should quit it." She pushed off against the bales and stood. "But it's got under my skin. It's a sick kind of love but it's all I got."

I wanted to say I was sorry, but there was a minefield between us and the slightest false step could trigger an explosion.

Delia rocked from foot to foot. "I guess that's me sayin' I'm sorry for whatever I said."

Shoving her hands deep into her pockets, she gazed around, looking anywhere but at me. "You must be the one cleaned up. Can't see those freeloaders lifting a finger without there being something in it for them. When

121

Ezekiel was alive they—" She shook her head the way you might to discourage a mosquito from landing on your ear. "But that's a story for another day. I got a cow to milk before we go to town."

We? Joy kindled in my chest. "You'll give me a ride?"

She blinked. "Unless you'd rather walk."

A little voice in my brain said I should stand on principle and do just that. That voice was drowned out by Gertrude Gorman's questioning asking whether I'd cut off my nose to spite my face. "I'll ride. Thank you."

"Don't thank me 'til we get there." She laughed and headed for the door, talking over her shoulder. "That truck was old when Moses was in short pants, the road's liable to be worse after last night's rain, and my driving—well, Ezekiel used to say the safest place was right out in front of me."

She disappeared from my sight, still talking. "I put a towel out by the pump for you—and I guess you know where the outhouse is."

The engine cranked and coughed, gears ground, and the truck grumbled off just as the greasy food I'd gulped down did the same in my stomach. Scooping up my wallet and comb, the shampoo, that flowered dress, flip-flops, and the yellow elastic belt, I hustled through the orchard. With fingers set to hold my nose, I opened the tilting outhouse door and gaped in surprise. The inside walls, painted a crisp white, seemed more vertical than I expected and, instead of spider webs, the two rafters were festooned with Christmas ornaments and bits of tinsel. A strip of flowered carpet covered the floor, and the hole in the bench was graced with an actual toilet seat, the lid down. Beside it sat a roll of toilet paper, a couple of catalogs, a vase of late-summer roses, and a bucket of dirt with a trowel. I assumed that was to temper the odor and made liberal use of it when I finished.

In a few moments I was at the pump, stripping off my

rancid clothing without hesitating. I scrubbed away yesterday's sweat with that caustic brown soap, then washed my underwear and laid it over the line to dry while I shampooed my hair three times and rubbed at my teeth with my fingers. The dress had a deep pocket in each side seam, long, snug sleeves, and a neckline that fell just below the points of my collar bones. It hung like a sack but I pleated it with my fingers and cinched in the waist with the wide yellow belt so the hem rose above my knees.

I'd come halfway across the country through no choice of my own and lost almost everything, but I finally had a dress that was in style.

Racing back to the barn, I stowed my possessions and last night's finds into the nightgown, and returned just as Delia came around the corner of the house canted to one side by the weight of a bucket. "Let me get this in the cold cellar and then we'll leave on out." She descended a narrow set of stone steps at the edge of the porch and disappeared through a skinny door.

My eager fingers fumbled as I stuffed my wallet in one pocket and my comb in the other and wriggled into my damp underpants. Plucking my soggy bra from the line, I decided it was too much trouble to undo the belt and work my arms out of the sleeves in order to put it on. No one in Stony Ledge knew me. More to the point, no one in Stony Ledge knew Gertrude Gorman. Feeling like I'd been let out to play after a long confinement, I stuffed the bra into my nightgown sack.

"You all set?" Delia wrestled a rickety wooden cage from the back porch and into the bed of the truck. "Going to get a block of ice. And some chickens. Used to have a nice little flock and didn't mind sharing the eggs, but that last bunch of tramps had themselves a fried chicken feast and that was the end of it."

She pointed to a spot in front of the cage. Put your bundle up against the cab so it won't bounce out."

123

I stowed the nightgown sack and then wrestled with the handle until it gave and the door opened with a shower of flaky rust and the groan of hinges. With a last glance toward the barn, I climbed in. The seat was cracked and cluttered with tools and bits of rope and wire. The interior smelled of oil, mildew, and manure—the floor on the driver's side was thick with dried clumps of it, some in a waffle pattern like the sole of a boot. "If Ezekiel ever wiped his feet," Delia said, "I never saw him do it."

She stomped on the gas pedal and twisted the key. With a deep shudder and a high-pitched whine, the engine came to life. Delia crimped the wheel and let out the clutch. Too fast. The truck floundered, gasped for gas, and died with a bang. "It's been a time since I was behind the wheel."

Fact, not apology.

"It's tough to get it just right," I said in a voice I hoped didn't sound condescending. "Dad told me to imagine there were eggs under the gas pedal and big rubber bands holding my feet up over the clutch so I'd learn to push down easy and pull back slowly."

"Eggs and rubber bands, huh?" Delia twisted the key again. Our takeoff was smoother but when she shifted the gearbox sounded like a plow biting into a pile of gravel and she tromped the brake with the same energy she used on the pump handle. I left a dozen handprints on that dusty dashboard before we skidded to the bottom of the hill and rumbled across the cattle guard.

Someone had propped a piece of brown cardboard against the mailbox and written on it with crayon: "Turn back. Ezekiel is dead."

Delia studied it for a second, chewing at her lip and I wondered if I should offer to get out and take it down. "Guess I'm done with travelers," she said, and pointed the truck toward town. "Some of them were interesting folk. And most of them did their part to keep the place up, helped me with the garden and shared the berries they picked. But that last bunch . . ."

I nodded, feeling that both of us had lost more than a loved one. We'd lost our communities, lost our faith that kindness would triumph over selfishness and even be rewarded.

"Don't mention that you were up here when you call the law about your car," she said after a bit. "Chigger Johnson's got no use for me. Tell him you were on your way to where you have a job waiting, tell him you heard how beautiful his county is, tell him you stopped to take a picture and someone drove off with it."

I nodded. I could manage that.

"They likely crossed the state line before you even found it gone. But sometimes, even when it seems pointless, you have to try."

Pointless. I nodded. I'd become far too familiar with that, but I was also familiar with trying and wouldn't abandon that habit. I wasn't the lucky type and I'd been raised to refuse handouts. Anything that came to me was through hard work. Sometimes I resented that, but I took pride in it all the same.

Gazing out the window, I was struck by how different the terrain appeared in sunlight. Two days ago, in the storm, this stretch of road seemed to tunnel through a dense forest of sodden trees, but now I glimpsed fields opening beyond the thickets that lined the road and stock ponds reflecting the sky. Cows and horses grazed beside houses with broad front porches, corn stalks bent with the breeze, and a pair of goats raised their heads and then went back to making a meal in the ditch. A brown and white hound ran alongside us for a hundred yards and then bolted down a drive toward a yellow house with a tin roof and towering stone chimney. A pale-haired woman came down the steps from the porch, hunched over a toddler who clutched her hands as he swung each foot to

125

the step below, trusting her to keep him upright.

Reminded of my own trust betrayed, I looked away and saw Delia glance through the grimy back window at my lumpy bundle. "I guess you'll be going back to New York."

I shook my head. "Chicago. Once I find a way to get there. Does a bus run through Stony Ledge?"

"Wouldn't know." Delia shrugged. "Never gave any thought to traveling after I come here. Why you goin' there?"

"I want to go to journalism school." I blurted out my dream, thinking that she was a stranger and I was leaving. "I want to be a newspaper reporter."

"Huh." Delia swiveled toward me and narrowed her eyes—a move that set the truck slewing across the road and made me grasp at the dashboard once again. "Didn't know there was a school for that."

"There are lots of college journalism programs." Had she finished high school? Would she feel I was talking down to her?

To my relief, she turned her attention to the road. "You've got a curious nature and you speak well. Seems like you could learn your way into a writing job, like you can with farming or laying up brick."

I shrugged. "I guess some people might, but I don't think I—"

"Thinkin' can get in the way of doing." She spun the wheel and we bumped into the post office lot and idled beside the phone booth. "I'll stop back to check on you in an hour or so." Her voice had a strange, wavering quality. "In case you change your plans."

Never!

I shoved the door open, slid out, and yanked my bundle from the back. "Thanks." Before I could say more, she drove off in a fog of scorched oil.

Nightgown-sack over my shoulder, I opened the

126

bright door to the post office. The woman behind the counter had on the same lace collar but with a dark blue skirt and blouse. "What a cheerful dress," she beamed. "And your hair shines like new money."

I felt myself flush as I fumbled a bill from my wallet and asked for a pre-stamped postcard and change for the phone.

"I'm surprised you're still here. I swear I saw your little car go by yesterday morning." She laid the card and coins on the counter and peered past me, her voice sharp with suspicious disapproval. "Did I see you drive up with Delia?"

Grateful for years of practice fending off small-town speculation back in Maplekill, I pocketed the change but didn't respond. "Thank you for the card."

The woman frowned, narrowed eyes glittering. "It sure looked like Ezekiel's truck and Delia driving." Words as sharp as razor blades.

Slipping the postcard into my pocket I ducked the interrogation. "Thanks again." Aware of her gaze, I gathered my bundle and walked to the phone booth. A sign pasted across the dial read: "BROKE."

Naturally.

I kicked at a furrow of gravel, and glanced behind me. The lace-collared woman stood in the window, watching. Remembering that Thoreau had once said he could live without the post office, I smiled, shuffled to the edge of the road, and walked toward the center of town. My memory of Stony Ledge was blurred by the rain, but I recalled a miniscule hardware/feed/farm supply store, a café, a service station with two round-shouldered pumps, and a long, low building with signs advertising groceries, dry goods, books, guns, bait, and tackle.

The idea of buying worms where you got your bread and milk and underwear seemed peculiar, but a place that had all of that would probably have a phone.

127

Stony Ledge was larger than Maplekill, but it had a raw and insubstantial feeling about it—as if the residents hadn't been here long, weren't certain they wanted to stay, and lacked the initiative, time, and energy necessary for civic improvements. Businesses were set back behind rutted parking lots and there were no sidewalks, only humps of weeds and anemic grass, clotted with litter and presided over by wood or metal poles holding aloft hand-painted signs with uneven letters.

No matter how I dug in my toes, the flip-flops slipped sideways and gravel bit into my heels. By the time I reached the store, my left foot was cramping and I vowed to dig out my sneakers as soon as I found a place to sit. I made a second vow to find a cup of coffee or a cola to tamp down the headache blooming behind my eyes.

A bell jingled as I pushed open a thick wooden door set between windows taped over with notices for events long past and sales yet to come. Flickering fluorescent bulbs encased in fly-specked fixtures shed miserly light across rows of shelves bowed beneath boxes with their fronts sliced away to reveal the contents. The store smelled musty, like the back of a hall closet where winter coats, still damp, had been put away.

When my eyes adjusted to the dimness, I spotted a grizzled man hunched over a glass case that displayed fishing line, bobbers, hooks, and boxes of ammunition. He glanced up from a magazine with a long-legged centerfold model and frowned as if he spotted an ant in his sugar bowl. "Hep ya?"

I forced a bright smile. "Yes, thanks. The phone at the post office is broken."

"Is that a fact?" He lifted the sandwich laid out beside the magazine. I stared as his yellowed teeth bit into sodden white bread encasing a gelatinous orange substance with red chunks.

I thought of caterpillar guts and swallowed to keep my

128

breakfast down.

"Pimento cheese," he said, his words sticky. "Got them over in the cooler."

I nodded, hiding a shudder. "Is there another phone in town?"

He thumbed to the right. "Gas station."

"Thanks. Where can I catch a bus going north?"

He took another bite and thumbed left. "Down at the interstate."

I remembered where April and I had turned off the highway and into the hills. That was a long way from Stony Ledge. "I, uh, my car—"

"Gas station." He thumbed right again, stuffed in another bite, and went back to ogling the model, tonguing a crust of cheese at the corner of his mouth.

Frustration sizzled in my throbbing head. "My car's not broken, it was st—"

"Gas station." He leaned on the words as if I was hard of hearing or mentally deficient. "Down the road. Gas station."

Recognizing futility, I retreated to the road and trudged to the gas station. A man who could have been the twin of the one I just met sprawled in a chair tipped against the wall between the service bay and a humming soft-drink machine. A picture of frosty bottles beckoned and I slid my hand into my pocket and fingered the coins. The man looked me up and down twice before his eyes settled on my chest. He shifted a lump of something from one cheek to the other. "You one of Ezekiel's band?"

In what I hoped was a casual gesture, I slung my left arm across my breasts and gripped my bundle as if I were giving my right hand a rest. "No."

"Sure look it."

"I'm not. I was told you have a pay phone."

"Did."

Another man saving his syllables. "My car was stolen.

I need to report it. And then I need to get to the bus station."

He spat a stream of brown liquid at a fat beetle, splashing the dispensing slot of the soda machine, murdering my thirst. "Most of that crew sticks their thumbs out."

Hitchhike? I'd heard horror stories about what happened to girls who hitchhiked. Granted, I'd heard them from Gertrude Gorman, but still . . .

He spat again and cocked his head as if trying to look up my skirt. "Should be somebody willing to give a pretty girl a ride. Do it myself if I weren't so busy."

Busy?

Thinking I'd missed something, I peered into the empty repair bay.

"Expecting a job in before too long."

And I was expecting April to return my car and apologize for being born.

"Most people needs a ride or got one to give puts up a notice over yonder." He thumbed to his right.

Feeling like Alice seeking directions from a host of strange creatures, I went on down the road to a two-story brown house with cranberry-colored trim, a deep front porch, and a bulletin board nailed up beside the door with a hand-lettered sign above it that read: "Community Events and Services."

I set my bundle beside a hydrangea bush and climbed the steps for a closer look. The board was thick with notes written on index cards and ruled three-ring-binder paper and scraps of brown grocery bags. "Cat lost. Dog found. Chickens for sale. Sweet corn. Bedsprings." I riffled through them—no rides being offered and I had neither paper nor pen to leave a note of my own.

I was about to hike back to the grocery store when the door opened and a man with silky white hair, eyes the color of the algae that grows on ponds, and a nose like a

130

fishhook stepped out.

"Time is money," he said, straightening a white tie covered with tiny red hogs and tugging at the lapels of a shiny gray suit. "When applicants arrive to see about an employment opportunity I don't expect them to laze around on the porch interminably. I expect them to knock sharply upon the door and present their qualifications."

I blinked. *This* was a man of many words, lengthy and confusing.

"Speak up, young lady. What qualifies you to be a reporter for the *Quarry County Clarion?*"

CHAPTER 14

"Ask her in, Dad," a male voice called from inside.

The man who'd confronted me rolled his eyes. "She's dressed like she's going to a costume party and she doesn't have an application. On top of that, she didn't have the sense to knock."

Didn't have the sense?

I'd been in Stony Ledge only twenty-five minutes and I was thoroughly sick of it and its residents. "I was just about to," I lied, planting my hands on my hips. "And I don't have an application because I wasn't aware there was a job."

"Ad was in the paper. Last three issues. Page four." He shoved the door, speaking over his shoulder. "A quarter page ad and she missed it. She's as dumb as they come."

That does it!

I toed out of a flip-flop and wedged it in the door, spotting my flushed face reflected in a small brass plate that informed me this was the Stony Ledge newspaper office, stationery supply, and print shop. "I missed the ad because I don't read your paper. Maybe a lot of other people don't, either."

Thoreau wouldn't have. He said he never read any memorable news in a newspaper.

The man's eyes narrowed and he put his shoulder against the door, mangling the flip-flop.

"But even if I saw it," I spat through the narrow crack,

"I wouldn't have filled it out because I wouldn't work for someone like you. You're even crankier than my grandmother and that's saying a lot."

The man yanked the door wide, pointed a finger, and opened his mouth, but a burst of laughter cut off his comeback. "Invite her in for an interview," the voice called. "I want to meet somebody who's not scared of your shadow."

The man turned to aim his scowl into the office, releasing the door. I hesitated for a second but then, fueled by curiosity and annoyance, slipped on my flip-flop and sidled past him into a room cluttered with desks, tables, file cabinets, and overflowing cardboard boxes. Bulletin boards covered one wall and on another two schoolroom-size chalkboards were filled with lists—one for what looked like advertising and another for articles. A younger man with the same silky hair but in light reddish brown hunched over an ancient typewriter at a table in the back, pounding away with two fingers.

He hit the return, thwacked a few more keys, and yanked the paper free of the platen. Leaping to his feet, he strode toward me, wiping his fingers on a handkerchief and tucking the tail of a blue shirt into his khaki slacks.

"Thaddeus Tolliver, Junior. That's my father." He nodded at the cranky man. "He uses every bit of his name, but folks call me Tad because I wasn't much bigger than a tadpole when I was born."

I slid my hand into one twice the size of mine and canted my head to take in sparkling hazel eyes, a freckled nose with a just a hint of his father's hook, and a brimming smile. "I'm Elizabeth Roark. You seem to have gotten your growth spurt and a share of someone else's."

The smile became a grin and he squeezed my fingers but didn't release my hand. "Six-six in my stocking feet."

"And all gut," his father muttered. "The boy eats like hired help."

"I *am* hired help. And the pay is lousy." He leaned close, his warm breath feathering my ear. "That's the way it is when you work for relatives."

A kindred spirit. I grinned with delight. "Don't I know it."

"Ah," he squeezed my fingers again. "Would that be the cranky grandmother?"

"When you're done with the social amenities," Senior grumped, "perhaps we could commence with the interviewing process and then send her on her way and return to the business of putting out a paper."

Tad winked, released my hand, and gestured toward a ladder-back chair that leaned almost as much as Delia's outhouse. "Have a seat and tell me about yourself."

"About your qualifications," Senior corrected. "*And* experience. *And* references." He shoved a scarred leather office chair out from behind a massive desk at the front of the room and towed it over.

For a few seconds we stood in a cluster, then Senior scowled at my designated chair and I realized he was waiting for me to sit. Surprised at this display of manners, I did, anchoring my feet, pressing my knees together, and smoothing the hem of my dress. "Well, uh, actually I . . ."

"Told you this was a waste of time," Senior snorted.

Tad brushed that aside with the back of his hand. Senior flipped his own hand as if signifying that I wasn't worthy. The ache behind my eyes expanded into a band of pain that tightened around my brain. I wanted to pinch the hook of his nose and twist until he begged for mercy.

"She's probably never worked at a paper in her life," he muttered, hurling himself into the chair with a jounce of springs and a creak of leather. "Probably never even *read* a paper."

I clenched my fists to keep my fingers off that beak.

"Why don't we see what she has to say?" Tad's voice sounded tired and mechanical, as if he interceded often, as if nothing ever changed around here and nothing ever would.

My anger ebbed and I felt a tingle of excitement, felt drawn into a conspiracy with Tad, the way Dad and I had colluded to avoid those dreadful beans and franks. But I had nothing to make his sticking up for me worthwhile— no experience, no references, nothing except a desire to find out if being a reporter was what I truly wanted. I plucked at my hem, thinking that lack of qualifications wouldn't have stopped April, liar that she was. And Diana wouldn't be fazed either; she'd bank on charm and acting skills.

Senior cooled to a muttering-under-his-breath simmer and Tad sat, turned to a fresh page in a notebook, grasped a pen, and offered an encouraging smile. "Tell us about your experience, Elizabeth Roark."

I decided on honesty embroidered with exaggeration. "Well, I was the editor of my high school newspaper. We took second place in the state competition." Remembering what Delia had said about Yankees, I left out which state. "Since then I've been going to community college to complete the basic curriculum so I can major in journalism."

Tad made a note on his pad. Senior mumbled. I rushed on. "I've been working twenty-eight hours a week at my grandmother's bridal shop and I handle all of her advertising." That consisted of renewing the same tiny ads that ran around Christmas and Valentine's Day in three weekly papers. "I've also written news releases for civic projects and our church bazaars." Three total, but I figured it wouldn't hurt to throw that in and mention religion at the same time. I'd heard that was important in the South.

"That's all?" Senior snorted.

I was about to nod when Tad cut his eyes toward a stack of newspapers on the corner of the table and mimed

135

opening one. "Uh, no, I keep up with the news. I read my local paper from front to back and between classes at college I go to the library and read the *Wall Street Journal* and—" I caught myself before I named a New York City paper. "—and I listen to the radio and watch the news on television to keep up with national and international events."

I turned to Senior and stared into his pond-slime eyes. "Every reporter has an obligation to do that, don't you think? It provides context for their own stories."

He made a face the way you do when you bite into something you hadn't expected to be sour.

"I agree," Tad said. "But I don't always have the time." He gestured toward the blackboards. "Getting this paper out eats up the hours."

"Makes it sound like he does it all himself," Senior groused.

"We divide it up," Tad told me. "I cover crime, government news, features, and the farm reports. Dad keeps up with the society news, obituaries, and all the advertising."

Senior coughed.

"And he writes the editorials," Tad added making his version of the sour-taste face. "We're looking for someone to take over my beat for the next six—"

"*Three* months," Senior cut in. "Maybe less."

Tad patted his father's shoulder. "Dad's having surgery."

Senior glowered as if Tad had sold state secrets to the Russians, but I felt a surge of elation. This job, at a tiny paper in a remote rural town, was only temporary. How many qualified journalists would be interested? My guess was "none." I sat up straighter and raised my chin a confident quarter of an inch.

Senior's glower gave way to a sly smile. "If you didn't know there was a job, then what in blazes were you doing on my porch?"

My brain froze up for a second, but then I decided on the straight story. "I've been traveling some and visiting in the area. I heard about the bulletin board and came to see if I would find a ride to catch a bus to Chicago. I'm enrolling at Northwestern." The straight story with a few holes—like a slice of Swiss cheese.

"Northwestern," Tad echoed as he made another note on the pad. "Great school."

I relaxed enough to smile, but then Senior squinted down that hook of a nose. "Who you been visiting?"

My stomach lurched. *Trapped!* "Oh, I—"

Bang!

"Was that a gunshot?" Senior stood and hustled to the window with Tad close behind. I hunched over, making myself small. I'd heard that sound just a few hours before up on Hog Run Ridge.

"It's that old black witch from up on the ridge," Senior said. "What the hell's she doing here?"

"Let's find out." Tad opened the door wide and I spotted Delia coming across the lawn, overalls flapping.

"You in there, girl?" she called. "I spied your bundle by the bushes."

Senior speared me with a glare. "If that's who you were visiting, this interview is over."

CHAPTER 15

"You in there, girl?" Delia called again.

"Are you looking for Elizabeth?" Tad stepped onto the porch, disbelief lofting his words.

"Girl in a flowery dress wearin' a pair of floppy sandals?"

Senior speared me with his eyes. "That's you."

Two could play the big-word game. "How astute of you to arrive at that conclusion."

I stood, mustering all the dignity a braless woman in rubber shoes could, and marched past him. "Thank you for your hospitality and for entertaining the idea of employing me." Not that he had. And why would I work for him? He'd make me every bit as miserable as my grandmother had.

"I'm here, Delia." I crossed the threshold, doing my best to pretend I didn't see Tad's arched eyebrows, didn't care what he thought.

"Was on my way back up to the ridge when I saw that bundle." Delia poked her chin toward the nightgown sack. "You find out about a bus?"

"Yes." My shoulders slumped. "I've got to get down to the interstate." I pointed to the community bulletin board. "But nobody's going."

"Well, leave a note. Somebody will by and by." A smile lit Delia's homely face. "Come on back up to farm and help me get the ice in and the door hung back on that chicken

138

coop. I'm fixin' to pick apples and make pies later on."

"Wouldn't eat her cooking if I was starving to death," Senior muttered.

Aware that beggars can't be choosers, I tweaked a smile at Delia and then peered past her to the truck and its cargo: a block of what I supposed was ice covered by the tarp and a squawking mass of chickens. Beaks and feet appeared and disappeared between the slats of the cage and even from this distance I smelled the result of cramming frightened fowl into a cage and then putting it in motion. I wondered what helping with the birds entailed and whether Delia would drink herself hateful as the day wore on.

"You never mentioned that you needed to get to the bus station." Tad touched my arm, creating a tingle of warmth. "I'd be happy to drive you there if you can wait until four. I'm meeting a fertilizer and pesticide expert for a story I'm working on."

Delia's wide lips drooped. "Well, there you go, girl. You got your ride." She cocked her head and the smile returned. "You take care of yourself until you come back to Hog Run Ridge."

Come back? I stifled a derisive snort. "I will. Thank you for . . . everything." Even those harsh words last night. Gertrude Gorman often said that what didn't kill you made you stronger. If that was true, I wondered how quickly that strength came on. I could use some.

Delia nodded. "Thank you for cleaning up my barn."

"You can't go gallivanting off with this . . . woman," Senior fumed at Tad as Delia strode to her truck. "I've got to go over to Brett Randolph's funeral. And we're on deadline."

"I've got an interview set up down that way, Dad. And we're always on deadline." Tad winked at me. "Amazingly the *Quarry County Clarion* gets to press on time every week."

Senior's face turned purple. "Don't get smart with me. You need—"

"—some lunch." Tad grasped my arm just above the elbow and led me down the steps, flinching just a little when the door slammed behind us. "I'd be delighted if you'd let me treat you. We have only one café," he said in a bright voice, "but you won't find better fried chicken anywhere."

Delia fired up the truck and took off in a billow of feathers. "On the other hand," Tad said as he batted one away before it could settle in my hair, "maybe we've had enough chicken for one day. How about a hamburger?"

"Anything's fine, as long as there's coffee with it."

"That's a given. I'm running about a quart low." He glanced at my crumpled bundle of possessions. "Is that, uh . . . do you need to, uh . . ."

My cheeks flamed and I reminded myself again that I was never coming back. "It's nothing anyone would want." I turned my back on it and trudged toward the road. "My car was stolen yesterday. They took everything but that."

"I'm sorry." He hustled to catch up. "Maybe the police will recover it."

A more optimistic view of law enforcement than Delia's. "Maybe. I haven't reported it missing yet. Delia doesn't have a phone. And the one at the post office is broken."

Tad rotated his wrist and checked his watch. "Well, Jimmy McCoy should be pulling up at the café soon. He's the deputy assigned to this area and the Thursday special's his favorite: barbecued pork chops, greens, and sweet potato pie."

I wasn't surprised Tad knew that. Superficial appearances aside, when it came to observing and categorizing others, Stony Ledge residents had a lot in common with folks back in Maplekill.

"It's right over there." Tad nodded to a two-story

white house with green shutters on the opposite side of the road. What had once been a garage had been extended and sported a row of windows facing the road. Tad cupped my elbow and guided me across the road.

I wondered if that touch meant he liked me and felt myself flush again. Probably just the Southern way, I told myself. Chivalry. Nothing personal. Still, I reveled in the way he towered over me—five inches beyond Ben's height. I felt delicate, feminine.

Faces turned to the windows as we trekked across the rutted parking lot. "Nothing they like more than minding everybody's business," Tad whispered as he opened the door. "They'll have the phone lines buzzing tonight."

I stepped up into a cloud of cigarette smoke and embraced the sizzle of hot oil and the aroma of frying pork and onions. "I know all about small-town gossip," I said without lowering my voice.

A woman with a blue checkered scarf over rows of skinny pink foam curlers frowned and rubbed at the lines between her eyes as if she could smooth them away. "With all the talk on the grapevine, I'm surprised anyone buys your paper."

Tad chuckled and, fingers splayed across my back over that spot where my bra would have hooked if I had it on, steered me to a yellow linoleum-topped table at the rear and plucked two grease-stained menus from between the napkin dispenser and a bottle filled with what looked like tiny hot peppers. He pulled out a metal kitchen chair with a red vinyl seat and held it for me. When I was settled he took the chair that faced the room. I suspected he'd shielded me intentionally and I liked him for it.

"It's a little informal. You put your order in at the window." He nodded toward a pass-through with a narrow counter beneath it crammed with bottles of ketchup and jars of mustard and relish in a pan of water and ice, pitchers of water, rows of glasses and mugs in a

141

rainbow of colors, and a pot of coffee steaming on a hot plate, "Minerva calls you when it's ready."

I decided this was explanation, not apology. With my belted-in dress and rubber shoes, he wouldn't think I was used to dining at fine restaurants. "That's practical. Saves steps. And the expense of hiring a waitress."

"If Minerva could find one she might. But most women are married and raising kids and tending their gardens." He slotted his menu. "I'm going to have the special. And coffee. I'll get us some now."

He scraped back his chair and strode to the narrow counter. I bent over the menu, trying to ignore the whispers behind me, and remembering all too clearly how I had speculated about strangers in Maplekill. The menu, with only a few items, offered little distraction: ham, tuna, roast beef, or grilled cheese sandwiches; fried chicken, hamburgers, beef stew, or the special; slaw, fries, pie, and ice cream.

"Here you go." Tad rested a tray on the edge of the table and unloaded two bright blue mugs of coffee, a bowl of sugar, a tiny pitcher of milk, and two spoons. "Have you decided what you want?"

"Not yet." My eyes lingered on the tuna sandwich, my mouth remembering the way my father mixed the fish with relish, onion, celery, and lots of mayonnaise and piled it high on toasted rye with lettuce and tomato. Tuna sandwiches elsewhere were often just fish and something that looked like mayonnaise but wasn't.

I made my decision. "Grilled cheese on whole wheat if they have it." Probably those oily, bright orange squares. Still, potentially less disappointing.

"That's all? No fries? No slaw?"

Slaw was also suspect—probably not the tangy mix of cabbage, carrot, and onion that Jo made and probably also awash in not-mayonnaise—but I hadn't had a vegetable for days. "All right. Slaw."

With the tray under his arm, Tad departed and I tried to ignore the stares I felt probing my back, busying myself with returning the menu to its slot, pouring milk into my coffee, stirring, and finally raising the mug to my lips. The coffee was better than most, rich and dark, within a few moments of the first sip my headache ebbed.

Tad slid into the seat across from me and checked his watch. "Minerva says Jimmy called to ask her to hold a special for him because he's running late." Raising his cup, he took several long swallows. "So, what brings you to Stony Ledge?"

I grimaced. "It's a long and humiliating story."

He arched his brows and grinned. "As humiliating as the time this town boy was sent out to milk his great uncle's bull?"

I giggled into my mug, feeling half safe, half relaxed. "Well, there were cows involved but Delia did the milking."

"Delia's tough as an old boot," he said in that matter-of-fact tone. "Had to be. Cyrus Cleburne worked her like a mule."

"Cyrus?"

"Ezekiel." He flipped his fingers. "Call him what you want, he was as lazy as the day is long except when it came to figuring the angles. If you ask me he came up with those visions just to get work done around the farm."

Tad raised the corner of one lip and crinkled his nose. "Some thought he brought in all those weird folk just to rile things up, like the time he spiked the punch at the church social. But he carried the name of a family that's been in these hills since time out of mind, so they let him be."

I blinked. Ezekiel was really Cyrus and Tad was dishing the dirt like ladies in the church foyer back in Maplekill.

He leaned toward me and lowered his voice to a

143

whisper. "The population of this county is the same color as the inside of a loaf of white bread so it was a scandal when Cyrus brought Delia back here a few years ago. He's a far distant cousin on my mother's side and blood is supposed to be thicker than water, but . . . Well, it seemed when he realized he was too old to keep up the farm and too poor to hire help, folks speculate he figured he'd get a slave by marrying one. Had to go north to do it."

I digested that with a swallow of coffee. "So Cyrus was—? "

"As white as you are." He raised his eyebrows. "You didn't know?"

I shook my head. "I never met him. He died before I got here."

His eyes narrowed. "I thought you said you were visiting Delia."

"I never said that." Had my life ever been so uncomplicated that explanations weren't necessary? "It's a long—"

"Tad," a woman's voice called. "Order's ready."

Frowning, he scraped back his chair. Glancing over my shoulder toward the pass-through, I saw that all eyes in the café were on me. I felt hot and cold and sick to my stomach. I wanted to bolt, but I was stuck until four.

"Stare them down." Diana's advice echoed in my mind. She'd coached me before an honor society presentation before the whole school. It hadn't been my finest hour. But I survived.

Stomach knotting I turned in my chair, picking the woman in curlers because she was the farthest away, and meeting her eyes with what I hoped was a quizzical gaze, a "can I help you?" expression. She squinted and I almost ducked my head and cast my eyes to the ground, but then I reminded myself that I'd be gone in a few hours, and intensified the stare.

She bounced against the back of her chair as if she'd

144

been struck by a baseball, and then scooped a shiny red purse from the floor and rooted through it. One down. The knots in my stomach tightened, but I transferred my attention to a man in a rumpled brown suit with a yellowing shirt and a thin black tie hanging like a dead snake around his neck. He swallowed, Adam's apple scaling his neck, and reached for the cigarettes in his shirt pocket.

"Hope you like this." Tad set an oval plate in front of me.

Grateful for the diversion, I squared my chair to the table and hunched over the plate, inhaling the aromas of toasted bread, melted cheese, and a pickle pungent with garlic. The mound of chopped cabbage was bright with slivers of red onion and carrot and garnished with chopped almonds. "This looks incredible."

"Minerva's got a way of taking an old recipe and changing it just enough so it seems new but still familiar." He set a packed plate at his spot. "And she's got the sense not to mess with success when she achieves it."

Drawing up to the table, he grasped a knife and fork and began to operate on chops glazed with a wine-colored sauce. "If you want to talk, I'm here to listen." He forked a chunk of pork into his mouth and followed it with the tip of a triangle of pie that looked like a paler version of pumpkin. "And I won't spread it around. You can trust me."

Trust? Would he use that word if he knew how mine had been betrayed? "Thanks," I said, polite without warmth.

Picking up half the sandwich, I bit into it. Cheddar. Melted around a meaty slice of tomato. I tried the slaw. Mayonnaise. I crunched down half the pickle and went back to the sandwich. After Delia's greasy breakfast, I should have been full for hours, but my hunger had nothing to do with calories and everything to do with

145

craving a feeling of well-being. I wanted to cram down this delicious food until my stomach swelled against my belt, to feel a Thanksgiving-dinner kind of fullness.

Then I thought of Thoreau who disdained gluttony and believed in savoring food.

I laid the sandwich down and breathed two dozen times, watching Tad sop up juice from the greens with a chunk of cornbread. Then I nibbled, chewed, and savored. I detected coarse black pepper in the sandwich and dill and an herb I couldn't identify in the slaw. Smooth melted cheese slid over my tongue and I contrasted that to the coarse texture of the bread.

The knot in my stomach unraveled; I found myself liking this spot in Stony Ledge and this man who'd been kind to me. Before I finished my sandwich I was telling Tad the story—but not the part about the money because that made me look like a fool and not the part about Ben dumping me for April because that hurt too much and made it seem I had no value. I made Ben a friend and April a friend of a friend and said I left home because Maplekill was too confining and I hated the bridal business and working for my grandmother. Tad nodded at that and scowled a lot over what April did.

Just as we were finishing, his eyes flickered toward the door. "There's Jimmy now." I turned to see a lanky uniformed man with black hair that twirled onto his forehead in a style from the 50s. "I'll get us coffee to go and ask him to stop in when he's done."

"Stop in where?"

He nodded toward the street. "Over at the *Clarion*."

I poked my fork at a last shaving of carrot, my contentment sifting away like sand through my fingers. "I don't . . . I mean, your father . . ."

"He won't be back for hours. Besides the fact that the world's windiest preacher is presiding at the funeral, Dad's a pallbearer. He's got to stay until they start shoveling."

I felt relief at that, but also guilt about taking up so much of Tad's time, and fear that—as Gertrude Gorman insisted almost all men did—he'd expect a return on his investment, a return promised by my bare legs, flowered dress, and the braless state he couldn't help but notice.

Realizing I'd chased the carrot sliver twice around the plate, I laid my fork along the edge and set to work shredding my napkin. "But he said you were on deadline."

Tad laughed, shoved his chair back, and flashed me a wink. "I finished up the piece he's worried about yesterday, but if he knew he'd say 'idle hands are the devil's tools' and find a make-work project—like filing the stuff that's been in the garage since before I was born." He set his plate on top of mine and gathered up the silverware and mugs.

"Gertrude Gorman says the same thing. Except instead of 'tools' she says 'workshop'." I stood, wadding my napkin and wiping a drop of glossy barbecue sauce from the table. "But you were typing something when I came in."

"Assignment for a correspondence course in psychology." He led the way to a large trash can where he dumped the pork chop bones and motioned for me to toss in the napkin. "When Mom died four years ago I quit college. Dad needed help running the paper and money was tight. But I want a journalism degree, so I've been getting it piecemeal."

He set the dishes in a huge metal tub on wheels. "Don't mention that, either. Dad never went past high school and doesn't understand why I want to know about history or math or how people's minds work if all I'm going to do is run the *Clarion*." He leaned in the pass-through and called to a stocky woman in a hairnet, "Two coffees to go, please."

"But you're going to do more than that, aren't you?

147

CAROLYN J. ROSE

With a degree and your experience you could probably go almost anywhere, maybe even be a foreign correspondent."

"Maybe someday." He shrugged. "But this place suits me for right now. I'm a pretty big frog in this little puddle."

The last sentence held a hint of smug arrogance that reminded me of Diana. I didn't like that he said it or that I drew the comparison.

Drawing a thin wallet from his back pocket, Tad took out a five and made change from the coins and bills in a fishbowl at the end of the counter. I wondered if anyone had ever cheated Minerva and decided that it would take a bold thief to defy all those prying eyes and the deputy mixing barbecue sauce into his pile of greens. When Tad stepped over to speak with him I slipped a quarter into the bowl, and met the eyes of a bushy-bearded man before I marched to the door.

"Jimmy will be over in a bit." Tad handed me one of the coffees and we hiked across the parking lot, the thin cardboard cup scorching my fingers. "In the meantime, you can write up a few sample stories for me to show Dad."

"Thanks, but there's not much point in that, is there?" I hopped on my left foot while I kicked a stone out of my right flip-flop. "After you drop me off, I'm getting the first bus out to Chicago."

"What about your car?"

"It's probably a long way from here by now." Halfway to California. "It could be months before the police find it."

If they ever find it.

I felt a profound sense of loss. Buggy was more than just a car.

He kicked a flattened beer can into a rut. "I guess I kind of hoped you'd stay. You don't have much

148

experience, but I bet you learn fast and we could have a lot of fun together."

"Thank you for saying that." A statement from the heart that brought heat to my own cheeks. No matter what April thought, I needed attention, too.

He turned to face me, a flush creeping up his cheeks. "And the truth is no one else applied."

I held back a satisfied smile. "But your father didn't seem to have much use for me."

Tad sighed. "That's been his way since Mom died—all bark and plenty of bite to go with it. I can't soften him up the way she did."

"You do the best you can." I touched his arm. "But I couldn't work for him. He's too much like Gertrude Gorman."

"The world is full of Gertrude Gormans." Tad took my arm as we reached the road. "They're rockslides on the highway of life. We can't get through them, so our choices are to turn back or figure out how to get around without going so far out of the way we lose sight of where we're headed."

He made it sound so simple, so possible. Smiling, I repeated the words to myself, intending to remember them. April was a rockslide. But I was around that now and in a few short hours I'd be back on the highway.

CHAPTER 16

Jimmy McCoy sauntered in before I had more than a few sips of coffee and settled myself in Tad's chair. The deputy looked me up and down, his eyes—so dark I couldn't see the line between iris and pupil—taking a snapshot and printing it on his brain.

Tad stood. "Jimmy, this is Elizabeth Roark."

Jimmy nodded, the twist of hair bobbling, bouncing against his forehead. "Pleased to meet you."

He pulled a tiny notebook from his shirt pocket, but before I could speak, Tad launched into an even more sanitized and skewed version of my tale than I'd delivered. I felt a brief anger—after all, it was my car—but then recognized that Tad's involvement gave me a better shot at getting something done.

Watching over the rim of my cup, I listened as Tad, without a single pause for thought, provided me with relatives in towns I'd never heard of and said I was heading that way when I stopped to take a picture and April begged for a ride. He told Jimmy that I was too good for my own good and that I'd driven her up to Cyrus' farm.

Turning me into a present-day version of the Good Samaritan, he described how I'd come across Delia searching for the cows and went into the woods to help, locking my car. Jimmy's face clouded when Tad told him April and others broke out a window and looted my belongings. I didn't know about Tad's journalism skills,

150

but his imagination was well beyond Diana's. He had promise as a fiction writer or con man.

When Tad finished up, Jimmy scowled and hitched at his belt. "It's time we went up there and cleaned out that nest of vipers and set Delia straight."

I gasped, my heart constricting with fear of what might happen—especially if she'd been topping off her tea and turned hateful on him.

Tad glanced at me from the corners of his eyes and patted the air by his side. Telling me to calm down? I gripped my cup so hard coffee sloshed over the side and splashed on the edge of Tad's table. I mopped at it with my sleeve.

"They cleaned themselves out," Tad told Jimmy. "Letting the cows loose was the last straw. Delia threatened to call the law and they took off like road-running lizards."

Jimmy threw back his shoulders and puffed out his chest as if his reputation alone was responsible for the exodus.

"All of that mess was Cyrus' doing. And now that he's dead things should be pretty quiet up there," Tad continued. "I ran into Delia this morning and she told me she was as sick of all those freaks as everyone else."

I gaped. Tad hadn't even said "hello" to Delia. He patted air again. "All she wants is to mind her own business. Any more travelers show up, she'll turn them away."

Jimmy hitched his belt again and rocked on his heels as if considering whether he needed to drive up there anyway. I held my breath. Tad patted air. Jimmy's eyes shifted to me. "You got your license, tag number, registration?"

"Yes." I emptied my lungs, filled them again, and fumbled my wallet from my pocket. Trying not to look at the photo of Ben I'd slid it behind, I worked a folded index card from a plastic sleeve. When I bought the car, Dad suggested I jot down all the relevant information in at least two places and now I was thankful. I handed the card over along with my license. "The registration was in the car, but everything's on here."

Jimmy copied a few things into his notebook and passed them back. "Got a number where we can reach you? What about your kin?"

"I, uh, this messed up my plans. I won't have time to visit them after all." Fingers chilled with fear, I worked the card back into my wallet. What if he insisted on a name and number? "Tad's taking me to the bus station this afternoon so I can get to Chicago."

"Chicago?" Jimmy tucked the notebook away and rocked on his heels. "You got kin there, too?"

"Uh, no. I'm planning to go to college."

"When you find the car, I'll get a message to her," Tad volunteered.

A phone jangled, startling me. It had been four days since I heard that sound and it made me feel even farther from Dad, even more alone.

"Excuse me a minute." Tad hustled to his father's desk. The squatty black phone rang again before he scooped up the receiver and clamped it to his ear. "You've reached the *Quarry County Clarion*, your weekly window on news and events." He used an official voice but rolled his eyes as if to say he'd be happy to dispense with the slogan.

Jimmy rocked once more. "Chicago? Seems like there are plenty of colleges for a girl closer to home."

Spoken like almost anyone in Maplekill. I bit back a caustic reply.

"No!" Tad's knuckles whitened around the receiver. The tone of that one word told me something had collided with his life. He dropped into his father's chair, his left hand over his heart. Jimmy stopped rocking.

152

After a long moment Tad whispered, "Thank you. I'll be there right away," and hung up.

He stood, hands clawing as if he'd been caught in a current of fast water. "Dad collapsed at Brett Randolph's funeral."

Jimmy pulled a set of keys from his pocket. "Let's go."

Tad crossed his hands on his chest. "It's his heart. They're taking him to Little Rock."

"We'll pick up his car and then go on down there." Jimmy strode toward the door. "You got spare keys?"

"Somewhere." Tad jerked open a drawer and pawed through it, coming up with a key attached to a length of braided orange and yellow plastic cords, fumbling with it, dropping it, turning to me. "I said I'd take—"

"It's okay." I scooped up the boondoggle keychain and pressed it into his fingers. "I'll be fine."

"But I promised I'd . . . I *wanted* to take you to the bus."

"I know you did." I was sure of that. "And if I haven't found a way out of Stony Ledge by the time you get back I'll let you drive me there *and* buy me another lunch. Now go on. Your father needs you."

He chewed at his lip. "But where will—?"

Jimmy was out the door, so I felt free to say it. "I'll go to Delia's."

"But how will you—?"

I put my hands on his shoulders and turned him. "I'll walk. I'm a big girl and thanks to you I had lunch enough to last me the whole hike. Now go!"

He took three steps and then spun toward his table. "My interview. The agriculture expert. He's expecting me at five."

"I'll call and tell him you can't make it. What's his name?"

"Um . . . I can't remember." He pointed to a stack at the edge of his table. "It's on a paper near the top. Clipped

153

to the story that's half written."

"I'll find it." I gave him a push and he went out across the porch on stiff legs, hands out like a sleepwalker. In a moment I heard a car door slam, an engine roar, and tires bite into gravel. Then I was alone.

A quick search of the heap of papers yielded the half-written story and a news release with a name and number at the top. I dialed and got Phil Buchanan who gave me his condolences to pass on to Tad, and offered to answer my questions on the phone and mail a couple of pictures he'd taken. I asked him to hold while I rolled a piece of paper into Tad's typewriter and skimmed his penciled notes.

I saw that he referred to *Silent Spring* and my heart jumped. I'd read that over the summer. This was no longer new territory and I had questions of my own.

As I hammered away at the sticky keys I imagined Gertrude Gorman's smug smile. She'd insisted I learn secretarial skills for the day when I'd certainly have to fall back on them. During my senior year of high school, partly to silence her and partly because I needed another elective, I took typing and found I enjoyed both the discipline and the speed with which I could record my thoughts. I never admitted that to her; the rules of engagement required that I keep mum about pronouncements that turned out to have validity.

When I was finished, I clipped my notes under Tad's, squared up the heap of paper, then unclipped the notes, unfolded the clip, and used one end to pry loose old ink and ribbon lint crusted inside the typewriter keys.

I knew I was just killing time—the shallow depressions in the letters would fill again in a few days— but I didn't want to leave this place where someone had been interested in me, where something had almost gone right.

Too soon the keys were clean and, with no reason to be there, I felt like a trespasser. With a last look, I pushed in the button on the knob and pulled the door closed behind me. The click of the latch sounded far off and final, like the sound of a pebble dropped into a well.

I picked up my bundle, walked halfway to the road, then traded my rubber shoes for sneakers and made faster progress. The surly grizzled man was still at his post in the grocery store and couldn't be bothered to smile even when I laid my carefully considered purchases on the counter: a toothbrush and toothpaste, shampoo, a safety razor, several candy bars and bags of peanuts, two dripping bottles of soda dipped from the rusty water in a squatty cooler that smelled faintly of bleach, a flashlight and batteries, a pen and a notebook.

I'd searched for women's underwear but hadn't found any and wasn't about to mention the subject to a man who spent his days drooling over a centerfold photo. But beneath a jumble of fishing gear I found a green canvas sack with a zippered pocket. One side was faded to beige as if it had once been displayed in the window and it was furred with dust, but its strap had a buckle that could serve as a bottle opener and the tag tied to that buckle read $1.99.

"Should be more," the man grunted. "They don't make 'em like this anymore."

"It's faded and filthy," I pointed out. "You should pay me to take it."

I pressed my arms against my sides. Where did that come from? When did I start saying what was in my mind without second thoughts and triple amendments? Half stunned, I didn't know whether to be proud or frightened of where this might lead.

The man glared, then punched a one and two nines on the adding machine and pulled the lever. He snatched a twenty-dollar bill from my hand and slapped my change on the counter. I stuffed it into my wallet, not taking the time to organize the bills in descending order and register

155

the meager amount left. Then I crammed my nightgown and its contents into the sack and piled everything except one soda and the pen on top.

With the sack over my shoulder, I trekked to the post office. It was closed for the day, but I spotted a slot beside the door marked "MAIL." Peering through the window I noted that letters pushed through the slot dropped onto the floor inside and guessed the busybody collected them in the morning. She would read my postcard then, but at least I wouldn't be standing in front of her while she did.

The card's edges were dog-eared but I doubted Dad would notice or care. Again I imagined him pacing near the phone. Would he assume that April and I had gone together? Would he go back and forth through the hedge to Jo's house hoping that she might have heard something from April? What kind of cold comfort would either of them get from Gertrude Gorman?

Shivering, I gazed back down the road toward the *Clarion* office, thinking about that squatty black telephone and the door I locked behind me. Stupid! Too busy thinking about myself.

I'd mailed a card on Tuesday. Surely he'd have it soon, maybe even tomorrow. I addressed and dated this one and wrote: "Pretty country here. Decided to stay a few days. Heading to Chicago soon. Love, Elizabeth."

I was about to poke it through the slot when I recalled the image of Dad sliding through the gap in the hedge to merge his misery with Jo's. In tiny letters I penned: "April went on to San Francisco."

The soda bottles were empty, the shadows were long, and I was dripping with sweat when I reached the spot where the tribe broke the window and stole my Buggy. Panting, I set my pack down and stopped to rest, staring at the cardboard boxes flattened in the ruts, a metaphor for my life. I kicked the nearest in disgust. It sailed a few inches from the ground, hovered for a moment like an ungainly bird, and then fell back, dust spurting onto crumpled fabric that had once been white.

Anticipation thudding in my chest, I bent and tugged two pairs of underpants and a bra from beneath the box. The second box sheltered another pair of underpants and two pairs of socks. I shook off the dust, giddy with heat and a rueful joy. As I jammed my prizes into the sack, I thought of what Thoreau said about life near the bone being the sweetest. Meager as it was, this discovery was sweeter than maple sugar.

"I guess you know what you're talking about, Henry David. But if I get any closer to the bone, I'll be inside scraping at the marrow."

Carrying on a one-sided conversation with a man dead for more than a hundred years, I climbed the rest of the way without panting and without stopping. When I crested the hill and spotted Delia's house, she was sitting on the front steps in a faded shirt and overalls, shading her eyes against the declining sun. As I got closer I saw a tall glass in her hand and braced myself in case she'd been topping it off from that jug.

CHAPTER 17

A wide smile transfigured Delia's homely features and she patted the stone step beside her. "Seems like every time I look out I see you coming up that hill. Take a load off and tell me how you missed out on your ride."

"Mr. Tolliver collapsed at a funeral and they took him to a hospital in Little Rock. Jimmy McCoy drove Tad down there."

She nodded and I shifted from foot to foot, wondering how to ask if I could stay. She seemed welcoming enough, but what was in that glass?

"Tad promised to take me to the bus when . . . when he can." That could be days, weeks. Or, between caring for his father and getting the paper out, he might forget me entirely. "But I'll try to find another way as soon as I can."

"Well, I expect right now you need some tea before your tongue cleaves to the roof of your mouth."

Delia lifted a pitcher from the edge of the porch, filled an empty glass, and handed it to me. "There's not a single drop of liquor in there. It's not calling me this evening and if it does, I vowed I won't answer."

Wondering if she had the strength to do that, I sipped at the tea. It was just a little sweet and not at all salty. I drank it down speculating about who she'd made it for. Because of her color and her marriage to Cyrus, Delia was a pariah, so I doubted anyone from town would come visiting. Was she expecting relatives? Should I, the

158

uninvited guest, find another place to stay? But where? In the tick-infested woods? Deciding I'd consider that when I had to and not one second before, I shuddered and slumped onto the step.

"Collapsed, huh?"

I shook myself back to here and now. "Tad said it was his heart."

"Didn't know he had one," Delia mused.

I almost agreed, but then thought of how kind Tad had been and held my tongue. He could speak the unvarnished truth about his father the way I did about Gertrude Gorman, but he'd earned that right. I hadn't.

"That old man brought it on himself," Delia said. "Angry at everyone who crossed his path and for not much reason. But he's tough as a granddaddy rattler. He'll pull through." She rubbed her chin. "As far as changing his ways, though, that dog won't hunt."

I cast my mind back over the scene on the front porch of the *Clarion*. Delia had said nothing to Tad or Senior and they'd said nothing to her. As far as I could remember, no glances of any degree of meaning had passed among them. "You know the Tollivers?"

She shrugged and refilled my glass. "Know *of* them."

I assumed that meant she'd overheard gossip, or witnessed an encounter between Senior and a target of his displeasure.

"With a slab of cheese or without?"

"Excuse me?"

"Apple pie. Came out of the oven an hour ago. You like yours with cheese on it?"

When it came to cheese, I doubted that I'd be lucky twice in one day. "Without, please."

Delia hustled into the house and returned with a quarter of a pie, two inches thick and oozing with reddish brown cinnamon-sugar juice. It smelled as good as any I'd ever had, but I forked off a bit of crust, expecting it to be

159

heavy, tough, or as greasy as the breakfast eggs and potatoes. Instead, it dissolved on my tongue with a flaky burst of butter. Once again, I stifled the urge to devour this offering in a few gulps and held back, savoring. "It's delicious. Thank you."

Delia waved that off. "How long you staying?"

"I, um . . ."

She waved that off, too. "Makes me no never mind. You're no trouble, you don't eat much, and you got fine manners. That's more than can be said about them others that set upon us like locust." She nodded toward the orchard. "As long as you help out and don't mind sleeping in the barn."

"I don't mind," I lied, thinking of that lumpy pallet of cast-off clothing.

Delia refilled my glass and glanced behind her. "My man had a powerful spirit and he wasn't near ready to go. Probably take him some time to cross over."

The skin on the back of my neck prickled. Was she saying Cyrus was haunting her? Had the spare glass been for him? I set it down with a sharp click, afraid to ask. "The barn's fine."

Sleeping on a lumpy bed was better than worrying about ticks and snakes or wispy wraiths floating out of a closet or down from the ceiling.

As a child I'd been alternately thrilled and chilled by ghost stories, from the Headless Horseman to local tales of an empty grave and a strange mist at a bend in the stream. Stories, nothing more. But the way Delia spoke made me wonder whether there was fact behind the fiction. Was Ben's uneasy spirit roaming the hills of Vietnam? Had it returned to Maplekill? Or was it here, searching for April?

Shivering, I hugged my knees to my chest, but then raised my chin. I had no reason to fear Ben's spirit, and if it materialized, I might get some of the answers I longed

160

for.

A cricket chirped in the weeds among the jumbled rocks beside the steps and Delia patted the porch. "Come on inside, Mr. Cricket, and bring me some good luck for a change."

I added my silent plea to hers before I recalled how Gertrude Gorman insisted crickets ate clothing. She hunted them down with a broom and squashed them flat. "I didn't know crickets brought good luck."

"If they're in your house. Bad luck if you kill one indoors, though."

As if it feared that I might have my grandmother's intentions, the cricket remained hidden, working up a steady rhythm, chirping faster, louder. Delia held up a finger. "Count 'em."

I glanced around. "Count what?"

"The number of chirps. Until I tell you to stop."

I set my half-finished pie down, thinking this odd behavior was evidence she had lied about refusing the call of liquor. "When do I start?"

She folded her finger into her palm. "Now."

I counted to myself, wondering how high she'd make me go and what the point was beyond being willing to prove myself a worthy guest. Ten. Twenty. Thirty. Forty.

"Stop." Delia peered at me. "I counted off fourteen seconds. How many chirps did you get?"

"Forty-three."

"That means it's eighty-three degrees according to Mr. Cricket. Cooler than last night. Drier, too."

I realized the sweat I worked up climbing that hill had evaporated, even from my armpits and under my breasts.

She pointed to the western sky where bands of wispy clouds were tinged with orange. "No rain tonight means a good day for picking tomorrow. Had to fix the chicken coop so I got just enough for one pie today. And I don't much like getting up on that ladder."

161

"I'm not afraid of ladders." I forked off another bite of pie. "As long as they're not too wobbly."

"I'll hold it steady."

I finished the pie and drained my glass, knew I should get to the barn before full dark, but stayed put as the western sky turned fiery red and bats darted across the pasture. Ben had held the ladder for me when we gleaned the misshapen fruit of those ancient trees back in Maplekill. When it was his turn to pick, he swung up into the branches, and tossed apples down faster and faster until I gave up trying to catch them and fell laughing to the grass.

Choking on the memory of the triumphant smile that crinkled his crooked nose, I filled my glass with a trembling hand, the pitcher rattling against the rim, and sipped tea now as warm as the air.

"It seems you were meant to stay here a bit longer."

I stiffened. That "meant to" part smacked of Gertrude Gorman's "God has a plan" speeches. If talk was turning to religion, I'd hoist my pack and go to the barn with Thoreau as my only companion.

Or so I hoped. My mind prickled with thoughts of ghosts and their intentions.

"I'm not one to wait a lifetime for revelation," Delia said. "I lack the patience and I like my meanings to be clear so I don't wonder. But I've seen it time and again that good balances bad. And the other way around, too, bad coming after good like a hawk after a flock of chicks."

She breathed deep and laid one finger on the point of my shoulder, pressing against the bone. "I don't know what went on before you came here, but it seems you're carrying a load that's pulling you down. Could be this is the place where you're meant to reach bottom, let it go, and start back up."

I imagined myself, my sack across my back, leaping off the lip of a ravine and plunging into a churning river of

162

dark water. "What if I reach bottom but it's mud? What if I sink so far into it I can't get out?"

"Some do," she mused. "Some get so used to their misery and their burdens, so proud of them even, they won't let go. And there they stay."

I glanced at her from the corners of my eyes, glad she seemed focused on the last bit of velvety blue on the rim of the world and not on me. Was I proud of my burdens and how close I held them? Had I become arrogant about my ability to carry them, haughty about managing?

I didn't want to tell Delia about Ben and April, Gertrude Gorman and my father, and the day Sebastian died. And then a single star winked and I thought I might tell her only the little bit I'd told Tad. But the light faded and dark came on with a rush of wind and the cry of a night bird and I wanted to tell her everything, *had* to tell her everything.

It came out like snowmelt down a hillside in a spring thaw, in a trickle and then a rush. Words tumbled over words until the sky glittered with stars and I felt clean and shiny and smooth inside, like a pan that's been scoured until the metal gleams and feels like satin beneath your fingers.

Delia said not a single word until I panted to a halt at the present moment and sucked at the last of my tea. "That feels better, don't it? Laying something out in words helps lay it to rest."

She stroked my hair, her chapped skin catching and pulling just a little. "I'm sorry about your man. Love can sure open us up for a world of hurt."

I nudged my head against her hand, craving connection. She twined my hair in her fingers. "And I'm sorry you ran up against that thievin' girl and that pack of travelers. It's always the innocents who suffer most. They're too trusting, they don't see wickedness until it's too late."

I frowned, not liking to be called innocent, but forced to acknowledge I was. Not that I'd been blind to April and not that I'd trusted her, because I hadn't. What I had been was unprepared for the extent of her treachery. Calling me innocent was a kind way, Delia's sober way, of saying I'd been a fool.

"Well, it seems you have a way to get home if you want to." She drew her fingers from my hair and patted my shoulder. "You're not like that girl with the scarecrow and lion and such."

"Dorothy," I said, remembering how I'd compared Delia's husband to the wizard when I first came to Hog Run Ridge. Two days ago. A lifetime ago.

"Right. The girl with the ruby shoes." She stamped her feet on the step below. "Sure didn't look comfortable to me. Looked like they pinched at the heel. I like my shoes with some give to them and rubber in the soles so my feet don't get so angry before the end of the day."

I laughed, for the first time considering those ruby slippers the way an innocent wouldn't.

"But it seems before you go on or go back, you've got to come to a place of forgetting."

I was glad of the dark that hid the roll of my eyes. How could I ever forget Ben or the shock of his betrayal? And how could I forget April and all that had happened since I left Maplekill? That was insane. Next she'd be telling me I needed to forgive them.

"I don't mean that you can forget the past. That will be inside your skin as long as you live." I heard a chafing sound and thought she might be rubbing her arms, rubbing at Cyrus' memory. "But if you mean to go on and make a life for yourself, you'd best leave behind how things might have been if they worked out the way you wanted."

I shook my head. "Leave behind my dreams?"

"Dreams, designs, schemes, might-have-beens." The

164

porch creaked and then the door hinges squealed. "You made them. You can make new ones."

The latch snicked and the bolt rasped home.

I listened to the cricket for a few minutes, then shouldered my pack and trudged to the barn to seek solace with Thoreau.

Following the narrow path carved out of the night by a quarter moon, I thought that dreams weren't cookies or dresses or houses. Dreams weren't mixed up from a recipe, cut from a pattern, or built on foundations set into the earth by an architect's design. Dreams were rare and elusive, magical things created from hope and possibility, nurtured by love and belief.

And I had so little of those ingredients.

CHAPTER 18

A cool breeze woke me at dawn and, after a stop at the privy, I made my way to the pump with my sack and scrubbed myself, the sack, and every bit of clothing inside with that corrosive brown soap. I shaved my legs, wrung out the largest of the T-shirts, wiggled into it and carried the rest to the clothesline, feeling another burst of joy as I surveyed my array of underwear. This was my new definition of wealth and luxury—enough so I didn't have to wash every day.

I brushed my teeth and then sat on the back steps, combing my hair and thinking about the candy bars and peanuts in my pack, trying to interpret what Delia had said last night. Did "you don't eat much" mean that she'd feed me in exchange for chores? The only way to find out was to wait and see, so I moved on to the bigger question: how long should I wait for Tad?

I left Maplekill early on Monday and leaving here at dawn on the same day a week later would give my journey a rough symmetry. But should I pursue my plan of going to Chicago or, as Delia said, make new dreams?

"What would Henry David do?" I quizzed myself.

"He'd march off to that different drummer."

"But what if I don't hear a drum?"

"Listen harder."

I cocked my head, but heard only the metallic buzz of grasshoppers, the twitter of birds, and a faint scuffling.

Then a bolt slid, hinges screeched, and Delia spoke in a voice thick with phlegm, "You're up with the sun."

I rolled my head and saw her framed in the doorway dressed in the same shirt she'd had on last night and a pair of cracked leather slippers with jagged holes for her big toes. "Did you let the chickens out?"

I'd cut through the corner of the orchard so I hadn't passed the coop. "No." I leaped to my feet. "Do you want me to?"

She nodded, opened a metal bin beside the door and dug into it with a coffee can, pulling it out half full of cracked corn. "Toss that in front and while they're pecking at it see if they laid us any eggs. Otherwise breakfast will be grits and cold biscuits. I'll get the stove going and milk Clover."

When I reached the coop, I saw that Delia had repaired the door with determination but little skill, setting the hinge back into the rotted spot it had fallen from, driving a dozen rusty nails around it, and bending them over to hold it in place. Dad would shake his head and laugh. I rattled corn from the can, listening to a chorus of clucks from within and thinking that I'd watched him often enough that I could fix the door if Delia had some solid lumber, a saw, and a chisel.

Jamming the heel of my hand under the latch, I braced myself on the narrow ramp, levered the hook loose, and tugged at the door. Chickens burst forth like water from a broken dam, squawking and scuttling across my feet, fighting for corn in a flurry of feathers. Inside, the coop smelled of straw and ammonia and I threaded my way around damp blotches. I found three eggs in the straw piled in racks on the wall, carried them back to the house, and tapped on the half-open door.

Delia emerged and peered into the can. "The girls did good their first night in a new place. I'll scramble those up with some cheese." She stepped back inside and in a

167

moment called in a voice that seemed more resigned than inviting. "Come on in. Coffee's about brewed up."

I hesitated, but the lure of caffeine was stronger than fear of imposing, and I crept inside. The kitchen, a rectangular room that stretched the width of the house, had two doors leading off it, both shut tight. The room was both run-down and kept up. The tan and brown linoleum on the floor and countertops was worn and cracked, but it was clean and the pine table was bleached almost white. Plates, glasses, and mugs shared newspaper-lined shelves with mixing bowls, utensils flowered from a brown pitcher without a spout, and scoured pots and pans hung on the wall beside a shiny black stove. A pot glugged, rattling its lid, and a percolator on the back burner hissed and gurgled.

Delia broke the eggs into a frying pan slick with grease and speared me with her gaze. "Who was you talking to out there?"

"Talking to?" I pushed my glasses higher on my nose. "I might have said something to the chickens."

"No. Before I first come out. You was talking to someone."

I held off on an answer, worrying it around in my brain. Gertrude Gorman always said talking to yourself was a sign of insanity—never mind that she did it all the time—and Delia likely held some belief of her own.

She squinted. "You didn't see Cyrus, did you?"

I shuddered and shook my head. If I'd seen Cyrus, I'd be halfway to Stony Ledge by now. "No. I was talking, uh, *pretending* to talk to Henry David Thoreau."

Delia rubbed her chin, then set out a bowl of biscuits, a plate mounded with butter, and a jar of jam the color of the morning sun. "Persimmon," she told me. "Picked last fall."

Her brow furrowed. "Thoreau did you say? No one by that name in Stony Ledge. He a traveler?" She tugged at

168

her lower lip. "And what do you mean 'pretending' to talk to him?"

I slid a stool from beneath the table and balanced on it, wishing the coffee was ready and I had at least half a cup inside of me to help my brain cells connect. "Well, Thoreau was a writer and he died a long time ago—1862. But he had a way of looking at things that makes a lot of sense to me and so I was wondering what he'd do in my situation."

Delia twisted a tuft of hair and salted the eggs. When her silence felt uneasy, I tossed in a few facts. "He lived back east, in Massachusetts. He once got thrown in jail for not paying his tax. He built a cabin by a pond out in the woods and lived there alone."

"Why'd he do that?" Delia plucked a knife from the pitcher, grabbed a hunk of pale orange cheese from an old-fashioned icebox with a wooden door, and whacked off uneven slivers. "They run him out of town over that tax thing?"

"No," I chuckled. "Someone paid that for him. He ran himself out so he could find out what was important. He said we need the wildness of nature."

"Wildness?" Delia cackled. "He could have come out here. I got a gracious plenty of wildness up on this ridge."

She tossed cheese onto the eggs and went at them with a fork. "Rather have a house with electricity and running water. Hmmph. Wildness!"

The repetition of that word brought an image of tangled leaves and limbs and vines, of Ben cradling one arm against his chest, then plodding with deliberate steps, listening for voices, sniffing for smoke, hoping to find an end to wildness.

Delia scraped the edge of the fork across the pan, shattering the image, making me feel as if I'd lost Ben yet again. "This Thoreau sounds like those crazy travelers coming up here to live rough and then going back to their nice houses and telling it like they was the first to ever wipe their bottoms with a handful of leaves. What do they know about real life?"

She snatched two plates from the shelf and slammed them on the table. "Didn't even pay his own tax."

I cringed, hating that Delia would equate Thoreau with April and the worst of her tribe, but trying to see it as she did. How could someone who struggled for all she had not resent those who turned their backs on simple comforts for philosophical reasons or because that was the current fad?

She shoved eggs onto our plates. "How long did that fool stay out there alone?"

"Not too long," I muttered. I didn't tell her that he had regular company at Walden Pond and walked into town often. I recalled that some criticized Thoreau for not getting too far away from society, and maybe being too interested in the impression he made on it. I didn't tell Delia about that, either, because it made Thoreau seem like all the rest of us who couldn't pass a mirror without pausing—even if only for a second—to study our reflections. "He stayed for a year or so."

"And then what'd he do?"

I felt myself flush. "He, um, went back to town."

"Ha! I knew it! Just like those travelers." Delia seized the pot I'd heard glugging and slopped grits beside the eggs. I was glad she didn't say, "Just like you could." She banged the pot back onto the stove. "How you come to know so much about him?"

"We studied him in school, and I've got the book he wrote when he lived by the pond. It's out in the barn." Delia tossed me a fork and poured coffee. I clasped my hands around the mug and took a deep sip. It was gritty and so bitter I choked.

"Takes cream," Delia said and got a bottle from the icebox. "Pot don't work right." She poured healthy dollops into my mug and her own, settled across from me, and stabbed up a forkful of egg. "So he wrote a whole book just about living by a pond?"

I shook my head and swallowed grits. "No, he wrote about lots of things—human nature and religion and progress."

She grunted, finished her eggs, and ladled more grits onto our plates. "Recite me something he wrote."

I buttered a biscuit and slathered on jam. After considering her apparent lack of education and the hardships of her life, I discarded Thoreau's thoughts about richness being proportional to what people could leave alone, his idea that when you're richest, life looks poorest, and his advice to cultivate poverty as if it were an herb in your garden. Delia would call him a fool again and call me the same for reading his book. "Um, he said that no matter how little you have, you should meet your life head on and live it."

She pushed her lips in and out, then nodded. "Well, he's right about that. If there's nothing to be done, then make the best of it. What else?"

"He, uh, said we need space between us when we're talking about important things."

"Huh." Delia drained her coffee and poured another cup. "Don't know if I agree with that. Seems you want to be close enough to read a person's eyes." She refilled my mug. "Bet he never had a sweetheart."

"I don't know." I filled my mug to the brim with heavy cream and stirred with my fork. "But I'm pretty sure he never married." I thought of a picture I'd seen. "He was kind of homely."

The second that slipped out, I felt as if I'd stabbed a friend in the back. I found his writing so beautiful that I'd been stunned by that picture, his long nose, unkempt hair, and the scraggly beard sprouting from his neck. I expected—no, wanted—him to look like a movie star, and I

171

was crushed to find that he wasn't handsome, at least not by those standards.

I remembered that I'd thought of Delia as almost ugly and felt even worse. Who was I to judge?

"There you go, then." Delia thumped her mug on the table. "No wonder he went off to the woods alone."

I ducked my head. Flawed as he may have been, I was even more flawed. I was shallow, superficial, no better than April.

Delia rose, set her plate and mug in a metal tub, and poured water from a bucket. "Well, pretty is as pretty does. Look at what that April did."

Put in my place, I gathered up the grits pan and my plate, slid them into the tub, and cleared the rest of the table so Delia could wipe it with a damp rag. "Seems like that Thoreau made a good point now and then. And seems like you learned a lot of it by heart like some folks do the Bible." She sounded proud of my accomplishment. "Never got past the sixth grade so I'm slow at reading. Never had much time for it, neither. But maybe I'll take it up. Maybe even read some of that Thoreau."

I didn't deserve that book. "I'll leave him for you when I go."

A smile lit her eyes. "That's kind of you, but it seems like if you and him have come this far you should go on together."

I shrugged. If nothing else, I would consider Thoreau—and myself—with new eyes.

"What's your favorite thing he said?"

I shrugged again and toed a crack in the linoleum, still beating up on myself for failing to be different, better.

Delia put her hands on her meager hips. "Must be something you'd want to embroider on a cushion. Though I can't imagine anyone as smart as you thinkin' that poking a needle in and out of a piece of cloth for show is anything but a waste of time."

If she intended that bit of praise to do the trick, it worked. A quote flashed in my mind and I didn't linger more than a second considering Delia's reaction. "I can't remember his exact words, but he said you can't kill time without doing harm to eternity."

Delia nodded and her eyes misted with a far-away look. "Never had enough time of my own to want to kill even a second of it. Seems like a bad habit to get into."

She tossed the rag in the tub and turned to the door. "Let's get going. Apples don't pick themselves."

After hitching into my father's old corduroy pants at the clothesline, I followed her to the orchard, thinking of all the time I'd killed waiting to get older, waiting to learn a little more, waiting for Ben to tell me that he loved me, to propose so we could marry and live happily ever after.

When Thoreau left Walden Pond he said he had more lives to live and couldn't spare more time for that particular one.

I had one life. Starting Monday I would stop killing time and live every hour of it.

CHAPTER 19

For the next three days we worked from sunup to sundown picking apples, pressing cider, cooking up applesauce and apple butter, and sealing canning jars in a cauldron of boiling water that sent up billows of steam and made the kitchen walls trickle with condensation. Delia worked in a sleeveless shift and I stripped to my underwear, ignoring Gertrude Gorman's voice in my mind telling me that was unladylike, tawdry. I gathered eggs and learned to milk the cow and, when I found tools and a passable piece of lumber in the barn, mended the chicken-coop door.

On the second day, Delia wrestled a tattered mattress from the attic, set it on bales of hay under the tarp in my stall, and covered it with sheets. She topped them with a quilt so worn and washed its colors and patterns were as indistinct as a desert landscape at noon.

We ate slabs of pie, ham and cheese sandwiches on brown bread, fried potatoes, and biscuits drenched in honey. We drank gallons of water and sweet and salty tea. And every day we drove that rattling truck across the pasture or down the hill and put in a few hours cutting wood to season and splitting and loading logs cut the year before.

Her body twitching with the strain of holding it, Delia took trees down with a snarling chain saw that belched fumes so noxious they made my head pound. "Pine to get

174

a fire going, oak to keep it into the night."

After she showed me how to hold my hands and keep my feet out of the way of the blade, I lopped off limbs with an ax. I was slow and awkward at first, but then Delia gave me something to meditate on: "Pretend that tree is April."

After that, the blade bit deep and true.

I wondered what Dad and Ben would think if they could see me. I often went with them to cut wood, but Dad restricted me to piling limbs and lugging logs. When I complained about being stuck with "women's work," he issued me a hatchet so small and dull I could have pounded my fingers to a pulp before I sliced one off.

When I asked Ben to show me how to use his ax, he backed away, index fingers crossed as if to ward off evil. "Don't put me in the middle. If you get hurt your father will chop me into kindling."

If I hadn't left, would things have changed? If I'd married Ben, would he have become as protective as Dad?

I lopped off a limb as thick as my arm with two strokes. They'd had good intentions. And I saw now that I was part of the problem—I'd given up and given in too easily.

But here there was no man to tell me what I couldn't do, and a strong woman setting the pace. If Delia didn't stop to rest, I didn't either. Determined to show her I wasn't the "city girl" she called me just a few days ago, I worked until I ached all over and then I worked on, feeling a swelling pride in my strength and endurance.

Despite my increasing comfort with her, I still watched Delia for signs that she'd uncorked the venom in that jug, knowing a few harsh words could undermine my fragile courage and faith. And whenever we had line of sight to the road, I found myself watching, hoping to see Tad coming for me. I told myself I was being petty and selfish—that he'd made a promise in a moment of stress, that his father had to come first—but I dreaded Monday and holding my thumb out. Who would stop? Someone like the grocery-store man who drooled over the centerfold? I shuddered. There were long, rusty nails in the barn; I'd carry one in my pocket and two in my pack.

"Worked all my life," Delia said Sunday afternoon as we unloaded the truck and stacked wood by the back porch. "Chopping weeds, picking cotton, doing laundry—anything to help out the family and get the little ones raised after my father died. Married when I was almost thirty and thought it would be different, but it was more of the same—cleaned my house every morning and then went out and cleaned for others to buy him fancy clothes."

She paused, cradling a log and gazing out over the pasture. "That man sure looked fine, but good looks don't mean a good heart."

I went on working, careful not to let her see the pity I felt. My life—disjointed as it had been for the past few weeks—was a bed of roses by comparison.

"Gambled away every cent, ran off with another woman, and left me with nothin'. But at least that was familiar ground." Delia dropped the log onto the stack and went for another. "Met Cyrus at a motel where I was doin' up rooms and was so damn sick of scrubbing for others I never gave a thought to how much doing for he expected and how lonely it is to live among folks who look right through me if they look at all. That's when the bottle called."

She hoisted two logs from the bed of the truck. "Well, this is my farm now. Cyrus willed it to me and I'll fight to hold onto it if I'm driven to that. I've got a bit of that social security for what I can't grow and to save up for the taxes. I'll run this place so it keeps me fed or it'll run me into the ground."

Thunk! Thunk! She dropped the logs and brushed her hands on her overalls. "But I'll run this place myself. I'm done with men."

I slammed a log of my own onto the stack, opened my mouth to say the same, and saw Delia raise a finger. "Never say never, girl," she cautioned. "Not while you're young. Wait until you see enough of life to know you won't have to back down off that never some day. Saves eating that humble pie."

I grimaced, thinking that the taste of humble pie was all that kept me from calling home.

Sunday, as night closed in, I felt a sense of loss—partly because Tad hadn't come, and partly because this hardscrabble farm felt like a second home, a home where I was sheltered from the world but also forced to face it. We sat on the porch at dusk, drinking tea, catching the evening breeze, watching a swelling moon rise, and counting the chirps of that same cricket or one of his friends. Seventy-eight degrees. Cooling off.

"I'll be up extra early," Delia said. "If you're going off right after breakfast I'd best make it a good one."

Had I told her I was leaving in the morning? Or had she assumed that, since Tad hadn't come, I'd take matters into my own hands? Perhaps she'd seen me washing my underwear and T-shirts and those found jeans that this morning slid over my hips and zipped with just a slight tug.

"You'll want a lunch, too." She poured more tea. "I'll make up some sandwiches. And there's plenty more pie."

All of that was all tucked up in a paper sack when I came into the kitchen the next morning wearing those jeans and a red T-shirt. The bitter coffee I'd gotten used to boiled on the back of the stove, grits bubbled like lava, a dozen biscuits steamed on a plate at the center of the table, and six eggs sizzled in a huge frying pan beside a brood of bacon slices. I got cream, butter, and jam from the icebox and set out a pair of plates, mugs, and utensils. "There's enough food here for an army."

177

Delia smiled. "Makes me feel rich to have more than enough. Never had that growing up." She poured coffee. "Any left over will keep for tomorrow."

Where would I be tomorrow? I dumped cream into my mug and spread butter and jam on a biscuit, bit deep and tasted the tang of baking powder and the sugary slick mix of jam and butter. "Thank you for everything, Delia. If you hadn't been here to hel—"

She brushed that off with the edge of the spatula. "You don't need no one to help you, girl. One day soon you'll figure that out."

There was no doubt behind her words, not like there would have been had Gertrude Gorman said the same thing. I got no sense of desperate hope, only certainty, and I felt a flush of pride as she carried the frying pan to the table and loaded my plate.

"Enough." I held up my hands. "I've got a long walk. I can't eat more than two eggs and a few slices of bacon or I'll be waddling like a pig. It will take me all day to get to Stony Ledge."

With a clang of metal on metal, she set the pan back on the stove and got the pot of grits, but paused a step from the table, her head cocked, a smile lifting the corners of her lips. "Oh, I expect you won't be walking."

My heart leaped. "You'll give me a ride?"

She ladled grits. "Was plannin' on it. But I won't need to."

I blinked and tried to make sense of that as she snatched a plate and a mug from the shelf and set them at the end of the table. "Company's coming. Go on around and invite 'em in for breakfast."

"How do—?"

She shooed me with her hands. "Go on."

Wondering if she'd put more than cream in her coffee, I took another bite of biscuit, put it down, then snatched it up again, split it with my fingers and crammed a slice of

178

bacon inside. If she was headed into a hateful spell, I'd settle for this and be on my way. Respecting the unwritten rule that I honor her privacy and never come farther than the kitchen, I circled the house, chewing on my sandwich.

As I reached the front I heard a dull rumble. Bad muffler. Even though she'd been frying eggs, Delia must have heard it when the car began to climb the hill. I marveled that her ears were so much better than mine. But then, she'd lived here for years, could screen out the usual sounds and listen for the anomalies.

With a ping of rock on metal and the crunch of gravel beneath wheels, a car grumbled up the final slope, towing a cloud of dust that spun like a young tornado. Gleaming white, the car was long and low with a hood wider than a double bed.

Tad was behind the wheel.

Joy and anger collided in my brain. He'd come. But he'd come after I'd decided to manage on my own. Self-conscious, I held the biscuit behind my back and stood straighter, sucking in the shrinking roll around my middle.

He waved and stopped the car a few yards away. The dust devil laid down like an obedient dog as he opened the door. "You're still here."

His smile was huge, eager, but I held mine in check. There were serious things to discuss. "How's your father?"

"Doing better." He swung out of the car. "It wasn't as bad as it could have been. He's still in the hospital and he'll need to rest for a good while," he crossed his fingers, "but he could be doing a little work by Christmas."

"That's great."

"Yeah." He grinned. "And in the meantime there's no way I'll be drafted."

Annoyance flashed in my brain. Ben hadn't looked for excuses; he'd gone out to meet his fate.

Annoyance turned to anger. Not at Tad, but at Ben

179

and his blind belief in honor and duty. If I could go back in time I'd try harder to make him see that there were other roads. But even as I wished that, I knew I couldn't have swayed him.

"But Christmas is a long way off," Tad chuckled. "That's why I'm glad you're still here."

I shook off the past, but lingering anger put an edge on my voice. "Why?"

He stepped back, furrowed his brow, and tugged at his blue-and-green striped tie. "I need your help getting the paper out."

That simple sentence, the assurance of my worth and importance, brought a surge of joy that smothered my resentment. It towered like a wave, then broke on the rocks of reality. "I don't have any experience."

"Your notes on that interview were terrific." He wiped away the protest with a flick of his fingers. "I never would have thought of some of the questions you asked. You're a natural."

"Thank you." I felt myself blush with pride. "But I was planning to leave for Chicago today."

He held out a hand, palm up. "You probably can't register until the next term. And I really need your help."

I studied his pleading eyes. Did he believe I could do the job well, or was he simply desperate?

He put the hand over his heart. "Couldn't you stay on? Just for a bit?"

Remembering dreams deferred for others, I dug my toe against a clump of grass. The biscuit crumbled between my fingers.

"It would be good experience," he wheedled. "It might help you get a job at a paper in Chicago. I'd write you a letter of recommendation saying you do everything except walk on water."

I stubbed the grass into the dirt. A glowing letter of recommendation, even from a paper as tiny as the *Quarry*

County Clarion, might be helpful. Right now I had only the bridal shop on my resume and not so much as a one-sentence recommendation from Gertrude Gorman damning me with faint praise.

"I'll pay you whatever you were making and more." Tad dropped to one knee and pressed his hands together. "Pretty please. I'll buy lunch every day."

I smiled at his pose and my mouth watered at the memory of that slaw.

No! Don't take this detour!

I swallowed, stiffened my spine, and grasped at the one straw I was sure would hold. "Does your father know about this?"

Tad's lips compressed and his gaze slid toward town. "Not exactly."

Meaning no. "Well, he didn't *exactly* like me. He'll have another heart attack when he finds out."

That bit of gossip would sizzle along the Stony Ledge grapevine at the speed of spite. People might hold back a day or two because of his condition, but then someone would want to be the first to carry the news to Senior.

Tad got to his feet, dusted off his knees, and kicked at the same clump of grass I'd abused. "I thought once he saw what you could do he'd change his mind."

I shook my head. First, because Tad had no idea what I could do, or even *if* I could do. And second because people like his father and my grandmother didn't back off from first impressions; their opinions set up harder every day, like footprints in concrete. "I appreciate the offer, Tad, but—"

"Never make big decisions on an empty stomach," Delia said.

Tad's eyes widened and I turned to see her in the shadow of the house. How long had she been watching? Listening?

"I've got a mess of breakfast inside. Why don't we all

go put it where it will do the most good?"

I glanced back at Tad. His lips pressed together, but then his eyes flicked across my face and he nodded just a bit and patted his stomach. "I haven't eaten since last night and that was a dried-up mystery-meat sandwich in the hospital cafeteria."

"No mystery about this meat," Delia chuckled. "Cured the bacon myself." She led the way around the house, calling over her shoulder, "Save that sorry biscuit for the chickens, girl, and get yourself a hot one."

Embarrassed, I tossed the biscuit away and wiped my hand on my jeans, knowing Tad couldn't help but notice but telling myself this wasn't as embarrassing as carrying that nightgown sack.

Inside, Delia nodded him to a cane-bottom chair I hadn't seen before and snatched a mounded plate from the oven. He stood until we sat, then lowered himself to the chair, tucked a napkin into his collar, leaned over the plate, and inhaled. His eyebrows arched with what I guessed was surprise and I wondered what he'd expected to find on Delia's table. Fried snake and boiled weeds?

"Smells great." Folding his hands, he bowed his head.

"If you're bent on giving thanks, I'm the one who's owed." Delia snatched up her fork and stabbed at her eggs, tines scraping against her plate.

Tad's brows arched again, but then he grasped his fork. "Thank you, Delia," he said in a voice without feeling but also without a trace of phony sincerity. He shoveled grits into his mouth, following them with egg and bacon, and making a soft humming sound as he chewed and swallowed.

Delia shoved biscuits and jam his way, and when he reached for the coffee, I intercepted him with the pitcher of cream. He shook his head. "I take it black."

I chuckled. "Not this coffee you don't."

He shook his head again and raised the mug to his

182

lips. Delia and I watched as his cheeks bulged and he fought to swallow. "It's strong," he choked, dousing it with cream. "But good."

Delia snorted. "Boy sits the fence like a man running for office."

Tad scowled just a touch and looked at Delia in a way that reminded me of the way cats size each other up when one crosses another's territory.

She buttered a biscuit, set the knife at the edge of her plate, and fixed her gaze on me. "Well, girl? You stickin' to dreamin' or you gonna start doin'?"

CHAPTER 20

I started doing.

My education began on the way down the hill. "Women around here," Tad said with a flush creeping up his cheeks, "are kind of old-fashioned in the way they dress."

I fingered the hem of my T-shirt and thought of the woman at the post office with her lace collars. "I noticed."

"I knew you had. A good journalist is observant." He ran his finger under his collar, undid the top button, and loosened his tie. "And flexible enough to see when personal standards might get in the way of doing the job."

I raked my fingernails across the weave of my jeans, missing them already. "You want me to wear a dress?"

"Or a skirt, or slacks. But nothing too . . ."

"Wild? Crazy?" I sounded as petulant as a child. "Modern?"

"I was going to say 'unprofessional.'" He touched my shoulder, sliding his fingers to my elbow before he hooked them back on the wheel. "It's just the way things are here."

My arm tingled from his touch but I didn't want him to know, so I didn't rub at my goose-pimpled skin. "It's not your fault. It's the way things are lots of places." I tried not to sound sullen, didn't succeed. "But all my clothes were stolen, remember?"

"That's why we're doing a story on plans for a church rummage sale." He twitched his tie. "That's where this

184

came from. There's no way I'd pay full price for these instruments of torture and I don't care who knows it."

A few minutes later, chortling like conspirators, we combed through bins and racks in a basement smelling of mold and lavender sachet while Tad tossed questions at two elderly women with tight gray curls. I emerged with a khaki skirt, a blue A-line shift, a lime-green shirtwaist dress, three blouses without a flower among them, a pair of loafers only a little too tight, a brown sweater, two pairs of slacks, and a canvas satchel for my pens and notepads. Tad found a tie with swirls of red and blue and paid five dollars for the whole lot.

The ladies followed us to the car, assuring me that they'd washed everything at least once, apologizing because the clothes weren't ironed, and pointing out a tiny gap they'd mended in the seam of the sweater. I thanked them for their trouble and they God-blessed me and told Tad I was "a cute little thing," polite and not at all what they'd expected from up at Ezekiel's place. Tad shot me a wink, reminded them what the Bible said about judging others, and hustled me to the car.

"They were so sweet," I chided him. "And you made them feel guilty."

"You bet. And they'll pass it along." He grinned and tugged at my hair. "What's the problem? I did it for you."

Having spent years beneath the iron blanket of guilt Gertrude Gorman laid upon me, I abhorred the idea of using it to manipulate others, even for the sake of turning prejudice back on itself. It seemed too easy to slide on from there to other purposes. Had Tad ever done that? Would he?

I pondered those questions as I changed into the skirt and a blouse in the downstairs bathroom and got settled at his table with a crisp new notebook he took from a stack in a box against the wall. He handed over a sheaf of notes and news releases and set me to work writing pieces he

185

called "light and bright." Wanting to prove myself, I tried too hard.

"Don't worry about literary value," Tad told me an hour later as I struggled to describe a triumph at the county fair. "Consider your audience. Everybody in Quarry County knows Miz Fulton makes the best pies around, so it's no surprise she won. What they want to know is who she beat out and if she's going to compete next year."

Later he laughed at my suggestion that I write a story about roadside litter and laws and penalties in other states. "It doesn't matter what they do anyplace else, Elizabeth, this isn't anyplace else."

As if that explained it all.

And maybe it did. As we wolfed down the lunch Delia had packed, I wrote "this isn't anyplace else" in my notebook with the rest of his advice.

Before the second day was done, Tad answered the phone and listened with a grimace that told me Senior knew I'd darkened his door. "I didn't take her on to upset you," he said without heat, without chill. "I flat-out need the help."

He listened, circling his index finger in an on-and-on gesture that made me smile despite the bitter acid flooding my stomach. "Yes, Dad, I know how you feel about women doing men's work. And I know she doesn't have any experience. But we ran that ad for a month and no one else applied."

I felt sorry-sick, missing the job already, and missing what Gertrude Gorman would call "a license to snoop." My grandmother and the well-worn routines of Maplekill had stifled my curious nature, but now curiosity was a requirement.

Tad listened again and rolled his eyes. "I know you used to, but the paper's a lot bigger now and I've got to sleep sometime."

186

He clenched his jaw. My stomach roiled and I pressed my hands against my gut. "That would be a big mistake," Tad warned, his voice frosty. "She knows a lot about civil rights laws. She could sue us and probably win."

With a surge of hope, I wrote "rights" on a fresh page of my notebook. I might need this information in Chicago. If I knew what I was entitled to, I'd be less intimidated. I'd never thought much about that before. Back in Maplekill things were just the way they were and I'd been part of a couple. But now I was alone and from here on I needed to pay attention and stand up for myself.

"I understand, Dad. It's clear as a bell." Tad gave me a thumbs-up that made my pulse race. "Only temporary. She'll be gone before you get back."

He smiled and made the on-and-on gesture again. "No, she's not using your desk, Dad." He frowned and then shrugged. "Sure. If you have the energy and it's okay with your doctor I'll bring a batch down when I come tomorrow."

"A batch of what?" I asked when he hung up. "Cookies?" I felt so happy about being allowed to stay I'd even bake them myself.

"Articles." Tad scowled. "He wants to review everything you write."

Joy gave way to a feeling of degradation and I responded in a child's petulant tone. "But you've gone over my stories and I've made the changes you want. And you said I was getting better."

"You are. You're learning faster than I did." Tad flashed a meager smile, then pinched the bridge of his nose. "I just won a round, Elizabeth, now I've got to let him have one."

Knowing Senior would read my work made me feel worse than embarrassed—it felt like I was sitting naked on the toilet and there was no lock on the door—but I had to agree or quit. I kicked at the table leg, then decided I

187

wouldn't let him drive me off. "Okay."

"It'll be fine," he said. "You'll see."

I nodded to make him feel better, but the next afternoon I cringed when he gathered a stack of stories from the corner of his desk. "I'm taking Dad's car down to the hospital." He handed me the keys to his, a junker with an old quilt covering worn spots on the seat and half a welcome mat catching dirt on the floor. I'd driven it the day before to interview a farmer who had piled bales of hay into the shape of a medieval castle. "You'll have to drop it down to second to get it up that last bit of hill."

"I can manage," I said, snippier than I intended, furious about Senior's interference and the criticism I knew would come.

He wagged a finger. "And don't let any hippie girls steal it."

"Maybe I'll steal it myself." Even snippier.

"Go ahead," he chuckled. "Hunting you down could be fun. At the very least it will get me out of Quarry County for a few days."

Despite what he'd said about being a big frog in this puddle, I wondered if he felt as trapped by obligation and expectation as I'd been in Maplekill. "I'm sorry I'm so crabby."

He shrugged and headed for the door. "You're entitled. But you have such a beautiful smile that I miss it when you don't let it shine."

The warm glow from that stayed with me until the next morning when he laid the stories out on the table and I saw paragraphs hemorrhaging red ink, Xs, arrows, and vicious cross-out lines slashed deep into the paper and annihilating entire sentences.

I felt sick and dizzy, like the time I'd passed a bad car wreck and seen mangled metal covered with blood and a body under a sheet. I hadn't imagined my work was so shoddy. "He cut almost everything."

188

"Yeah. He didn't leave much except the punctuation marks." Tad shuffled the pages together and set them back on the corner of the desk. "You ready to go get the square dance club story?"

I blinked. "Shouldn't I rewrite those instead?"

"That would be an enormous waste of time." He pushed the knot of his tie into place and got the camera from the bottom drawer of his father's desk.

His casual attitude toward my humiliation lit a fuse. "Why? Because I wouldn't get them right the second time, either?"

I snatched up the sheaf of papers and whacked it against the desk. "They're my stories and I'll get them the way they should be if I have to write until my fingers are bleeding and I can't pound another key."

"I admire your fire." He hooked the camera strap over his shoulder. "But before you blow that gasket all the way, maybe you should look closer."

Teeth gritted, I studied a page, deciphering words barely visible beneath clots of red ink. "This isn't mine." I shuffled to the next page, rage turning to confusion. "This isn't mine, either." I riffled through the stack. "None of these is mine."

"Very good." Tad patted my head as if I were a tiny girl who'd gotten a gold star for a first-grade worksheet. "I wrote them years ago."

"You didn't give him anything of mine?"

He rocked on his heels, twitched his tie, and smiled like the Cheshire Cat. "Nope."

I admired him for being clever and confident enough to pull off the deceit and yet, to my astonishment, I felt a pinch of pity for his father. "That's sneaky."

"Yeah. I've had lots of practice at being sneaky since Mom died. I'm getting so good at it sometimes I amaze myself," he said without a trace of remorse.

Snatching the sheaf of paper from my hands, he

189

dumped it into the wastebasket. "Dad's not a great writer and he's a terrible editor, but it's his paper."

Just like that bridal shop belonged to Gertrude Gorman. "And he's afraid of losing it," I whispered. Frightened about his failing health. Scared Tad was doing a better job. And terrified of how empty his life will be without the paper.

A curtain seemed to open in my mind and I saw my grandmother, older, shrunken, sitting alone in that big room upstairs with no dresses to sew and no meals to cook, with no one to try to bend to her will.

I sniffed back tears, sorry for every tiny deceit. "When you go next time, take him what I've written."

He gaped. "You're kidding!"

"No. It's okay."

His gape turned to a scowl. "But it's stupid. They've got him on a lot of medication. We can get away with this for weeks."

The word "stupid" triggered another burst of anger. Recalling how Jason had called me "Miss Do-What's-Right," in his derisive tone, and how the tribe had "gotten away" with my car, I decided I'd rather be nauseatingly honest than a cheat or a thief. "I don't want to 'get away' with anything. Besides, if I can't stand up to a little criticism here, what will happen when I get to Chicago?"

Tad's scowl smoothed out and he placed a kiss in the center of my forehead. "You blow me away, Elizabeth. You're the sweetest, smartest girl I've ever known."

My breath caught in my throat and I was aware of nothing but the searing heat of that lingering kiss, of his body inches from mine, and of a sense of overwhelming awkwardness and confusion. "We're late for our interview," I blurted, scooting under his arm and bolting to the door and the safety of the next task.

The next few days passed in a blur of details,

deadlines, and demands. Evenings, when there wasn't an event to cover, I earned my keep, stacking wood that Delia hauled from the hillside, milking Clover, churning butter, or shoveling out the chicken coop. After dark we sat on the porch, drinking tea and talking, watching as the harvest moon grew fat and full and then slimmed down again. Delia seemed thrilled to hear about where I went, who I interviewed, and what I learned about the art of writing it all down. And I was delighted to share and flattered when she pored over the paper I brought home and read each of my articles twice.

One night, over my protests, she heated a flatiron on the back of the stove and pressed my rummage-sale clothes and the others that I'd salvaged.

"You'd char them to cinders," she chuckled, testing the bottom of the iron with her finger. "This old iron takes some getting used to. Can't have you going out with scorch marks on your seams. You don't get but one chance to make a good impression on folks around here."

I looked up from sprinkling the blouses and rolling them tight as she'd showed me. "That's exactly what Tad says."

"Boy's clever." She gave me a hard look. "Studies people like you study books."

"Journalists are trained observers," I said, feeling proud to call myself a journalist, preening because Tad noticed right away that I was observant.

"Looking and learning is just fine." She took a blouse from my pile, shook it out, and set the iron to it. "But what a person does with that can be a thing apart."

A thing apart?

Not wanting to display ignorance, I didn't ask what she meant. Conversations up here had a way of coming around again and she might illuminate her remark the next day.

But that night she took up the bottle again. An

191

insistent mumbling brought me awake. I clicked on the flashlight and saw her sprawled on my makeshift sofa with a tall glass in her hand. She shaded her eyes with her free hand and squinted into the light. "What you doin' in my barn?"

"Sleeping." I tried to make that sound more factual than sarcastic so it wouldn't rile her up. At the same time, I almost laughed at the state of my life—wearing cast-off clothes, letting nasty old men assault my writing, sleeping in a barn on a lumpy mattress squirrels once nested in, bathing outdoors in frigid water pumped by hand, and listening to the rantings of a drunk. It was beyond anything I could have imagined a month ago. "Sleeping on a bed you made up for me."

"I'm drunk, not blind." She slapped the bales. "What I'm asking is, 'Why are you wasting your life with me. Why aren't you with that young man?'"

I scavenged my brain for an answer that a drinking woman would find logical, not incendiary. "Because it's late."

I shone the light on my watch. "It's after midnight. People would gossip their tongues off if I was still down at the newspaper office." Where Tad's bedroom, I discovered when I went upstairs for a fresh dish towel from the linen cabinet, was just above the table where I worked. Where his double bed was made with corners tucked so tight the quilt was as flat as a cloth laid on a table. Where loose change lay on his dresser, a tie hung from a closet knob, and the wall was covered with photographs of faraway places: the Taj Mahal, the Great Wall of China, the Grand Canyon. I would have had the same pictures on my walls if Gertrude Gorman hadn't forbidden me from pushing thumbtacks into the plaster.

Delia laughed and took a long swallow. "They gonna talk anyway, girl, you're a fool if you think not."

I cupped the flashlight with my hand so she couldn't

see my face. I might still be a fool about a lot of things, but I wasn't ignorant about the way small towns worked. I saw the knowing glances in the café, and yesterday I again stared down the woman who never seemed to take those curlers out of her hair.

"But no sense in throwing gas on a fire." Delia's head lolled back and she was quiet for so long I thought she'd gone to sleep. I was about to click off the light when she spoke again. "What you doin' up here wasting time with me?"

"I'm helping you get your wood in for winter." I tried to ease her thoughts down another path. "How many cords do you think you'll need? What do the crickets say about the weather?"

"Crickets don't say shit. It's squirrels you gotta watch." She lurched to her feet, smashing her glass against a supporting beam. "And I don't need your help. I don't need help from anyone. You can get along out of here."

"I will," I shouted back, sick of tiptoeing around her moods. "First thing in the morning."

"Sunup," she yawped, staggering out the door and pulling it closed with a thud. "Sunup you be gone."

For a few moments I lay there trembling. Where would I go? Could I find a room in town until Christmas, or should I leave for Chicago? My stomach churned, but then I reminded myself that uncertainty was the nature of my new life. In strange and unexpected ways, things seemed to work out. I rolled over, drew in a few deep breaths, and went back to sleep.

Long before dawn, the door banged open and I saw a wavering light and heard Delia's gruff voice behind it. "You, girl. You still here?"

I sat up, every muscle tight. Had she gone deeper into the liquor and her vile mood? Had she decided morning wasn't soon enough to run me off?

Grasping my wallet, I tossed back the quilt and closed

my fingers around the flashlight. She shuffled toward my bed, a kerosene lantern in one hand, a stout cane in the other, her misshapen shadow spread huge and terrible across the ceiling. "You gone, girl?"

I slid my feet into my sneakers. Once fear propelled me past her, I had the whole ridge on which to hide.

CHAPTER 21

"I guess I was hateful again." Delia set the lantern on the floor, leaned on the cane, and rubbed at an oozing cut on her shin. "Don't recall what it was I said, but I knowed I musta been in a bad way when I found myself fallen out on the steps."

"It's okay," I muttered.

It wasn't in the least, but I feared she might snap from being contrite to contentious in a second if I challenged her.

"It's not anything like okay," she snarled. "You're looking at me like a cornered rat."

"It's okay," I repeated, my voice patient but weary.

"Not a rat." She shook her head, her enormous shadow ballooning between the rafters. "Nobody likes a rat. You ain't no rat. A rabbit, maybe."

Tears glistened on her cheeks. "The point is I'm a lonely old woman and I don't mean you any harm. You've been a comfort to me." She wiped her nose on the shoulder of her shirt. "A deep and abiding comfort."

Until that moment, I hadn't thought of her as grieving for Cyrus. She seemed strong and complete, proud of going it alone. But now I saw how difficult her life would be on Hog Run Ridge—eking out a subsistence living amidst those who had no use for her. She had no champion like Tad to make them take a second look.

"Can't understand why you want to spend time with

195

someone as mean and miserable as me when you got the whole world out there."

That's what she'd been driving at earlier.

Laying the wallet and flashlight on the bed I closed the distance, stretched out my arms, and then hesitated, afraid Delia would see this as pity and swing back to drunken rage. "Because you're my friend," I whispered.

She stared for a second, then smiled that transforming smile and let me gather her in.

The next day I talked around it with Tad—not telling him about Delia's drinking or her "hateful" talk, but commenting on how isolated she was, and wondering if that would change.

"Not likely," he said. "Attitude runs deeper than law. Most think she should go back where she came from."

"I'm sure they think the same about me." I made a joke of it.

"It's not the same, Elizabeth." He looked at me as if he wondered why I didn't see that. "Cyrus flaunted the law when he married her up North. Nobody challenged that, but lately I've heard some folks question whether she should have that farm. Cyrus had a third cousin whose kids carry the family name and . . ."

His voice trailed off, but I got the picture. Green nausea swept over me and I gripped the edge of the table, understanding why Delia said she'd fight if she was driven to it. I knew firsthand that when all you have isn't much, you hold on tight. "That farm is all she has. She's not going to just give it away no matter—"

"Hold on, firecracker." He flung his hands up. "*I'm* not the one saying that. I'm just telling you the way it is."

In a moment I nodded. "Sorry," I muttered. "For taking aim at the wrong target."

"Accepted." He brushed at the air. "I think we both need a break from all of this. From the paper and Stony

Ledge. Why don't you ride down to Little Rock with me tomorrow and we'll go to a movie and have dinner?"

A date? My heart thumped harder, but the rest of me went numb with fear. No matter how comfortable I felt with Tad, this was a tall hurdle to leap. I felt disloyalty, too—because lately I had gone hours without thinking of Ben and hoping he was safe—and I felt guilty because he might be dead and forever deprived of small earthly pleasures like movies.

I touched reality like a talisman. "What about your father? Doesn't he expect you to spend the day with him?"

Tad's lips compressed. "He'll have plenty of other visitors over the weekend. But I'll need to drop in. If you don't mind waiting . . ."

"I don't mind." My lips betrayed me. "Maybe there's a bookstore nearby." I hadn't been able to read Thoreau since Delia and I had our discussion and I was too exhausted at the end of most days to do more than pen a postcard to my father and grandmother—because ever since I pictured her alone I added her name to the address—and gaze up at the stars for a few minutes before I flopped on my derelict bed. But Delia said rain was due and lots of it, and books would pass the time.

"I haven't noticed any bookstores around the hospital," he said, "but we'll get a phone book and find one."

After the chores were finished late Saturday morning, I scrubbed myself with a bar of lemon soap excavated from the back of a dusty shelf in the dry goods store and shaved my legs and armpits. I let my hair dry in the sun, fluffed my bangs and, using my reflection in the washtub, brushed on eye shadow and mascara I bought at a tiny drugstore down the road past the garage where that work bay was still empty.

After long consideration, I put on the jeans because

they made me feel thinnest and a blouse with blue, yellow, and green vertical stripes that helped the illusion. Back at the barn I riffled through my wallet, thumbing the fifteen ten-dollar bills Tad gave me yesterday for two weeks work. I slid six of them and a handful of change into one pocket and poked a comb into another.

Delia was on the porch peeling apples when I came around front to wait for Tad. "You look like a spring flower."

Chagrined that my primping was so obvious, I flipped my hand. "It's just jeans and a shirt."

Delia nodded, eyes narrowing. "That young man won't be able to keep his hands off you."

I felt my cheeks flame, recalling Tad's breath against my ear, that kiss on my forehead, recalling what April had told me after I'd found her in bed with Stash. I wouldn't solicit affection from strangers like she had, but that didn't mean that I didn't need tenderness. Besides, Tad wasn't a stranger. I'd known him for two weeks.

Delia's eyes widened and she grunted, shook her head, and pointed a finger at me as if about to say more, but just then Tad pulled up and I ran to the car calling, "See you later," over my shoulder.

When he started down the hill, I stuck my head out the window and looked back. Delia raised her hand but kept it still—the way a minister does when he gives a blessing. I waved and in another second she was out of sight.

When Tad and I had been together in the car before, we'd been heading to an interview or driving up and down the ridge. The eyes of the community had been on us, guaranteeing certain restrictions and inhibitions. But today those walls were down and I felt exposed, every fault magnified ten times, every thought as huge and apparent as if a skywriter blazoned it across the vault of blue above us.

I hugged the passenger door, but the air between us crackled and we made small talk in voices as bright and brittle as new ice: "Don't those cows look like they're reading that billboard?" "Wow, there must be a thousand pumpkins in that field!" "What kind of a hawk is that?" "Does an automatic transmission really use more gas?"

Tad turned on the radio and we sang along with the Beatles and the Stones and tried to harmonize on "California Dreamin'" and laughed when we made a mess of it. Then the Temptations doing "My Girl" brought Ben's memory too close and tears clogged my throat. I was glad when a sharp bend in the road wiped out the song with a burst of static.

When Tad dropped me at a collection of shops I felt a shameful sense of deliverance. As soon as he turned back onto the street, I breathed to the bottom of my lungs, flexed my fingers, and rolled my shoulders to ease knotted muscles. Was it anticipation that made me so tense?

I browsed a dusty bookstore, lingering at the science fiction shelves in homage to Ben, silently telling Bradbury and Vonnegut and Heinlein that one of their most loyal fans was missing in action—perhaps forever. I held my breath, fighting back tears, knowing this was the biggest reason I hadn't called home or put a return address on my cards—if there was bad news, I didn't want it. And if there was good news, it belonged to April.

April!

The fury her memory provoked dried up my tears like the Sahara sun. Turning my back on science fiction, I stumbled on to true crime and mystery. Thoreau would have had little use for such "light" reading. He felt that once we learned to scan a written page, we should read only the best in literature, the classics. Two weeks ago I would have agreed, but now I craved something that didn't require deep thought.

I glanced at *In Cold Blood*. No. Reading about murder

on an isolated farm while sleeping in a barn at an isolated farm was just too creepy. I chose two of Agatha Christie's mysteries because they were dog-eared and splotched by readers who apparently couldn't put them down during dinner. The descriptions on the backs of Rex Stout's tales about an overweight detective who hated to leave his house intrigued me, so I bought three of those.

Down the way I came across a lingerie store with a huge "SALE" sign in the window. I bought a lacy bra and three pairs of nylon panties in blue, red, and black. Then, blushing, I fingered through the nightgowns, my nails whispering against nylon and lace and coming to rest on a lilac gown with thin straps and a scalloped hem. I took it from the rack and held it against me, noting that it fell far short of my knees. Gertrude Gorman would tut in disapproval and say it would be cold in winter and make me sweat in summer. Diana would wink and make a comment about bedroom activities that made a couple sweat any time of year.

Only when the clerk had wrapped it in tissue paper and tucked it into a white paper bag did my cheeks cool. But when Tad glanced at that bag as I tossed it into the back seat, I flushed again. "Books," I said, although those were clearly inside the used brown paper sack.

Tad nodded. "How do you feel about Elvis?"

I hesitated. We'd been so focused on reporting we'd had no time for discussions of likes and dislikes. For all I knew, Tad thought Elvis hung the moon.

"Just checking," Tad chuckled. "I thought we'd see *Fantastic Voyage* instead."

I felt another jolt of disloyalty to Ben who'd read me an article about that movie when he was home on leave. When I joked that he was more interested in Raquel Welch than in the premise, he tossed a sofa cushion at my head saying, "That's why they call these throw pillows."

How easy it had been between us. How open.

200

"Unless there's something else you want to see," Tad said.

"No." I shook off the memory and manufactured a smile. "That sounds like fun."

Provisioned with buttered popcorn, chocolate bars, sodas, and a stack of paper napkins, we found seats in the back row, an armrest between us, and lost ourselves in the darkness and the improbable tale. After the popcorn was gone, Tad wiped his hands and slid his arm along the back of my seat. His fingers trailed through my hair and then rested on my shoulder.

I tensed, but then relaxed as much as I could, breathing in the scent of his aftershave. I'd bought some of that kind for Ben once, but he said it was too sweet and smelled like some kind of weird soda-fountain drink.

Tad nuzzled my glasses up and kissed the end of my eyebrow. Then his lips trailed across my cheek and he breathed into my ear sending a current racing through my veins that made my fingers and toes numb.

Swept on that current, I tipped my head, offering my lips. He pressed his to mine, advancing and retreating, as if he knew exactly how frightened I was and would go only as far as I wanted and no more, as if he could read things in my mind I hadn't admitted to myself. Was I the second girl he'd kissed or the twenty-second?

Remembering that revealing nightgown, I pulled back, ashamed, and settled my glasses into place. Had I bought that gown to wear for Tad because of how I felt about him or to prove I wasn't the uptight prude who left Maplekill three weeks ago? Tad hummed a little and stroked my hair as if I was a kitten. I imagined us, some day in the future, lying on a soft bed, in an elegant room with white curtains fluttering in a balmy breeze, soft shadows waltzing on the wall. I imagined him telling me that he loved me, sliding the straps of that nightgown down my arms, revealing my breasts, saying I was

201

beautiful and somehow making me believe it.

I held the image in my mind as he kissed me again.

We emerged from the theatre with our arms around each other. Night had closed in bringing billows of smothering clouds. Thunder rumbled far off, and the air was sodden with rain to come. Within minutes perspiration beaded on my forehead, and the skin of my midriff grew hot and sticky where his hand lay against it. In my dreams and imaginings about romance, sweat didn't exist and the sheer amount of it now made me uncomfortable. It was too earthy, too animal, too embarrassing. Glad we were nearly to the car, I blotted my forehead with the back of my hand and tried to sound casual. "Where are we going now?"

"How about in here?" He swung me into the deep shadow of an alley and pulled me tight against him, feeding on my lips. His hands cupped my hips, pressing me to him. He moaned into my mouth as he stiffened against my stomach.

I tensed, not ready for this, wondering if I ever would be. It seemed crude, obscene. He pulled me even closer.

Heels tapped along the sidewalk, stopped. "Young people today have no modesty," a woman's voice complained. "And no morals."

Tad's grip relaxed and he moved his hands to my waist but kept his mouth on mine. Flushing with shame, I closed my eyes, told myself I didn't know these people, didn't care what they thought. I had morals. I wasn't cheap.

And yet I was here.

I shoved against Tad's chest. He grunted, slid his hands to my back, pulled me to him again.

"They could at least get off the street," a man's voice agreed. "They've got no respect for themselves or for others."

The heels tapped on. "I've got a good mind to call the police. Teach them a lesson."

The police!

I shook my head. "We should go. Those people said—"

"Forget them. They're gone."

Walking backward, he drew us farther into the alley. I struggled for breath and glanced over my shoulder at the empty street shrouded in mist stained by the light of distant neon signs. "But they said they'd call the police."

"They won't."

"You don't know that." A drop of water struck my arm. "Besides, it's starting to rain. We need to go."

"Not yet. I need another kiss." He rubbed against me, letting me feel how hard he was, and chuckled low in his throat. "And you need to do something about this. Any ideas?"

I didn't want to answer, didn't know *how* to answer. I wasn't flip like Diana, wasn't experienced like April. Raindrops pattered on the lid of a garbage can farther along the alley. "We need to go."

His mouth eclipsed my protests. I pushed my hands against his chest, but he grasped my wrists and pinned them behind my back. His free hand slid from my hips to my breasts and I thought of what Delia had said, "That young man won't be able to keep his hands off you."

I struggled, but his fingers circled on my damp blouse, then slid inside, teasing my nipples through my bra. Without my consent they grew rigid. A puddle of warmth formed in my groin. My legs trembled.

"You like that," he whispered. Rain spattered my glasses as his hand slid down my stomach and squeezed my crotch. "How about this?"

I felt fouled, dirty, and tried to twist aside. But he jerked at my wrists, holding me off balance, sucking in my pleas that he stop, insistent fingers rubbing at the seam of my jeans until my body betrayed me and I heard myself moan.

"I want you so bad." His voice was husky and his fingers stirred ripples of warmth, making me shudder and gasp. He released my left wrist and guided that hand to the zipper of his slacks and the throbbing hardness beneath. "There's a motel on the way out of town. It's not the nicest place, but they don't ask if you're married."

Revulsion corkscrewed in my gut. The strange journey from Maplekill hadn't changed me that much. This was my first time, and I wanted more than a sleazy motel and sex with a man who had been there before.

I shoved at his shoulder and clamped my legs together. "No. I won't go to a motel with you."

"Okay." He laughed, a dark and dangerous sound, then jammed his knee between mine. His fingers fumbled at my jeans, prying the metal button from its hole, tugging my zipper down. "Then I'll fuck you right here."

That word. That horrible, dispassionate, loveless word.

Humiliation burned my cheeks like acid. "No." I clawed at his groping fingers. "Stop."

He batted my hand away as if it were a moth and yanked at my jeans. "Don't jerk me around, Elizabeth. You were begging for it a minute ago."

"I wasn't begging." I tried to hammer the heel of my hand into his groin but he squeezed my fingers together so hard I yelped.

"Don't fight me." Pinning my wrists in one hand, he snatched them above my head, and slammed me against a rough brick wall, knocking the air from my lungs. "You owe me."

"Stop," I gasped. "Please stop."

"You teased me all day." Panting, he jerked my jeans to my knees and slid his fingers into the waistband of my panties. "You can't change the rules in the middle of the game."

CHAPTER 22

For the first time ever I was grateful for those white cotton underpants. The fabric clung to my sweaty skin as if it, too, was fighting for my virtue. But inch by inch, no matter how tight I locked my legs, Tad worked the elastic down.

"I know you want it," he grunted from between gritted teeth. "Stop fighting and just enjoy it."

Never!

I opened my mouth to scream for help, realized it was Ben I wanted to call for, and felt more lost and alone than that horrible day when I understood that my mother was gone forever. I had only myself to depend on.

And only myself to blame for this!

Each twist and kick worked in Tad's favor, so I let myself go limp, dead weight hanging in his grip, glad of every extra pound packed on my frame.

"Damn it." He tried to jerk me upright but wasn't strong enough to hold me up and rip my clothes off, too. He released my wrists and I fell to a litter of broken bottles and mangled newspaper.

Too late, I saw my mistake.

He dropped beside me. "If you want it in the dirt, that's the way you'll get it."

I flung myself away. "No! Leave me alone!" Something sliced the heel of my hand but I ignored it and got to my knees, tugging at my panties and jeans, scuttling deeper

205

into the alley.

Another mistake. It ended at a blank wall. I spun, searching for a way out, rain pelting my face.

"Come on, Elizabeth." He strode toward me, unbuckling his belt. "Give me what I need and I'll buy you a steak dinner."

I almost laughed at the idea of trading my virginity for seared beef and a mealy baked potato with a dollop of sour cream and a sprinkling of chives. Seizing the lid from a garbage can, I anchored myself against the wall. He'd have to beat me senseless before he raped me.

"What the hell is your problem?" Tad fumbled at the placket of his undershorts. "Come on. I need—"

A siren whooped.

"Shit." Tad tucked at his shirt with frantic fingers.

I could have hugged the condemning couple who passed us earlier.

Lights brightened the end of the alley as I replaced the lid, fastened my jeans, and wiped my bloody hand on my thigh.

A patrol car nosed into the mouth of the alley, emergency flashers pulsing through the mist.

"Let me do the talking." Tad clutched at my arm. "Don't say a thing."

I tore myself from his grasp. "Don't tell the cops you tried to rape me?" On juddering legs I wobbled to the rim of the headlight beams.

"It wasn't rape," he whined. "You led me on. It will kill my father if I get in trouble because of you."

I waded into the light. "You should have thought of that five minutes ago."

"It'll be your word against mine." He stayed just behind me, his voice a snarl. "My family's been here for generations. I run a business. You're a Yankee hippie in cast-off clothes living with an old nig—"

"Don't say that word."

"I'll say what—"

"Guess you don't have sense enough to get in out of the rain," a deep voice boomed from the patrol car. "Or out of sight of folks in town for a church convention."

"Sorry, officer," Tad called. "We got carried away. We've only been married a week."

I wanted to scream that I wouldn't marry Tad if he was the last man on earth, but the cautious voice in my head warned me to keep still. Tad's lie, I saw, cloaked us both in mock morality. Holding my breath, I waited to see how it played out.

"You're a lucky man," the cop said. "Wish my wife was built like that."

Feeling like a piece of meat, I crossed my arms over my breasts and sidestepped away from Tad, squinting into the headlights, seeing only the low hulk of the car in a corona of rain.

"Where you live, son?" the cop asked.

"Stony Ledge. I run the paper up there. We came down to see a movie."

"What's your name?"

"Thaddeus Tolliver, Junior."

"Where's your car?"

Tad pointed through the rain. "Down at the end of the block."

The cop was silent for a few seconds, then grunted. "You run get in your car and get right home. Don't even think about stopping along the way."

"Thank you, officer," Tad said. "We won't."

He reached for my elbow but I kept my arms crossed tight as I passed the patrol car, my skin crawling when the beefy, balding cop looked up from his clipboard, ran his eyes over me, and winked.

"Don't touch me," I hissed when we were clear. "Don't you ever touch me again."

"Don't worry." Tad unlocked the passenger door but

didn't hold it for me. "I have no use for cock teases like you."

"Fine." I yanked the door open, dropped inside, and slammed it against the rain, hugging the handle.

Tad stabbed the key at the ignition. "And don't think you still have a job."

"I'd eat my shoes before I work another day for you."

He gunned the engine, crimped the wheels, and jerked the car into the street. "I ought to make you walk."

I thought of the miles between here and Delia's farm and felt a frisson of fear. Would he force me out along the freeway or the road into the mountains? Would he try again to rape me? Or worse? I shivered. Delia was the only one who knew I'd gone with him. Would anyone believe her?

Glancing over my shoulder, I saw the cop keeping pace behind us, raindrops falling like dimes through his headlights. Should I jump out now? "That cop's still behind us."

Tad's gaze darted to the rearview mirror.

Good. He was worried. "He wrote your name down. I saw him."

Tad scowled as we rolled up the ramp to the freeway with the cop car almost nudging our bumper. I half turned in the seat and waved, spotting my sack of books as I did. Stretching, I gathered them to me, gathered up that bag of filmy daydreams, too, vowing to dump it in Delia's privy where desecrated illusions belonged. "I got his name off his badge," I lied. "Officer Rex Christie. I'll call him if you put me out or try to hurt me again."

"Shut up!" Tad's jaw clenched, and his hands tightened on the wheel. "I'll take you home. Just shut up."

I did.

Before his car came to a full stop at the top of Delia's hill I tumbled out, slammed the door, and bolted to the outhouse. Stuffing that white sack through the hole, I relieved myself on top of it, cursing at the way I'd squandered my money and my trust.

Delia, a black slicker across her shoulders, a lantern held high, intercepted me as I threw myself against the pump handle. "Big storm's coming. I put the cows in the barn and— You okay, girl?"

A gush of water splashed from the spout, stinging the cut on my hand, washing off grit from the alley. "Yeah." I cupped my hands, sucking up water, rinsing my mouth, spitting out the taste of Tad's lips, the bitterness of shame. "I'm fine." I seized my toothbrush from a hook beside the pump, raked the bristles across that mushy brown soap, and scoured my tongue and gums until my mouth foamed.

"Don't appear fine to me. Slamming doors. Trying to scrub the skin off your tongue with lye soap." Delia edged the lantern close to my face. "That boy didn't hurt you, did he?"

Did he? My shoulder blades ached where he'd thrown me against the wall, and the cut on my hand burned, but those would heal. I bent, spat out soap, and rinsed my mouth with pump water until it was numb. What wouldn't heal was the hurt I'd done myself. I *had* led him on. But everything he'd said and done made me think he cared, that he'd be gentle and kind.

Then I remembered how he manipulated the women at the church and how he fooled his father with those old news stories. I remembered that he was studying psychology.

I threw my toothbrush to the concrete slab. He'd studied me, knew I was hungry for affection. He used that.

I couldn't bear for Delia to know. "He didn't hurt me."

She held the lantern high, kerosene sloshing. "I don't mean a hurt I can doctor with some salve. Did he hurt your heart?"

I shook my head, but choking sobs punched my ribs.

"Can't do much about that." She pinched her lips. "A trusting heart puts itself in harm's way time and again. And a heart that hasn't healed through breaks easy."

"And he fi—" I couldn't tell her that he fired me. That made my shame worse. "I can't work with him anymore."

"Don't expect I could neither." She picked up the sack of books. "Let's get out of the rain and get you warmed up."

Strangling on tears, I followed her into the kitchen and slumped on my stool as she prodded a blaze in the stove and checked that the kettle was full. She took two mugs from the shelf, measured tea into a pot, and set out a plate of oatmeal cookies. The first one tasted of soap, but I gagged it down. The second was okay. The third was sweet spicy with nutmeg. I ate a fourth. When I was fat, no one had been attracted to me. Except Ben.

Delia poured hot water into the pot and set it on the table to steep. "Most men aren't like your Mr. Thoreau. They don't sit by and ponder. If they don't get what they need they . . ." She shrugged.

They leave like Ben, or— I shuddered. What was more humiliating, to let yourself be screwed in an alley or to be abandoned? "Well, I'm through with men. If you don't need one, then I don't either."

Delia frowned. "Who said I don't need a man?"

"You did. The first day we were cutting wood."

"Can't remember." She rubbed her chin. "But anyway, that's me, not you. And maybe that's me lying."

I wanted to believe in her resolve so I could believe in my own. "You didn't sound like you were lying." I reached for another cookie.

Delia frowned. "You've got a bad cut there."

"Just a scratch."

"Are you sure he didn't hurt you?"

"I'm sure." I poured tea, avoiding her eyes. "I did this myself—caught it on the edge of a rack in a clothing store."

She shook her head, but held her cup to be filled instead of challenging me, then took the jug down from a high shelf, topped off her mug, and set the liquor between us. "Well, put some of that in your tea and things will look brighter in the morning."

"I haven't noticed that it makes them look brighter to you." Harsh words. I wished them back.

Her eyes tightened. "Who are you to know what's inside of me?"

I thought of a dozen answers, but raised my hands in surrender. "No one. I'm no one." The rough bottom scraped against the table as I pushed the heavy jug closer to her, "Drink all you want."

She shoved the jug so hard it wobbled. "Maybe I don't want."

"Then don't drink another drop. It's your business, not mine."

"You got that right." She scowled and I gave it right back, sick of her, of this place, of my life. Rain pounded on the roof and the kettle gurgled on the back of the stove. Those homey noises scraped my raw nerves. I gritted my teeth and glared so hard I thought my eyes would pop from their sockets.

Delia's chest heaved. She slapped a hand over her mouth and then dropped it, releasing a pealing laugh. "Look at us. Growling and hissing like two skunks tied tail to tail."

I felt my glower sliding off, held on to as much as I could.

Delia stood, opened the door and tossed out her spiked tea, then stashed the jug on its shelf. "A giant of a storm's whipping up. Gonna rain all night and all tomorrow and then some."

I thought of my first conversation in Stony Ledge, not even three weeks ago. "A toad floater?"

"Be some snakes floating, too. Glad I'm up on this

ridge. Never saw a snake float uphill yet."

That image made me give up what was left of my frown.

"You scurry on out to bed." Delia laid a hand on my shoulder. "Have yourself a good long cry. Tomorrow we'll just laze around and stay dry and on Monday you'll find yourself another job. Feed store has a sign up that they're hiring."

I shook my head. "I can't stay. Not after . . . Not here."

"Sometimes when you think you can't stay that's exactly the time you got to dig your heels in and hold your ground."

Easy to say. Hard to do. I stared into my mug, thinking that she meant well and spoke from her own experience. If I took advice like that to heart I'd still be in Maplekill. And would that be worse than this?

"You think about this while you're having your cry." Delia raised her fists and jabbed the air. "If you leave, he wins."

Wins what? The chance to stay in Stony Ledge and work for his father? And what did I lose? The chance to have people stare and talk behind my back?

I stood and placed my mug in the metal tub. "Thanks for the tea and cookies. Thanks for caring about me." Collecting my books I trudged out into the rain.

CHAPTER 23

Despite Delia's prescription for a good cry, I was too angry to allow myself that release. All night I thrashed in the tangled quilt, listening to the gentle chuffing of the cows and the swelling patter and drip of rain, wishing the streams would rise high enough to wash Tad from the face of the earth.

Fury swirled on into Sunday, jangling my nerves so I couldn't concentrate on my new books, the checker game Delia laid out, or her lesson in how to tell when boiling fudge reached the point where it would set up grainy instead of sticky. She showed remarkable patience, talking about her life, attempting, I suppose, to make me examine the state of my own and pronounce it better than most.

But my turmoil didn't ease and the storm amplified it. Trees bowed before a raging wind that stripped and shredded their leaves, tossing them like confetti. Sheets of rain fluttered across the pasture and slapped the house so hard it shuddered. I imagined Tad caught in a vicious current, sucked under, felt a flash of smug satisfaction.

"If I had electricity or a telephone, the lines would be down by now." Delia tossed more firewood into the stove. "That's one blessing to being poor." She glanced up at a spreading brown splotch on the plaster ceiling. "If the roof holds together until dusk, the worst will be over."

The roof held, the storm blew itself out, and my rage burned down to a sputtering smolder, leaving me weak-

213

kneed and nauseated, hunched over the table with my chin in my hands.

By then Delia had used every pot and bowl in the kitchen to catch drips, holding back only a frying pan to cook bacon and corn fritters. "I guess you're bent on leaving. But I'll sure miss your company." She set out a jar of honey, a wedge of cheese, a round of butter, the pie pan of fudge, and a pitcher of milk. "You brought a ray of sunlight to this Valley of the Shadow."

A perfect name for Stony Ledge. That's how I'd think of it from now on—dark and forbidding except for Delia's hilltop. "I'll miss you too." Improbable as I would have thought it three weeks ago, we had forged a bond. "I'll write when I get settled."

She smiled, eyes glossy with tears. "Make sure you put that letter in a thick envelope or everyone will know what you have to say before I do."

I remembered the nosy woman at the post office and anger flared. She certainly read the cards I sent to Dad, knew how thrilled I'd been to work at the paper.

"Best put tape on the flap, too." Delia winked. "Wouldn't put it past some to use a little steam to find out who's sending me mail that wasn't a tax bill."

She wiped at her eyes with the hem of her flannel shirt and forked bacon onto a strip of newspaper to drain. "This here's about the only good use for Mr. Tolliver's paper."

I felt a stabbing sadness for the pleasure Tad had plundered, then hatred cauterized the wound. "Put the rest of that paper in the outhouse."

Delia shook her head. "Don't want him that close to even that part of my skin. Expect you don't, neither."

My stomach spasmed and I traced the grain of the table with my fingernails, head down so she wouldn't see the stain on my cheeks.

"You'll get some distance from it, girl. Won't ever be gone, but it will be just a glimmer in the past. Good things will come to outshine it."

I doubted that—my life had been slipping downhill since April got off the bus in Maplekill—but I gave Delia the nod she'd worked for and raised my head to watch her divide the bacon between two plates loaded with fritters.

"Since you taught me that eggs and rubber bands trick I feel like I almost know what I'm doing in that old truck." She set a plate before me. "Honey's good on those fritters. Butter, too. Or both."

My stomach growled approval and saliva pooled under my tongue but, punishing my body for betraying me with this appetite and others, I took neither. Just to be polite, I'd eat a few bites of a dry fritter. Nothing more.

Slicing off a lacy edge that had browned too much, I jabbed it into my mouth. It dissolved with a burst of onion, salt, and sugar and a hit of heat from the dried chili pepper she'd crumbled into the batter. I swallowed greedily. Betrayed again.

Delia cocked her head. "Is that passable?"

"It's delicious," I muttered, hating myself for my lack of will power.

"Get more of it on your inside, then." She bit into a strip of crispy bacon. "Starving won't solve a thing. And making decisions on an empty stomach is as smart as making your bed an anthill."

She munched bacon and then cut off a slice of cheese as thick as my little finger and wedged it between two fritters. Giving in to hunger, I did the same, adding a strip of bacon, reminding myself to savor, not stuff.

"What I meant," Delia said later as she nibbled off a bite of fudge, "is that with all you taught me I feel like I could do okay out on the big highway."

"Sure you could," I lied. Her top speed was about what I could achieve in an uphill dash wearing flip-flops. "Just check the rearview mirror and pull over if you're leading a parade."

215

"How many times you think I'll pull over between here and the bus stop place?"

My heart swelled and tears prickled my eyes. "You'll take me there?" I jumped to my feet and hugged her, feeling the knobs of her shoulders, smelling the brown soap in her wiry hair. Riding with Delia, fraught with peril as it might be, was far better than hitchhiking. "Thank you. Thank you so much."

"Don't thank me until we're off this ridge." She canted her head toward the rafters and the withering howl of the wind. "Put on your old clothes when you get up. I expect there will be a lot of road to clear."

The wind had faltered to a gusting breeze, but the orchard lay in tatters when I let the chickens out and hauled my duffel bag to the house.

After a breakfast of eggs and leftover fritters we walked aways down the hill, stringy clouds spitting cool rain into our faces while we surveyed the situation. Toppled trees and torn limbs lay atop a carpet of shredded leaves that obscured deep gouges clawed by rushing water. Moraines of gravel fanned out where torrents had turned aside or run their course. "Worst I've ever seen it," Delia pronounced. "We'll clear just what we have to. I'll worry about the rest some later day."

As we loaded shovels, rakes, axes, rope, and the chain saw into the truck, I felt a pang of guilt. No matter how urgent my desire to get out of Stony Ledge, I shouldn't leave her with this burden.

"And don't you think about staying one more minute." She leveled a finger at me and then hoisted herself into the cab. "Mighta had to cut more wood for winter anyway. This saves me deciding what to take down."

Her voice was bright, but there was weariness in the set of her shoulders and I didn't believe a word. Still, I'd learned arguing did no good, so I wedged my duffel bag onto the floor at my feet and we bumped along to the first roadblock, a pair of young pines that had toppled into an embrace and dropped with their crowns pointing uphill. Saw snarling, Delia limbed them and cut them into lengths. I packed the smaller limbs into the trench where water had coursed around them and, wiping sweat from my eyes every few minutes, raked loose stones on top.

We jounced on to the next barrier, a half-rotten oak split down the center by the storm and so sodden that the chain saw bound up, smoked, and stalled out. After that we tackled a string of pines like fallen dominoes. Beyond were dogwoods, redbuds, and more oaks, a blur of shattered trunks, broken branches, and channels knifing deep into the road.

When my muscles screamed and it felt like someone was holding a welding torch to my back, I thought about Tad and used rage like liniment to burn away the ache and then salved it by imagining the byline I'd have one day. Once I dug my wristwatch from the pocket of my tattered khakis and then laughed. I had no idea when a bus might leave, and no idea how long this task would take. Knowing the exact time right now had no relevance.

The rain had stopped and the sun was rolling west from its summit when we reached the cattle guard and found it filled to the rails with debris left by sluicing water. No cow would find it frightening now.

Recalling how I'd explained the principle to April the day I came to Hog Run Ridge, I realized I'd filled my life with cattle guards, insignificant, self-created stumbling blocks that became intimidating, insurmountable obstacles. I'd run myself down before others got the chance, deferred my dreams, burdened Ben with my hesitancy.

I drew in a shuddering breath and squeezed back tears. Things could have been different, so very different.

"Have to fix that so I can get your letter." Delia

pointed at the mailbox canted over the ditch, its post undercut by the current. Pulling a shovel from the truck bed, she bent to the task of shoring it up, but then leaned on the handle, and heaved an enormous sigh. "I gotta stop for a bit."

I peered past her, down a tunnel of road crisscrossed with shattered limbs. So close. Once we got to the next mailbox, someone else would have done the heavy work to clear their own way to town. I squinted in the opposite direction feeling an upwelling of hope. Perhaps someone was working this way and would help us. "Who lives farther up the road?"

"No one."

I felt tears behind my eyes and told myself again that time had no relevance. I'd get there when I got there. If not today, then maybe tomorrow.

"Cyrus used to butcher hogs by the pen up there." Delia leaned the shovel against the fender and got a sack and a jug of water from the cab. She let the tailgate down and spread out lunch: ham and cheese sandwiches on thick slices of homemade rye bread with sliced tomatoes and pickles wrapped in waxed paper, potato chips, and fudge. I layered tomatoes and pickles into my sandwich and told myself I'd eat only because I needed the energy.

But the first bite set a match to the fuse of my hunger; I gobbled it and dug into the chips. No savoring today.

Delia matched me bite for bite, now and then glancing up that abandoned road. "Didn't care much for the killing. Or the butchering. But raising them hogs was easy." She took a long swallow from the water jug. "Fed 'em kitchen and garden scraps and they run wild until cold weather. Might could do that again if someone would do the rest for a share of the meat."

Her wistful voice reminded me again that she was isolated geographically and socially. I was leaving, Cyrus was dead, and travelers would come no more to seek their

218

fortunes. She'd have only an occasional trip to an unwelcoming town to break the tedium of chores and lonely hours. And every night that jug of fiery liquid on the kitchen shelf would sing its siren song of forgetfulness.

Guilt stabbed at my heart and I popped a piece of fudge in my mouth and told myself Delia could sell the farm and find a friendlier place to live out her days.

"Well, let's get back at it before I get so stove up I can't move." She stood, stretching her arms and legs, joints popping so loud I worried that a bone would snap. "I'll have more than enough time to put my feet up after that bus pulls away."

I squinted up at the sun and then along the road to town. It might take us hours to clear our way to Stony Ledge, and then there would be the slow drive from there. Night would be closing in before we arrived. Had Delia ever driven in the dark? Could she? And what about the cow that would need milking? "Let's start fresh tomorrow."

"No." Delia wrapped up the remaining pickles and fudge. "You want to get on your way. And . . ." She cocked her head and stared down the leaf-strewn lane. "Well, I feel like we need to get down this road quick as we can."

"It's your call." I went to work, channeling my concerns into hard labor, trying to sweat them away.

The first hundred yards were the worst. After that the steep shoulder of the ridge had broken the force of the wind. There were plenty of branches down but they were small enough that we could drag them to the side without getting out the saw. Water had overrun the road, but hadn't chiseled the ruts much deeper and in places had deposited debris to fill them in.

We worked without saying more than, "I'll take that side," or, "You got it?" My back ached and my legs wobbled. Several times I saw Delia stagger and fling an arm out to catch her balance or lean against the truck with a hand over her heart while she sucked water from the jug.

I kept watch from the corner of my eye, ready to catch her if she fell, but each time she stared down the road, pursed her lips, and went back at it, breath coming in ragged gasps.

It was five when we tugged the last limb from the road just above the next mailbox. "Pretty clear from here on." Delia grunted and clambered back into the cab. She squinted off into the trees to the right of the road, rubbed her eyes, and peered again, twisting a tuft of hair slick with sweat.

"What's wrong?" I stood on tiptoe, searching for a clear view through the leaves, getting only glimpses of sky and rippling water. "What do you see?"

"Nothing, I guess." She shrugged and tapped a gauge on the dashboard. "Have to stop for gas."

I hoisted myself into the truck and patted the canvas satchel in which I'd stuffed tissues, comb, makeup, two books for my journey, and my wallet. "I'll pay to fill it up."

"That's a kind offer, girl, but you keep your savings for Chicago. I expect living in that city you'll spend more in a month than I do in a year."

"I'll find a job." Voice quavering, I fingered one of the many rips in my khakis and glanced at my sodden shoes. When I was certain there was no more road to clear, I'd change out of them. "I know I will."

"I know you will, too." Her voice rang with the confidence mine lacked. "You do what needs to be done and you don't hesitate much once you're convinced."

She fired up the truck and we trundled along, twigs raking the undercarriage and snapping beneath the wheels. The yellow fields were silvery with standing water lapping close to the houses we passed. Cows and horses stood on knobs of sodden soil gazing balefully at drowned pastures. The goats that I'd seen grazing along the ditch perched atop an open shed munching ears of corn. Far beyond them loomed the chimney of the yellow house.

"Sweet Christ in Heaven!"

Delia stood on the brake and clutch, bouncing me off the dashboard. "I cannot let that stand!"

She shook a fist at the sky and then shoved me against the door. "Save that baby!"

My eyes slewed to the road ahead of us, seeing only a jumble of storm debris. Was she having a seizure? "What baby?"

Delia pointed out the passenger window. "There. Over there."

I stared at water, hummocks of flattened grass, and a barbed wire fence atop a rimple of dark earth curving toward the distant house. "Where?"

"Beyond the fence. In the water." She shoved me again. "I'll get his mother and father."

"There's no baby." I grasped her fingers, chilled despite the heat and her labors. "You're exhausted. You're imagining things. Let me drive you home."

"Forget me," she screamed, tearing her hand from mine and pointing across the field. "Run! Save that baby!"

"There's no—"

"Run!" Delia slapped my cheek. "Now!"

She's gone crazy! Get away from her!

I wrenched the door open, slid to the road, and reached for my satchel. Just as my fingers touched it the truck jolted forward and the flapping door slammed my elbow. I howled in pain. Heedless, Delia churned off through the debris.

Cradling my arm, I stared after the truck for a few seconds, then decided to get to the yellow house, find someone to help, and get Delia seen to. It was maybe half a mile by road, closer if I crossed the submerged field and followed the fence. And my shoes and slacks were already soaked.

Plunging into the ditch, I fought through a current

221

that reached my thighs, scrabbled up the other side, and almost fell against two strands of rusty barbed wire. I threaded myself through and sloshed into a field awash with dead and dying insects, twigs, leaves, and chunks of bark. My feet sank into muck invisible beneath turbid water that lapped against my knees, but I managed a slow-motion run by leaning forward and pumping my arms. Halfway to the berm I stepped in a hole and sprawled across a grass-tufted mound. Air exploded from my lungs.

Wheezing in short breaths that cut like razors, I groped at greasy grass, struggled to my knees, got one foot under me.

Something bumped against my hip and I glanced down.

A snake as thick as my forearm raised its head and stared back.

CHAPTER 24

I froze, heart hammering, breath binding in my chest.

The snake opened its mouth to show the white lining that let me put a name to it—cottonmouth moccasin.

Eyes glittering, it drew its head back.

I braced for the strike, looking away a bit so I wouldn't quite see, watching the breeze herd a row of ripples across the field. The snake bobbed on the swells. Its tail twitched. Then, with a swirl of water, it swam off.

Wiping sweat from my eyes, I bolted for the berm, yelling, splashing to frighten other snakes adrift on the flooded field. I clawed my way to the fence and slithered beneath it, tearing the right leg of my slacks from knee to ankle, emerging onto a narrow path, a minefield of saturated cow plops.

Slick footing. No time to pick my way.

I set my course for that remote chimney and ran, hoping speed and adrenaline would keep me on my feet, that someone would be home, that the phone would work, that they'd listen to—

I caught movement at the edge of my vision, swiveled, froze once more.

Ten yards away the tow-headed toddler from the yellow house stood in water up to the bottom of his diaper. He held a bit of leafy branch in each hand. As I watched, he poked them at a snake even larger than the

223

one that bumped me.

I drew in breath to scream, but then clamped my jaw. Sudden loud noise might upset the fragile balance between boy and snake, life and death.

How long had he been poking at it? Was he old enough to understand if I told him to move back or was he too caught up in his game to listen?

"Save the baby!" Delia's words rang in my mind. "I'll get his mother and father."

Tearing my eyes from the boy, I peered toward the yellow house. A line of trees obscured all but the chimney and a slice of roof. Were his parents coming? Or did they think Delia was a madwoman?

I glanced back the way I came. How had she known?

"Heeeee!" the tiny boy crowed.

I swung around in time to see him raise the branches and whack the snake. It recoiled, lifted its thick, triangular head, and displayed its fangs.

"Heeeee!" He lifted the branches high, waving them like battle flags. "Heeee!"

Delia spoke inside my head, the words as clear as if she stood beside me, "You do what needs to be done and you don't hesitate much once you're convinced."

I'd already hesitated too long.

Trembling, I slid down the berm and into the marshy field wondering again how she'd known the boy was here. Had she heard him over the rumble of the truck engine and rush of water in the ditch?

The toddler glanced my way, grinned, and fluttered his leafy flags. Even if he was too young to understand my words, he could recognize a soothing tone. That might keep him calm, maybe keep me calm, too. As if that was possible.

I cleared my dry throat. "Hi there, sweetie. Hi there."

The snake swung its head toward me, the inside of its mouth spectral white. Its fangs curved back. They seemed

224

far too stubby for their purpose.

Muck clutched at my shoes as I sloshed closer, raising rings of ripples. I was careful not to splash even as I wondered if I should charge in and try to frighten the moccasin away.

"Don't hit the snake, sweetie," I called in a singsong voice. Eight yards to go. "Snakes don't like to be hit. It makes them mad and then they hurt you. You don't want to get hurt, do you?"

"Heeee!" He waved the branches and then smacked them on the water. The snake lashed out.

"No!" I strained against sucking mud. The snake whipped back and reared its head again, a shred of leaf impaled on one fang.

Missed!

"I'm coming, sweetie. Stay still now. I'm coming."

"Heeee!" The boy raised his flags.

Two yards to go! Mud rose to my ankles. Twisting against it, I bent low and scooped water with both hands. "Get back! Get away from him."

The snake's head swung my way, so close now I saw individual scales, elliptical pupils. Its mouth opened wide. I splashed again. "Get back! Go away!"

"Heee!" The boy dropped his flags and dug his hands into the water.

The snake's head bobbled his way.

I lunged, ripping my feet from my shoes, stretching my arms, gathering the boy to my chest.

The snake hit my calf like a hammer. I tottered, spun sideways.

Don't look! Keep going!

The toddler squawked, flailed his arms, and kicked at me, but I managed one plodding step and then another.

"It's okay. Don't cry. I've got you." I wrestled him about, clutching his sodden diaper with one hand and sliding the other beneath his arm. His skin was slick and

225

soft. His fine hair smelled of sunlight and shampoo. I told myself to think about him, not the faint burning in my leg or my fear the snake would strike again. "You're okay. That bad snake didn't get you."

He grasped a handful of my hair in one fist and thumped the other against my shoulder. "Who you? Who you?"

"I'm Elizabeth." I smiled into clear green eyes ringed with curling lashes. "Liz. Can you say that? Liz."

His brow furrowed. "Ith."

"Close enough." I labored to the lip of a furrow, my heart thudding against my ribs, and skidded down into the next depression.

He wiggled and I clutched him tighter. Tipping his head, he let loose a yowl that echoed back at me from across the field. No, not an echo. Three people splashed toward us: Delia, a stocky man with a gun across his shoulder, and a pale-haired woman who seemed almost to run atop the ripples, screaming, "Danny! Danny!"

"There's your mommy." I turned the boy so he could see her and plunged on, chanting to contain my fear. "There she is. You're okay."

His yowls ebbed to throttled sobs and then, "Mommy. Mommy!" Sniffling, he stretched out chubby fingers.

"I'm here, Danny," she called. "I'm coming."

I tasted hot metal and cold mint in my mouth, swallowed, and felt electrical current racing along my nerve endings. Adrenaline, I told myself. "You're okay," I chanted. "We're okay. I'm okay."

The woman floundered over a grassy hummock, went down on one knee, came up like a rocket, her green dress dripping. "Danny!"

"He's okay." I held him out to her, arms quivering, leg ablaze.

"Thank you. Thank you." She snatched him and spun toward the house.

226

The world seemed to spin with her, the dome of sky, trees, field, fence, and water revolving. I windmilled my arms, trying to balance. The man charged past, eyes tight, mouth a grim line, the stock of a double-barreled shotgun braced against his shoulder.

"I'm coming, girl." Panting, eyes wide and stark against ashy skin, Delia closed the distance.

The shotgun thundered. Something thrashed in the water and the gun thundered again. The spinning world lurched to a stop and started up the other way, making the ground swell and go slack again like a sail in a fretful wind.

Delia flung out an arm and reeled me against her. I smelled sour sweat and the turpentine of pine pitch, felt rigid bone and stringy muscle. "Which leg? How many times?"

"Just once," I whispered, pointing with fingers that wouldn't quite straighten, that fluttered like leaves.

Supporting me with one arm, Delia bent, shoved up my torn khakis, and touched my burning skin. "Not as bad as some I've seen."

She straightened and smiled a little, her brown eyes glowing like polished stones beneath a skim of sunlit water. I stared deep into them and knew it all. "Cyrus never saw the future. It was you. Always you."

She stroked my cheek with a callused finger. "Yes, child."

"And . . .? Will I—?" I couldn't say the word.

"You'll be good and sick. Nothing I can do about that." She hugged me against her and stroked my hair. "But you changed that baby's fate. You won't cross over today. Sweet times are coming, child. Sweet times will be here soon."

Fire spiked up my leg and the world shimmered and swayed once more, but Delia held me up. Fear slipped from my shoulders like a snow-covered cape tossed aside on the threshold of a warm and welcoming room.

CHAPTER 25

Pain blurred my vision and earth and trees and sky ran together like watercolors in the rain. Everything felt rounded off and I couldn't balance, felt myself falling, falling. I closed my eyes, concentrating on Delia's promise—"sweet times"—settling against those words as if they were pillows just fluffed.

Arms lifted me against the rough weave of a shirt that smelled of sweat and gun smoke, fingers found my pulse, voices thanked me again and again, and then an engine started up and Delia held me against her side and crooned, "You're getting to the big highway, just not the way we planned."

A wallowing series of jolts gave way to the hum of tires on smooth pavement, "Lots faster than my old truck. We're going seventy miles an hour," Delia marveled. "Never went that fast in my life. We're flying, girl. Flying."

"Ungh," I grunted, keeping my eyes closed and building imaginary walls to hold back waves of pain, walls that crashed to rubble almost as fast as I got them up. My leg throbbed to the beat of my heart and I remembered what else Delia had said, that I'd be good and sick, that there was nothing she could do about that. I swallowed a moan and built another worthless wall.

Then arms lifted me again and fingers prodded my leg, felt my throat, and pried up my eyelids and shone a beam of light that made me wince. I smelled antiseptic and felt a sting overlay the burning in my leg. A cool round of metal lay against my chest and a thin cylinder slid beneath my tongue. Needles pricked, my last wall gave way, and a rolling tide of pain bore me under, rolled me deeper into a sea of fire.

"Come on up from there," Delia ordered. "Get up on top of that pain. Ride it like a skittish horse."

I groaned. What did I know of horses? Only what I'd seen on Saturday-night TV westerns.

"A big horse," Delia crooned. "Brown as fresh-turned earth with eyes the color of new grass and a white blaze like lightning down his face. He's got a wild streak, but you'll gentle it out of him."

She tied my hair back and threaded my arms into the sleeves of a gown that smelled like bleach. "Keep your hands on the reins and your feet in the stirrups. When he runs, lay your head down along his neck. When he walks, you sit tall and look around and thank him for carrying you through the desert."

I shuddered, remembering the geography text stolen with my car. Deserts were harsh and forbidding places. Places of death.

"Don't you worry about where he takes you." Delia sponged my face and neck with cool water, settled me against a pillow, and curled my fingers around the top of the sheet. "Just stay up on that horse and you'll be all right. I'll be right behind you all the way there and back."

And maybe she was.

But I didn't look—couldn't look—for fear I'd fall. The horse twisted, danced to the side, and then drew his lips back, thrust his head forward and ran. I clenched my fists around the reins, squinched my eyes tight, and hung on.

He ran for what seemed like a week, and then slowed to a rolling gait that made me queasy. I remembered what Delia said, straightened my spine, and peered around.

A desert landscape opened before me, a place where

the sun glinted off mica-flecked sand, where tiny tumbleweeds skittered like frightened cats and sluggish snarls of barbed wire rolled their dawdling way through steep-sided arroyos. I heard Sebastian bark and he ran beside me for a bit, young again. And then he was gone.

A mirage shimmered between me and the smudge of horizon, and sometimes I thought there was another rider out there and sometimes I thought I was mistaken, and more than once I was certain it was Ben. I tried to raise my arm to wave, but I couldn't.

Later I came half awake, felt Delia's fingers woven through mine, and wanted to ask her the question that brought me to Hog Run Ridge. Then I remembered that, dead or alive, Ben was lost to me.

I drifted back to that desert and rode on.

After a while I saw the little boy playing in the silvered water of the mirage. He waved his branches and crowed in triumph and I smiled, remembering how it felt to hold him and breathe the smell of his hair and skin, how he'd tried to say my name. "Ith," I whispered.

"You come down off that horse now," Delia said. "Feel the pillow under your head and the sheet atop. Come on down and sleep deep until morning."

I woke up to the taste of alcohol and a nurse in a rustling uniform sliding a thermometer under my tongue. She put a finger on her lips and nodded toward a chair by the window where Delia snored beneath a white flannel sheet, her skin gray as dust. "How are you feeling?"

I took stock. My leg burned and felt tight within its skin, my left arm ached at the inside of the elbow where a needle attached to a length of thin tubing jutted from beneath a wide strip of adhesive tape. My head throbbed, my mouth felt like the desert I'd ridden through, and the smell of toast wafting in from the hall made my stomach roil. "I think I'm okay," I croaked.

231

She raised her brows, but then studied the thermometer. "Well, this says you're about back to normal."

Normal?

I choked back a laugh. The way I'd once defined normal was a long way from this. I ran my parched tongue across fuzzy teeth. My breath must be rank. "Could I have some water?"

The nurse nodded, raised my head, and slid a straw between my lips. "A little at a time," she warned. "Or it will come right back up."

I sipped and swished it around my mouth. A man and a woman appeared in the doorway, the toddler cradled in his arms. I spoke around the straw. "How's Snake Boy?"

"Full of piss and vinegar." The man grinned. "Thanks to you."

The woman blotted a tear with her sleeve and, when the nurse motioned her closer, came to the bedside with faltering steps and a smile to match. Her pale hair was braided into pigtails and she wore a red-checked dress that set off her sapphire eyes. "He was taking a nap. I don't know how he climbed out of his crib or got out the door without me seeing. And down the steps without taking a tumble."

She brought her fingertips to my hand in a feathery touch. "You saved his life. You didn't even know us," she said, her voice brimming with awed amazement. "I'm . . . I'm Amy Shelby and that's Pete."

"Pleased to meet you." I offered my hand and, when she touched my fingers with that same tentative touch, grasped hers hard enough to let her know I wouldn't break. "Thanks for getting me to the hospital."

"There's no need to thank us. If that snake had struck Danny I . . ." She clutched my fingers like a drowning woman. "There's no way we can ever repay you."

I nodded to the chair by the window. "I just did what

Delia told me to do. She's the one you should thank."

"We intend to." Pete juggled Danny to his shoulder and raised his right hand as if taking an oath. "Every day for the rest of her life."

"We brought your bag from her truck." Amy squeezed my hand and let it go. "So you'll have fresh clothes when the doctor lets you go home."

Home?

I choked back a laugh. Under my revised definition of "normal," home was a leaky barn. I guessed Amy didn't know that.

The nurse checked her watch. "Doctor will be in any time now."

"We'll be downstairs waiting." Amy flushed and glanced at Pete who nodded. "And we're paying the bill," she said in a rush.

"No arguing about that," Pete added. With a sharp grunt, he shifted Danny to the other shoulder. "What have you been feeding him, Amy? He weighs more than you do."

Amy giggled, took possession of her sleeping son, and scooted out.

"We'll be in the lobby." Pete turned to follow. "I'll bring the car around front when I see you two coming. Oh, and tell Delia I milked her cow this morning."

"Thank you," I told the empty doorway.

"Nice people." The nurse busied herself swabbing the thermometer.

"*Good* people," I corrected, my eyes on Delia. "Fine people."

The nurse shrugged, as if the adjectives were all the same. Maybe she never thought about the difference.

Delia opened her eyes when the gray-haired doctor with a clipped beard came to listen to my heart. She tossed aside her sheet, stretched, and came to his side as he prodded my leg, nodding when he pronounced me fit and issued a tube of ointment and warnings to watch for signs of spreading infection, drink plenty of water, and get lots of rest for the next few days. When he was gone, I swung my legs over the side of the bed.

An earthquake rocked the room.

"Careful, child." Delia clutched me to her side. "Lean on me until your knees stop wobbling and then we'll get you dressed." She took my chin between her thumb and forefinger and peered at me. "I believe it's time you call your father. He'd be worried sick if he knew what happened."

I blinked back sudden tears, longing to hear Dad's voice, but knowing I couldn't call now, not weak and worn down as I was. "That's the best reason *not* to call. He'll want me to come right home. Or he'll drop everything and drive out here and—"

"What's wrong with that?" Delia pinched my chin. "You're his baby. His only baby."

I batted at her hand, my arm rubbery. "I'm not a baby."

"You are to him." She chuckled and patted my cheek. "Some fathers are like that with their girls their whole lives long."

I pondered that as Delia helped me into my clothes. Being thought of as a baby felt like being confined to a cage, but at the same time it made me feel comforted, cherished, safe. But safe was too . . . well, safe. "I'll call him when I'm stronger. When I'm well enough to leave for Chicago."

"See that you do. Or I'm liable to do it for you." She smiled, but her eyes were steely and I didn't doubt that she would.

Pete drove us back to his farm in a rusty station wagon and insisted on following us to the top of the ridge in his truck. "You might get stuck in a rut. Truck's got the

234

horsepower to get you out."

"Thinks he'll have to push us even if we don't mire down," Delia laughed. "You see the way he looked at my truck? Like he thought we should dig a hole and bury it." She patted the dash. "Bet it's got as many years left as I do."

And how many was that?

I glanced at her from the edges of my eyes. Delia had looked ancient the night I'd met her. How many years would she live? Did she know the day that she would die? I shivered and set that thought aside.

Pete turned around at the top of the hill and drove off with a wave. Delia pulled up close beside the front porch. I slid from my seat, bracing myself against the door, and pondering the state of my jelly-like legs. "I think I'll sit down for a while before I go out to the barn."

"Forget the barn." Delia bounded up the steps, flung the front door wide, and returned to take my hand. "I'll show you why I prefer the back of the house."

She led me across the threshold into a room out of the past century. Horsehide loveseats squatted on either side of the hearth, spindly chairs and scrawny tables drooped in the corners like wallflowers at a dance. Peeling pink flowered wallpaper peeped from behind sepia-toned photographs of men and women, raptor-eyed and disapproving, even those clad in wedding dresses and fancy coats. "Cyrus' kin on the wall there," Delia said. "And family furniture handed down forever—about as comfortable as a gallows."

She opened a door into the second room at the front of the house, a bright bedroom with a tall four-poster bed covered by a crazy quilt pieced in hues of green, blue, and yellow that reminded me of spring meadows. A broad-seated rocker with a blue velvet cushion sat in the corner between two windows and the walls were decorated with landscapes constructed with twigs and wire, rock and tufts of dried grass, leaves, flowers, nutshells, and bark, all glued to lengths of weathered board. Fanciful works that could have been made by elves. "Those are beautiful."

Delia beamed. "I make 'em in the winter to pass the time. Cyrus called them 'kindling.'" She raised the window sash and a sweet breeze swelled into the room. "Well, let's get you into that bed so I can see to the chickens."

I fingered a bit of satin worked into the quilt. "Here? I'm staying here."

"That's what a guest room is for. Can't keep an eye on you if you're out in the barn, now can I?"

I smiled. "No." A week ago I would have seen that gruff comment as a mark of how much trouble I was to her, but now I knew that was just her way.

"Woulda had you in here sooner, but . . ." She turned back the quilt, revealing crisp white pillowcases. "Truth is I didn't want to get too used to your company. Didn't want to be wishing you back once you were gone."

I hugged her, kissed her rough cheek, and then, with my last bit of strength, kicked off my flip-flops and hauled my throbbing leg up onto that glorious quilt.

The room lay deep in afternoon shadow when Delia shook me awake. "That young man's comin' this way in a bit. He's wantin' to see you for his paper."

Never!

I pulled the pillow over my head. "Tell him I'm not here. Get your gun and run him off."

"That would give me great pleasure," Delia chuckled. "Revenge is sweet. But resolution is meat."

I mulled that saying for a moment, then sat up. "Who said that?"

"Me, I guess." Delia shrugged. "You've done a lot of growing up, girl, but you got more ahead."

I raked my fingers through greasy, gritty hair. "Are you telling me to turn the other cheek?"

236

That was Gertrude Gorman's stock-in-trade advice but, thinking about it now, I realized that she had a smug and aggressive way of presenting that cheek. She didn't do it meekly for the sake of peace as Reverend Campbell interpreted the verse, but as a way of setting herself beyond the person who'd done her injury.

Delia slung my duffel bag onto the end of the bed and dug out my shampoo. "I'm telling you to show him how far you are above the dirt he crawls under."

I imagined a worm with his face and felt stronger. "You're right. He's just a slimy, stinky, dirt-eating worm from my past."

"But even a worm serves a purpose on this earth," Delia reminded me. "Let's get your hair washed and get your war paint on. You got the high ground. Don't give up an inch of it until he waves a white flag."

When Tad's father's car chugged into view we were on the porch sipping tea. I'd started to put on the blue shift from the church rummage sale, remembered Tad bought it for me, and slipped into jeans and a dark green T-shirt. Delia tamed her hair and changed into gray slacks that almost fit and a pink short-sleeved shirt that made her skin glow. She rolled my right pant leg to my knee to protect the salve rubbed into the wound, and brought out a stool to elevate my foot so the leg didn't throb as much.

Tad took a long time opening the door, reaching back for the camera, light meter, a notebook, and then a pen. Once he got out, he stretched and peered around, as if he'd never been on the ridge before and was admiring the view.

When he turned to the house I felt sick and so cold that goose bumps rose on my arms. I hugged myself, wanting to hide from the shame of his hands on me. "I can't do this," I whispered.

"He's just a worm." Delia patted my knee. "And I'm

237

right here to help you squash him flat if need be. All right?"

I nodded and she stood, shading her eyes with her hand. "Why, it's Mr. Tad. How you doin' today?"

He approached with dragging feet, looking everywhere but at me. "I'm doing well, Delia. And you?"

"Middlin'. Expect you came to see Elizabeth."

He flushed. "Uh, yes." He held up the camera, his eyes fixed on Delia. "For the paper."

"I see." She parked her hands on her hips. "Just for the paper? If you'd'a asked me Saturday morning I'd'a said there was more between you two than paper stories."

Tad bent his head and she shot me a wink. "Shows how wrong an old lady can be."

"Looks can be deceiving," I agreed.

"Don't I know it, girl. My first husband was a lot like this boy here. Looked like a million dollars walking." She leveled a finger at Tad and her voice fell away to a hiss. "And didn't have a penny's worth of principle to his name."

Tad flinched and made a show of flipping the pages of his notebook. Delia sat and sipped tea. "Sometimes there's a nasty old snake in that picture-pretty pond, isn't there, child?"

I raised my glass. "And sometimes it's just a big worm."

Delia grinned and clinked her glass against mine.

Tad flushed the color of beet juice and glanced back at the car as if he wanted to bolt. Then he faced about, but kept his eyes on the edge of the porch. "I, uh, the wire services want the story. I already talked to Pete and Amy."

"Have you? Well, good, because I'm pretty tired." I feigned a yawn. This was a big deal for him; his story would run in other papers. It would be an even bigger deal if he couldn't deliver an interview with me—an enormous smudge on his reputation as a journalist.

238

"Saving babies from snakes is exhausting." I yawned again. "Why don't you come back tomorrow?"

He scowled and kicked at a tuft of grass. "But I want—*They* want it today." His lips compressed and his cheeks puffed out. He sounded like he had in that alley when he thought I was at his mercy, thought he could bully me. "Come on, it will only take a few minutes."

"An apology will take even less," I pointed out in a sweet singsong tone.

He kicked the grass again. "Damn it, Elizabeth. This has nothing to do with—" His eyes darted toward Delia who raised her brows. "And anyway, this isn't the place to discuss it."

"This is the perfect place. And there's nothing to *discuss*."

Loathing myself for having been taken in by his nice ways, I gripped my glass, longing to shatter it against his handsome face. "It's simple. Either you're sorry or you're not."

CHAPTER 26

Tad chewed his lip, eyes swinging from me to the camera to Delia, who studied him with the unwavering gaze of that snake. He winced and huffed out a sigh. "I guess I'm sorry."

"No 'I guess' about it," Delia snapped. "If you use that word, you better mean it. And you'd better look her straight in the eyes when you say it."

I didn't want to look into his eyes and I thought that no matter what tone of voice he used or how much conviction it carried, his concession would be counterfeit—in the way of his world he had nothing to apologize for. But the set of his shoulders, his clenched fists, and the flush on his cheeks told me he knew that this wasn't about humility. This was about humiliation.

Tad's shuffling feet raised puffs of dust and he glanced back at the car again, but then smacked the notebook against his leg. "I'm sorry," he half whispered, his glance slanting across my face.

I didn't accept that, just let it hang until he cleared his throat and tried again, focusing on my chin, droning, "I'm sorry, Elizabeth. I apologize for presuming that you—"

I raised a hand to save myself from reliving my dishonor. "That's enough." It wasn't even close, but I wanted this over with, wanted him gone. "Delia knew the baby was in trouble and sent me to find it. She's part of the story. You'll have to take a photo of us together."

Tad's brow furrowed. "You can't tell me how to—"

"I just did," I snapped. "If you don't like it, then get in that car and go."

Delia chuckled and patted my knee. Tad mouthed a word that would have sent Gertrude Gorman stomping off for a bar of soap, glanced at the car one more time, then took a reading with the light meter and got the camera ready.

I'd learned about cropping photos while I worked for the *Clarion*, and arranged Delia close beside me on the steps, my arm around her shoulders and hers around mine so he couldn't slice her out cleanly. I'd also learned about interviewing and made mine the toughest of Tad's life, answering in monosyllables while words cascaded from Delia's lips. She described the storm and the battered landscape with as much skill as Thoreau, but glossed over her premonition, calling it only "a bad feeling."

When he drove away with a final glower, Delia gave me a hug. "You made me proud, girl. You'll always be your father's baby, but to me you're all growed up now."

Growing up had been hard work and nothing like I expected. I felt pride swell in my chest, but declined the sin of showing it. "I guess."

"You're a woman now. But that boy's gonna be just a boy for a good long time." Pointing at the dust settling on the road she cackled and slapped her knee. "He thinks his old daddy's gonna kick off soon and he'll get the paper, but that old man's as tough as a boar's snout. He's coming back in a month, coming back like vengeance wearing spurs."

I giggled, imagining Senior with chaps and a ten-gallon hat, riding a black horse and wielding a whip.

"There's your revenge," Delia said. "And you don't have to lift a finger."

"You're not making that up, are you? You see that for

sure?"

"Every bit."

I thought of how she'd sent me after Danny and changed his fate. "And nothing will change it?"

"Not a single thing. No one's gonna come to that boy's rescue."

I sighed out my last bit of anger. "Did you always have the gift of sight?"

"If I did, do you think I'd'a married that gamblin' man?" She laughed in the bitter way you do when something is too true to be funny. "No, I took a fall and knocked myself cold one day not long before Cyrus checked in to that motel where I was working. I wore real thick glasses before that, but after everything was sharp as noon except for these little pictures kinda floating by in the air. I was bringin' Cyrus fresh towels when I saw a picture of his car all wrecked up. Told him he'd best park it around the back. Drunk driver hit the one that took his spot."

Her deep sigh seemed both lament and valediction. "Sometimes wish I hadn't spoke up, but then I wouldn't have the comfort of this ridge."

"Did you love Cyrus?" I cringed at my boldness, wiped at the dusk between us to erase my words. "Sorry. That's not my business."

"Can't fault you for asking. I've wondered myself." The chair creaked as she shifted. "Seems I wanted a change, and he wanted to get at my gift—though I didn't see that until later. Tried to make me see beyond what was just a bit ahead. Used me so hard that by the time he died them little pictures had about faded away."

Her fingers wove through mine. "I couldn't see how April would do you, taking your car and all. Feel I owe you for that."

"No." I knelt beside her, ignoring the pounding in my leg. "If I hadn't been stranded here, that snake might have

242

got Danny."

April's selfish act had saved a life. A month ago I never would have believed that possible. I felt a swelling sense of awed amazement, like I had the first time I stepped back from a painting by Monet and understood how all the tiny dots worked together to make a picture. Even the dot that was Tad had a reason for being on the canvas of my life.

"If she hadn't stolen my car, I wouldn't have gone to the *Clarion* looking for a ride and I wouldn't have had a chance to write stories and find out that I really *do* want to be a journalist."

I thought of how Gertrude Gorman's doubts and uncertainties reflected and magnified my own. "I know I won't look back and say I wasted an expensive education following a daydream."

"Seems that worm had a purpose then."

"But that doesn't make him any more than a worm."

"And a sorry excuse for one at that. Other worms likely laugh at him."

I giggled at the image and twined her fingers in mine. "But most of all, I would have missed out on knowing you. That's worth more than the car or the money that was in it."

Delia stroked my hair with her free hand. "Bless you for that, girl, but lotsa folks around here don't think I'm worth knowing."

I pounded my free hand on the railing. "They're the ones not worth knowing. They're small-minded, prejudiced—"

She laid her fingers across my lips. "Don't pile up stones to throw until you walk in their shoes. And don't go thinkin' I'm that special. I'm the one got you snakebit."

"No you didn't." I squeezed her fingers." If I'd listened to you instead of arguing, I might have gotten to Danny before the snake showed up."

243

"Maybe." She gazed off into the blue distance. "Saw that baby in the water and just assumed he would go by drownin'. Wasn't until I was to that house that I saw the snake, saw you in that hospital!"

"You did the right thing. The only thing." I reached up and put my hands on her shoulders. "I'm big enough to take the bite, but Danny's tiny. You did the right thing."

An enormous burden of responsibility came with Delia's gift. The cold weight of it pressed on my heart and I released her shoulders and rubbed my arms. "I'm glad I don't have the sight. What if I saw that you were going to—?"

"You'd tell me, girl, 'cause we might could change the day or the way. Not everything I see has to be." She took my hands and raised me to my feet. "You proved that when you went off with that worm."

I gasped and felt my face flush with shame and anger. "You saw what he—?" I ripped my hands from her grip.

"Saw his intention," she said in a rush. "Told you and you took it as a compliment. And then it felt like if I said more you'd think I got the words from the bottle and that I'd drive you closer to him."

Like a movie, it played out in my mind: Delia saying Tad wouldn't be able to keep his hands off me, me running to his car, Delia standing with her hand raised as if giving a blessing as we drove down the hill.

She was right. I wouldn't have listened. I might even have been so angry at her that I'd let him— I shuddered. "You did the right thing," I told her for the second time that evening. "The only thing."

She stood, nodded, and opened the door. "And what's done is done. Now let's get some dinner inside of you and get you back into bed. Big day tomorrow."

I assumed "big day" meant another round of harvest-season chores, but when I limped into the kitchen I found

Delia, dressed in a long white apron over pressed gray slacks and a plum-colored blouse. She'd slicked her hair flat and tied it down with a wide yellow ribbon and was peeling apples to fill three pie pans already lined with crust. "Company's coming."

I nibbled at a biscuit, trying to recall what she'd said about her family. Was a brother or sister on the way? "Who?"

"Good Samaritans. They musta took that hard look you was callin' for." She eyed the biscuit in my hand. "Looks like you're getting your appetite back. I was worrying you'd be nothing but bones soon."

I patted my stomach. "Bones with a thick layer of fat on them."

"Not hardly." She tweaked the back pocket of my jeans, tugging at loose fabric. "You can't see it 'cause looking at myself don't help my hateful moods so I put the mirrors under the house."

"Don't get them out on my account." Pride in my appearance helped lead me to that alley.

"Point is: you need to think better of yourself. Not be prideful and admirin', just be satisfied with—" She cocked her head and grinned. "Hear them?"

I swallowed my bite of biscuit and held my breath, but caught only the whistling of the kettle. "No."

"You will." She poured a mug of coffee with a huge dollop of milk and handed me a plate of scrambled eggs and grits with chunks of melting cheese. "Get out from under my feet. Take these out on the porch. Soon as I get the pies in the oven I'll be out to check your leg."

I dragged a chair into a puddle of sunlight on the east side of the porch, marveling at the change in the weather. Before the storm I would have sought shade, but now a cool breeze brought autumn smells of dust and drying leaves. The grass in the pasture had a yellow tinge and the sky wasn't as bleached out.

245

I picked at my eggs, thought about what Delia said about being content instead of conceited, and then cleaned the plate, finishing just as I detected a roaring rumble. Not a car. Something bigger. I carried my plate to the kitchen. "Whoever they are, they've reached the hill."

Delia closed her eyes for a second, then opened them with a yelp of joy. "Bless their hearts and souls!"

She hustled to my room and made the bed, then steered me to the porch and down the steps. Standing on her tiptoes, she began waving in welcome a full ten seconds before a gray and red tractor clattered around the final bend, Pete at the wheel, Danny tight between his knees. Behind them came a string of cars and trucks.

"Going to clear your road and get it graded," Pete called. "Brought a few friends and relations to help." The tractor chugged to a halt and he swung Danny into Delia's outstretched arms. "He's learned to say snake."

"Thnake." Danny giggled and wiggled stubby fingers at me. "Ith. Heee! Thnake."

I held out my thumbs for him to grasp, watching what looked like half the town of Stony Ledge pile out with shovels, rakes, and chain saws.

"I measured that monster. Four feet, nine inches." Pete's face clouded. "If he bit Danny . . ."

"Get yourself out of the anxious seat." Delia kissed Danny's cheek and handed him to me. "This little fellow's gonna have a long, long life."

"I hope so." Pete knuckled one eye. "And I hope you'll be part of it."

Delia ducked her head. "I'd be pleased and honored."

Amy slid out of the rusty station wagon lugging a picnic basket and a jug. "I brought cider and sandwiches."

"Boloney and egg salad." Delia squinted at the basket. "And I believe I see you eating potato chips, Elizabeth. The barbecue ones you like so much."

"How did you . . .?" Amy gawked for a second and

246

then blushed. "Silly me! Anyone who can see a snake through a mound of earth can spot boloney in a basket."

"Heee!" Danny agreed.

Everyone laughed and got to work, dividing out the tasks as if fixing Delia's road was a chore they all pitched in to do every fall. And though I couldn't see the future, I suspected that's exactly the way it would be from now on.

That night we sat out on the porch studying a slim rind of moon, counting cricket chirps, and watching bats cast flitting shadows on the eaves as they captured insects drawn to the wavering flame of a beeswax candle. Its aroma made me feel safe and warm, the way I used to when I was tiny and my father would carry me up to bed.

I was exhausted from "keeping my company face on" as Delia called it and suspected she felt the same, but neither of us budged. We marveled again at the amount of wood sawed into lengths and laid up to season, discussed what she'd bake for the roofing party Pete had vowed to organize later in October, speculated about the spices in the cookies Minerva sent up from the café, and hashed over opinions expressed about Tad Tolliver.

"Full of himself. Has been ever since he was old enough to talk," Amy told me. "Said he fired you because your work wasn't good enough, but anyone who can read knows that's a lie, so no one believes him. After he got his picture of Danny I told him to shut his mouth and get gone or Pete would tan his hide like he's wanted to do since grade school."

"That boy's dug himself a hole," Delia told me, "and the whole town's lining up to kick dirt down atop him."

"That's what happens to worms who think they're big frogs in little puddles."

"Well, don't you be too smug about it." She leveled a finger at my nose.

I did the same back at her. "And don't you be too

247

smug about all that oohing and ahhing they did over your landscapes."

Amy, who spotted Delia's artwork when Danny bolted into the guestroom, insisted the other women come and see. They oohed and ahhed and Delia, with a smile as wide as the Mississippi, gave away every one of her creations.

"That storm brought down plenty of bits for me to work with," she told me. "And I'll have me a lot of long nights alone."

"I'll bet not all that many. That baby spent more time in your lap than his mother's. Like it or not, I think you've got a family."

"Can't say as I don't like it," she muttered.

I rocked back and set my heels on the railing, already missing these peaceful evenings that unsnarled my thoughts. If Gertrude Gorman hadn't been so busy running the house and her business, we might have had evenings like this. Maybe when I returned to Maplekill to visit, I'd insist she take a few minutes to sit with me at the end of the day.

"When" I returned, not "if." I once thought I'd never return, but I'd put away dreams of what Ben and I would have done together and now dread of seeing him with April wouldn't keep me from my home.

I'd reached that place of forgetting Delia told me about. I would always have the past that Ben and I shared, that sweet and innocent time. April would have the future and all its uncertainty.

"What did you see when you were up on that horse?"

I glanced out at the cows, dark silhouettes beneath the trees. "Horse?"

"When you rode down the pain," she prompted. "In the hospital."

Closing my eyes, I recalled that stark landscape. "I saw a desert and rolling tumbleweeds and huge balls of barbed wire. I saw my dog, alive and running beside me."

248

"Fever dream," she said in a voice that implied these things were as common as sun or rain. "What else?"

"I thought I saw Ben." I sat up, clutching the edge of the chair. "He was riding through a mirage. I waved at him but he didn't wave back." Cold fear knifed into my heart. "Does that . . . Does that mean he's dead?"

"Can't say, child." Delia took my hand. "Could mean lots of things—that he's far off, that he can't see you, or maybe that he's still lost. Dreams are different from visions."

"Can you look and see if he's alive?"

"Doesn't work that way," Delia sighed. "At least not for me. If I've never met someone, I can't see *for* them."

I broke her grip and smacked my feet to the porch. "I have a picture. Inside. In my wallet."

She shook her head. "I can't see from a picture."

My shoulders slumped and a moan sifted between my lips. I felt like I lost Ben yet again. "What if you looked for *me*? Look at when I go back to Maplekill to visit next summer. See if he's there."

"Wish I could. But I've got what you might call a nearsighted gift."

"But you told Pete that Danny would have a long life."

"Told him what he wanted to hear. What I hope will be true." She winced. "Words were out before I could call them back."

The weight of her gift was even greater than I realized last night. Now that people knew she had the sight, even chance remarks would be interpreted as prophecy.

"Cyrus thought I could build up my gift, like it was a muscle. Thought he could use it to make himself rich." She spread her arms to the night, then drew them in as if hugging darkness to her chest. "Never did see that he had more than most, had all he needed right here. Kept on wantin' until it ate him up."

Scraping back her chair, she stood and shuffled to the

249

door. "I'm going to bed."

I understood the moral to her words, but Delia said she owed me and I felt cheated. "Well, do you at least see me finally getting to Chicago?"

She glanced back and I cringed. I sounded every bit as testy as Gertrude Gorman on a bad headache day. "I'm sorry. I . . . I just—"

"It's okay, child. I can see that you're hungry for knowing how it turns out." The guttering candle flicked shadows across her face. She closed her eyes tight and sucked in a breath. "I see you laughing. Laughing long and hard."

She pressed her fingers against her eyes, but after a moment shook her head. "That's the best I can do tonight. I'm worn to a frazzle. I'll try again after I've had my coffee in the morning. Things are sharpest then."

She melded into the darkness of the doorway as she had the night we met, leaving me alone with the crickets. I thought of Thoreau and how he said his greatest skill was to want little. Delia had that same skill. But I wanted more. Not fame and adulation as April had, but a career, a place for myself.

I rubbed my aching leg. One more day of rest would be enough. Then I'd be on my way. And no one, least of all Thoreau, would hold me back.

CHAPTER 27

"You sure you can't wait 'til tomorrow?" Delia dished up fried ham, applesauce, and a block of steaming cornbread. "Startin' a journey on Friday's bad luck. Monday, now, that's luckier."

"Apparently not for me." I split the grainy bread and set a cube of butter in the cleft to melt. "I left home on a Monday with bad luck riding shotgun and going by April's name."

Delia chuckled and poured coffee. "But, see, you ended up here."

"That was *your* good luck." I forked off a bit of ham and dredged it in applesauce. "If I hadn't, you'd still be trying to figure out how to drive that heap of rust and treadless rubber you call a truck."

She poked her fork at me. "You didn't dare sass me like that when you first come."

I grinned, feeling content. Delia loved me, wanted me to stay. It was ironic that love made leaving difficult but also gave me the confidence to go. "I didn't know then that I could talk back and live to tell about it. But I figured out you're all soft inside like a marshmallow."

"Marshmallow that's been left too long in the fire." She sprinkled cinnamon on her applesauce. "I can be a scary old woman, can't I?"

"When you're in the bottle." I felt my cheeks flame and applied myself to my cornbread, wishing I'd kept up

251

the light banter instead of plunging into treacherous territory. It wasn't the way I wanted to leave things between us. "I'm sorry. You've got a right to—"

"But no more reason." Delia slapped her spoon on the table. "Look at me, child."

I peered through the top of my glasses, expecting a scowl, seeing a magnificent smile instead. "Don't ever apologize for speaking the truth. Helping you helped me. I don't have the sight when it comes to myself, so I couldn't see how it might work out that way."

She reached across the table and squeezed my hand. "I sure see it now. I'm glad you came and I'm grieved to see you go." She pushed back her chair. "But you're bound to be gone. All packed up?"

"Since before dawn." I drained my coffee, finished the buttery bread, and took one last look around the kitchen where I ate meals as good as any I ever had and came to see my life, and Thoreau's, from a fresh angle. "What about the dishes?"

"They'll be here when I get back. Never seen any run off yet."

She shooed me to the guest room for my gear and then hustled us to the truck. Now that I was seeing it for the final time, it appeared even more forlorn. I tossed the duffel in the back and hoisted myself up into the warm scent of manure and mildew.

"Still favoring that leg," Delia observed. "You sure you don't want—?"

I slapped the fly-specked window and yanked my door closed. "I'm fine. Stop fussing. It's not like I have to walk to Chicago."

"Have it your way." She slid the key into the ignition and turned it. I heard a click and a mechanical groan, then nothing. She tried again. Only the click.

Damn it!

I pounded the fissured seat. Was I doomed to be stuck

252

on Hog Run Ridge forever?

"Never did that before." Delia pumped the gas and turned the key again.

I yanked at my hair. Why hadn't I asked Pete and Amy for a ride?

"Working up a mad won't get us anywhere," Delia snapped.

I shot her a glare, stopped fuming, and started thinking. "The battery might be dead. If that's all, we can roll the truck and pop the clutch."

"Pop?" Delia gawked as if I'd spoken French.

"Just let off the clutch real quick—the way you used to do it. Don't ride the brake or you won't be going fast enough for the engine to catch."

She shook her head. "Only a fool takes that hill without the brake."

"You can use the brake when—" I slid toward her. "Get out. I'll show you."

Delia cocked her head and peered down the hill. "Hold off a bit. I believe someone's coming."

I craned my neck but, as usual, saw and heard nothing. "Who?"

"Don't know him." She rubbed her eyes. "He's come about your car."

Buggy! They found Buggy!

A wave of elation swelled, then broke against a shoal of anxiety. The man coming might be Deputy Jimmy McCoy. Tad's buddy. I shivered, remembering the way his black eyes had swept across me, fearing he knew Tad's version of events in that alley.

I dragged breath into my lungs and raised my chin. I'd stared down Tad. I was grown up now. "Did April wreck it, or will I get it back?"

Delia chewed the corner of her top lip. "I can't see that much."

I felt a flash of anger. Wednesday night she promised

253

to try to see my future, but she put me off again Thursday morning, claiming the moon going dark sapped her strength, telling me only that a wish made on Friday's new moon would come true within a year. I slapped the dashboard. "Well, what *do* you see?"

With a scowl and a sharp grunt she opened her door and dropped from the seat. "I see me clearing those breakfast dishes, Miss Snippy."

Before I could frame an apology, she turned her back and stomped into the house. Cheeks burning, I got out, limped to the porch, and sat on the steps.

For a long while I heard nothing except the wind soughing through the pines, dry leaves skittering along the road, and birds twittering in the orchard. A bee hummed past heading for butterfly weed by the pasture fence. The sound lingered in my ears, became the drone of a distant engine, fractured into a soft rattle that shattered to a clattering cough as familiar as my own.

Hugging myself, I stood on tiptoe, searching for the plume of dust, finding it, spotting the rusty nose of my car. My feet danced and my heart thrummed with excitement and a wild feeling of independence.

Sun glinted off the windshield as the car struggled up the final incline, wheels slewing in the freshly graded earth. I waved, pointing to a spot beside Delia's truck, jogging that way, the ache in my leg down to a twinge.

Buggy swung past, the glaring sun on the windshield obscuring the driver, giving me an impression of a man's jutting chin, sunglasses, the bill of a hat pulled low. With a final mechanical hiccup, the car halted and the driver's door sprang open without its usual creak. A rangy man in a work shirt and jeans unfolded himself from the seat. His head bobbed as he looked me up and down.

I crossed my arms over my breasts. "Thank you, deputy," I said in an arctic voice.

"Deputy?" the man croaked. He hooked his fingers

254

around the bridge of his sunglasses and slipped them off. "Deputy?"

I squinted into the shadow of his hat.

A name bloomed in my heart. "Ben?"

He swept the hat aside revealing eyes crimped with strain and underslung with bruised shadows.

"Ben!" I yelped. "Ben! You're okay."

"Mostly." He opened his arms and I leaped into them, pressing myself against him, feeling bone too close beneath the muscle of his shoulders and ribs ridged along his sides.

"I was a long crawl out of that jungle," he said. "Then they stuck me in a hospital for a few days before they shipped me home."

He spun me about, his deep, full laugh a little jagged, as if he hadn't used it often. I kissed his sunken, stubble-covered cheeks, his eyes, his crooked nose, his lips. He responded with such intensity I thought my teeth would shatter. Then he drew back, his kisses like milkweed down on my lips.

I felt myself falling, merging, melding. It was as if we'd never been apart, would always be together.

And then what was right turned around and was all wrong. To get my car, Ben must have found April, the girl he was promised to.

What I felt for him was real.

It just didn't belong to me.

CHAPTER 28

"Stop." I pressed my hands against his chest, struggling to break the kiss. "This is wrong."

"It feels right to me." He held me tighter, forced his mouth against mine.

That lit the fuse on rage building since the day we got word he was missing in action, the day April brought out that ring. I dug my fingers into his cheeks, shoved his head back. "Well it's not. You're engaged to that bit—" I clamped my jaw.

Ben lifted one eyebrow. "Bitch?" he asked in a mocking tone as he unwound his arms and set me on the ground. "Were you going to say bitch?"

"Yes." I stood my ground, my cheeks flaming with spite, wanting to tell him about Stash and all the rest, my conscience carping that I shouldn't be vengeful and malicious and hurt him for seeking love I hadn't given. I was still acting like a child whose romantic bubble had burst.

I breathed deep. "But maybe if I'd gotten to know her better we—"

Ben's roaring laugh and the pounding of his fists on the roof of the car overrode the rest. "That's like saying you should have sat down to tea with that water moccasin."

"If you feel that way, why did you propose to her?" I blinked in amazement. "And how do you know about—?"

"Heroine saves toddler." He mimed opening a paper.

"I read about it in Kansas City."

"Kansas City? But that's . . . What were you doing there?"

"Getting your rattletrap car fixed. New battery, belts, wipers, and a window. Even oiled those squeaky door hinges you kept saying you'd get to."

"But how did you find the—?" I stopped. Each answer raised more questions.

He slung an arm around my shoulders. "I'll explain it all if you lead me to that porch and get me some water. I spent two weeks living on roots and grubs and bad water and throwing you around took the last strength I had, Littlebit." He pinched my hip. "Even though there's not much left to throw."

I blushed, pleased that he'd used my pet name, ashamed of being thrilled he noticed I'd lost weight.

We were halfway to the porch when Delia emerged carrying a tray laden with sandwiches and a pitcher of tea. She'd changed into brown slacks and a pale blue blouse. "You must be Ben," she said with a smile like sunrise.

"And you must be Delia." He released me and executed a deep bow. "I'd know you anywhere."

"He saw the newspaper article," I told her. "In Kansas City."

Ben pulled me close again. "Before that all I had to go on was a postmark. I was planning to knock on every door in Stony Ledge. That paper saved a lot of wear and tear on my knuckles."

"Kansas City. Imagine that," Delia marveled. She set the tray down and fixed her gaze on me. "Told you that worm might serve a purpose."

"Worm?" Ben pulled my hair. "Did you get bit by a worm, too, Littlebit?"

I cut my eyes toward Delia, who pressed her lips together with thumb and forefinger. "No, just slimed up a little," I said.

257

And that, I decided, was all I'd ever tell him about Tad.

We climbed the steps and Delia moved the best chair to the railing, saw Ben settled with a napkin on his knee, and offered a fancy china plate of sandwiches sliced diagonally and displayed like a pinwheel with a pile of bread-and-butter pickles in the center.

I eyed her presentation with suspicion. How long had she known he was on the way?

"You're looking awful puny," she told him, pouring tea. "Got a crumb-topped peach pie in the oven that will put some flesh on your bones."

I'd seen a jar of peaches on the kitchen counter. And now I remembered seeing sacks of flour and sugar out, too. She'd known for hours, but kept still and let Ben surprise me. I resented that even as I admired her restraint.

"Peach is my favorite pie." Ben grinned and bit off half a sandwich.

Delia twinkled at him. "So Elizabeth told me."

I perched on the rickety railing, one foot anchored on the porch, thinking back, certain I never mentioned Ben's preference in pie. Delia winked and dropped into the chair I'd come to think of as mine. How far could she dip into my mind? A few weeks ago that would have made my skin prickle, but Delia had seen me naked, proved she was my friend. What did it matter if she harvested a few thoughts to make Ben his favorite pie?

Ben swallowed and held off on wedging the rest of the sandwich in his mouth. "I'm glad my girl found a good friend."

My girl?

I flushed with pleasure, but then remembered the question he hadn't answered. "What about that engagement ring you gave April?"

He flipped his palms open and shrugged. "Wasn't

258

from me." He took my left hand and stroked my fingers. "I've been saving up since I turned twelve to give you a rock the size of one of those lima beans you hate so much."

I imagined a diamond on top of a heap of those hideous gray-green mealy beans and giggled. I *was* his girl! Just like always. "Why would April lie about being engaged to you?"

"It's the nature of worms," Delia said. "They can't help themselves."

Ben nodded. "I think she's been making up stories so long she can't stop. If I knew how much grief she'd cause, I would have kept walking when I saw her panhandling outside that café with the cops bearing down on her." He sighed and gave me a weak grin. "But she was dirty and hungry . . . and you know how I am about strays."

I patted his head. "You were the patron saint of every dog and cat in Maplekill. Not to mention squirrels and raccoons."

"I should have stuck with four-legged creatures. She reeled me in like a farm-raised trout with a story about her aunt ripping off her inheritance and the police persecuting her." He waved that away with the back of his hand. "Said she was trying to find a job so she could go to nursing school. And I was about to ship out. I had no time to check out her story, no time to think." He took a deep drink of tea.

"So you nev—?"

"Never touched her except to put cash and a bus ticket in her hand."

I almost cried out with happiness but kept my face still. His tightened to a grimace. "Asking you and Mom to look out for her—that was like asking a couple of newborn rabbits to help out a fox."

"You just followed your nature," Delia said.

"And it's okay now. She's gone." I pirouetted along the

259

porch, chanting, "I don't know where, and I don't care."

"Utah as of last night," Ben said. "She called Mom and said the two of you were in a car accident. Wanted five-hundred dollars for the hospital."

I halted my dance, wondering for one second if April was really hurt.

Ben pointed at me. "She claimed you drove off and left her by the side of the road."

My fists clenched. "That lying little piece of—"

"She's all that," Ben agreed.

He turned to Delia. "My mother's more soft-hearted than I am, and she apologizes for everything, but that was the last straw. She told April I was back and we knew about her lies. Then she called her a parasite, a leech, and a whole lot more."

"Way to go, Jo!" I did two more pirouettes, remembering how I'd put April's face on the ticks lying in wait for me in the woods. I saw that what I had perceived as freedom to go wherever she wanted hadn't been that at all. Like a tick, she'd made her way mostly at the whim and expense of others.

"That girl won't never change a lick," Delia muttered.

I wondered if she saw that or was just guessing.

Ben snagged another sandwich and scratched the stubble on his chin. "Why was my key in Buggy? Did you lose yours?"

"No. She stole yours."

"And then stole that car," Delia said. "Smashed out a window while your girl was helping me chase down my cows and took off with everything except a few scraps of clothing and Mister Thoreau's book about that pond."

"Thoreau, huh?" Ben shot Delia a wink. "Littlebit always liked older men."

I raised my fists, poked the air in front of his face. "How did you find Buggy?"

He stuffed a chunk of sandwich into his mouth and

260

talked around it. "Police in KC had it towed from a no-parking zone. They called your house the day after I got back." His eyes narrowed. "Gene wanted to come, but your grandmother's headaches are worse. I told him this was my fault and my job."

Not "your father," but "Gene." And not asking but telling. Ben had made his own journey to adulthood.

"He's been frantic since the day you left, Elizabeth."

I hung my head, bending my shoulders beneath that yoke of guilt. "I sent postcards."

Ben snorted. "You should have called."

"I know. But I was afraid if I heard his voice I'd go back and then I'd never get to Chicago, never be—"

Ben drew me into his lap and kissed the top of my head. "He knows, Littlebit. He said he sheltered you too long and didn't do you any favors by it."

I snuggled against Ben's chest, feeling connected to my father across all the miles, happy he'd had Ben to talk to.

"He's a wise man," Delia mused. "Love's like a bird. Leave it free to fly and when it soars up high it's so beautiful your breath catches in your throat."

Ben glanced at the sky above the pasture, smiling as if he caught a glimpse of that bird, and then tugged my hair. "Your grandmother wanted to call the police and have you hauled home. But Donnie told Gene if that was the way you came back then you'd never come back again."

Donnie. I'd almost forgotten about her and my selfish jealousy. Now I was glad she'd been there for Dad, thrilled that she'd taken my side. "If I go back before I'm twenty-one, Gertrude Gorman will try to lock me in my room."

"Only because she loves you."

Loved me, feared for me, and wanted to protect me. "I know," I sighed. "And I love her."

He nuzzled my neck. "If you were locked up, I'd climb in your window every night and we'd snuggle."

261

I expected the image of that sorry motel room to rise in my mind, but instead I saw myself in bed with Ben, naked and unashamed. I took my emotional pulse and felt not the tiniest flutter of trepidation. "I'll expect a lot more than snuggling."

Ben blushed and cleared his throat. Delia scraped back her chair and bounced to her feet. "I'd best check on that pie before it cooks to a cinder. You two have things to say an old lady don't need to hear." She closed the door with a firm click and her steps thumped across the living room.

Lips to lips we giggled like children and then kissed again in the way that made me feel there was no me, no Ben, only us.

"Ummm. What a perfect day. You *and* a peach pie." Ben grinned but his eyes were filmed with tears. "You kept me going," he said, his voice fracturing like a skim of autumn ice. "Through every brutal mile."

I'd never seen Ben cry. I felt weak, frightened, and took refuge in bantering. "Really? Even though I can't make a decent pie."

"Don't I know that! I was the one who ate your mistakes, remember?"

He tousled my hair and gazed out over the pasture. "I'd recite the list a hundred times a day—that salty apple pie, those burnt pancakes, the soggy dumplings, the cake that didn't rise." His voice grew harsh. "And I'd laugh. Laugh like hell, but all inside so they couldn't hear me if they were around. That was important—laughing—it meant that right then I wasn't giving up."

I felt cold, sick, helpless horror. He put a finger to my lips—needless, I had no words.

In a moment he cleared his throat, reached for his tea, and drained the glass. "And I pretended you were next to me and if I stumbled, you'd help me up."

Tears scorched my eyes—tears of sadness, guilt, and

262

shame. He'd found solace in my image, but I hadn't sustained myself with his. I buried my face in his shoulder.

"When I made it to a base, called Jo, and found out you'd gone off, I felt like I was back in that jungle. I couldn't sleep or eat worrying."

"I managed okay," I insisted in voice both bold and hollow.

"I see that now." He tilted my head back and kissed the tip of my nose. "But what I don't see is why you took off. That just wasn't like you."

Wasn't like the old me. "I thought I'd lost you to April, to that stupid war. It hurt so much. And then Sebastian died."

I felt a frisson of fear. What if the old me was who Ben loved? What if we'd grown too far apart to be together? "I had to leave."

"Okay." He scratched his stubbly cheek. "But why did you take April?"

"She blackmailed me." In a rush of terse words I told him about the condoms, how I tried to shake her off at the diner, how she convinced a cop to chase me down, and how she hijacked my journey to try to see her future.

"It might take me until I'm a hundred," he sighed, "but I'll make it up to you, Littlebit. I swear I will."

"It's not your fault." I kissed the corners of his eyes. "I needed to break loose and she forced me to do it. Besides, I dreamed about you in Vietnam and I wanted to know . . . I *had* to know if you'd come back."

Tears glossed his eyes but a smile danced on his lips. "So, you still loved me."

"I'll *always* love you." I slid from his lap and knelt between his knees. "I thought you betrayed me but I was the betrayer. I doubted you because of what happened—what *didn't* happen—in that motel room. I thought you wanted someone who wasn't so uptight, someone like

263

April."

He brought my fingers to his lips and kissed each one. "You're the only one I've ever wanted."

I felt warm, special, wanted to stretch this moment out to forever. But there was more I had to say. "I know that now. I know more about betrayal than I ever thought there was to learn. More about a lot of other things, too." I cupped his face, then let my hands drop to the arms of his chair. "I'm not the same person who left Maplekill."

"Neither am I." His voice was sharp with pain. "But I'm the one who broke faith with you, Littlebit. I never told you how much I love you." He squinted as if looking into the past. "I never said the words."

"I never told you either. Diana said the rule is that a girl never says it first." I ducked my head, feeling like the ultimate fool for playing such a stupid game. "I assumed you knew."

"Assumption!" His laugh was brittle, like glass crushed underfoot. "The military taught me a hard lesson about assumption. And betrayal? Well, this government wrote the book on that subject by putting us in a war we can't win—not the way they're going at it."

The frantic anguish in his voice felt like a cold knife twisting in my gut. I seized his hands. "You're out of that now."

"I'm on leave. They could send me back."

The cold knife twisted harder, deeper. "They can't. You could have died."

"I'm just a pawn in the war game, Littlebit. And pawns are sacrificed."

I gripped the chair arms as if that could keep him here and whole. "What do we do now?"

"We start over and we do it right." He pushed my glasses down my nose and peered deep into my eyes. "I love you, Elizabeth. What do you want to do now? What do you *really* want?"

I searched my heart and mind and found my love and my dream like twin flames, neither engulfing the other. I wanted both. But I had never asked for it all before, never believed I was allowed to, that I had the right.

"I love you, and I want to be with you." My voice trembled and I raised my chin. "But I don't want to go back to Maplekill to stay. I want to apologize to Dad and your mom and my grandmother for sneaking off and worrying them."

I winced, both at the thought of delivering that apology and at what I had to say next. "And then I want to go to Chicago and study to be a reporter."

"Hmmm." He rubbed his chin with a soft chuffing sound and gazed off into the blue distance.

Was this where our roads parted?

My heart grew cold and heavy and I almost wavered. And then I realized I hadn't asked him the question he'd put to me. "What do *you* really want?"

"That's easy. I want to fall asleep beside you every night, laugh with you every day, and read the stories under your byline." He lifted one eyebrow. "And until this country comes to its senses, I want to be part of the minority that clogs the system."

"What does that mean?"

"It means I read *Civil Disobedience*. It means your friend Thoreau had some pretty good ideas." He grinned. "I guess Chicago is as good a place as any to protest the way things are going."

Protest? Ben? "What about honor and duty?"

"That's my duty now," he said as if he'd read my mind. "And Chicago's only a hop, skip, and a jump from Canada."

I felt weightless and dizzy, as if I'd slipped the gravitational pull of earth and was adrift in space. "You'd desert?"

"Well, your friend Thoreau said if I put my head in the

fire, I have only myself to blame. I'm sure not going to do that twice."

"Pie's ready," Delia called from the house.

"We'll be right there." Ben leaped from his chair and drew me into his arms. "I'll go with you if you go with me."

"It's a deal." I stood on tiptoe and kissed him long and deep.

For just a second I wondered if Delia knew how our lives would turn out.

I decided I would never ask.

Carolyn J. Rose grew up in New York's Catskill Mountains, graduated from the University of Arizona, logged two years in Arkansas with Volunteers in Service to America, and spent 25 years as a television news researcher, writer, producer, and assignment editor in Arkansas, New Mexico, Oregon, and Washington. She lives in Vancouver, Washington, and founded the Vancouver Writers' Mixers. Her hobbies are reading, gardening, and not cooking. For more information, surf to www.deadlyduomysteries.com

Also by Carolyn J. Rose

An Uncertain Refuge

Hemlock Lake

Consulted to Death

Driven to Death

Dated to Death

By Carolyn J. Rose and Mike Nettleton

The Big Grabowski

Sometimes a Great Commotion

The Hard Karma Shuffle

The Crushed Velvet Miasma

The Hermit of Humbug Mountain

www.ingramcontent.com/pod-product-compliance
Lightning Source LLC
Chambersburg PA
CBHW061557170626
46811CB00001B/237